At the end of the day, we're all fucked.

Plumb fucked.

Unapologetic Horror

www.plumfuktpress.com

This edition published in 2022 by **Plumfukt Press, LLC** (Kansas, USA).

Copyright © 2017, 2022 David Owain Hughes

Cover Art © 2022 Kevin Enhart

All rights reserved.

No parts of this publication may be reproduced, stored in a retrieval system, or transmitted in any form or by any means (electronic, mechanical, photocopied, recorded, or otherwise) without the prior written permission of the author. The scanning, uploading, and distribution of this book via internet or any other means without permission of the author is likewise illegal and punishable by law. Please do not encourage piracy—purchase only authorized electronic and print editions.

The works contained within this collection are fiction. Characters, names, places, and situations are fictitious or used fictitiously. Any resemblances to actual persons (living or dead), locales, events, or business establishments are entirely coincidental.

ISBN-13: 978-1734185751

** CONTENT MAY BE DISTURBING TO SOME INDIVIDUALS DUE TO HARSH LANGUAGE, GRAPHIC SEX AND VIOLENCE, AND GORE. YOU HAVE BEEN WARNED.**

PART I

CHAPTER ONE

SQUEAKING WIPERS. GREAT, THAT'S ALL I NEED, Rigs thought as rain lashed the windshield. Lightning illuminated the sky, tearing through the clouds and aiding the poor visibility on the motorway. Thunder crashed on.

"Jesus! It's coming down as though the world's ending. I can't see a bastard thing out here."

The CB radio crackled and spat static, catching his attention. He picked up the handle and said, "Is anyone out there on this piss-poor morning?"

He kept hold of the receiver, waiting for a reply. The squealing wipers bit into his senses, close to driving him mad. A tick developed at the side of his neck and a headache started to form behind his eyes.

"Hey, Taff," came an answer. "Quite the distance from home, aren't ya, boyo?"

Rigs ignored the Englishman's banter and replied with an even tone. "Yeah, and a mother of a morning it's been so far, too. Whereabouts you heading, Bristol?"

"The accent gave it away, eh?" The man cackled.

Rigs couldn't help but chuckle. "Oh, aye, you could say that. You flying solo, Rose?" Rose was the name he gave to all the English truckers he spoke to.

"Always flying solo, me. Most of us guys do. Why, you got company?"

Rigs looked over at Iain in the passenger seat and smiled. His mate's head was pressed tight against the glass, his peaked hat down over his eyes. Strings of drool clung to his lower lip. His breathing was rhythmical.

"Pretty much alone out here too, Rose," Rigs said. "Some weather this is, hey?"

"It sure is, Taff. I can't see shit. It's coming down in sheets!"

A gaudy orange sign out on the road flashed on and off, cycling between two messages: "Don't Drink and Drive" followed by "Feeling Sleepy?" *No, but a coffee would be nice*, Rigs thought. "You heading home or dropping off?"

"Heading back to the motherland, Taff. You?"

"Same. Heading back after dropping off a few tons of lumber in Newcastle."

"I . . . you . . . careful . . . you . . . was . . ."

Rigs replaced the handle as the Bristolian's voice broke up. "Ah, fucking thing."

He turned his attention to the stereo and hit the Power button. A man's monotone voice blasted from the speakers, delivering the morning headlines. All local stuff, nothing of interest. He thought of changing the channel, but the news ended and a song kicked on. Freddy Mercury's soothing voice filled the cab and set Rigs off singing to "Ride the Wild Wind."

"God, remember this one, Iain?" he said, looking over at his companion, who was still asleep. "You've got to be shitting me. With all this noise, you're still flat-out kipping!" He laughed and increased the volume to the radio, continuing to sing.

The old but gutsy Foden 3335 growled and grunted its way along the M4 as Rigs shifted through the gears. The diesel engine sounded in great form as its chunky tires rolled through pools of water. The murky liquid splattered against the cab's body and mud splashed against the doors and mudguards.

They'd left Newcastle two hours ago, after getting the last of the cargo out of their container and into Greg and Sons Timber Warehouse. The factory only had one fork truck in use, with two others out of action, so it took longer than expected. Rigs had hoped to be home by mid-afternoon, but that wasn't going to happen now. Besides the weather and the setback at the lumber merchant, the traffic on the way up had been horrendous, with accidents and jams most of the way to Birmingham and beyond. A five-hour journey had already turned into seven hours.

Rigs punched the accelerator. He didn't *need* to be home. He didn't have a wife, no girlfriend. Just Coal, his six-year-old Staffordshire bull terrier. The mutt was either sitting by empty food and water bowls (due to a shitty neighbor who couldn't look after herself let alone a dog), or fast asleep on the sofa farting and yawning.

He hoped for the latter, but it was more than likely the former.

But it wasn't Coal pushing him to get there. The pooch was used to solitude. Rigs just *wanted* to be home, to kick off his size thirteen Caterpillars and strip to the waist, maybe guzzle down a half-dozen bottles of Hobgoblin beer while slumped in his favorite chair listening to the rain splash against the roof. He wanted to drift off to sleep in front of the box while Coal lay at his feet and licked his toes.

It sounded like heaven and he wanted it. Badly.

Rigs turned the radio up a few clicks. Roy Orbison was singing about driving all night. *How apt*, Rigs thought. He sang along to the track while tapping the thick steering wheel with both hands. One booted foot thudded the floor beside the clutch.

"I drove all *niiiiiight!*" Rigs belted out, flashing his pearly whites and fluttering his eyelashes in the rearview mirror. He was pretending to be ol' Roy himself, singing to a stadium full of screeching women.

"What. The. Hell are you doing?" Iain said.

Rigs stopped mid-word. "What, you got a problem with my crooning?"

Iain wiped the saliva from his chops, rolled his head on his muscular neck, then oohed and aahed as his bones clicked and crunched. He stretched his arms and arched his back. "No, no problem here. I just find your poofy singing hilarious."

"It could be worse, ya know. I could be howling out a bit of One Direction."

"Now *that* would be a crime against humanity."

They both laughed.

"Where the hell are we?" Iain asked, looking at his watch. "It's gone eleven o'clock, mate."

"I'm not sure, but I think our exit is coming up pretty soon. Can't see jack in this weather, butty."

"Want me to get the Tom-Tom on the go?"

"No thanks, *ma'am*. I can get us home." The remark earned Rigs a powerful thump off Iain, which caught him on his left shoulder. The assaulted area began to deaden. Rigs chuckled. "Bitch," he said. "You could have waited for me to get my handbag out."

"True. With all that make-up you carry in it, you probably would have brained me."

Rigs snorted.

"Any chance we can pull this tub over for a few? I need coffee and a stretch of the legs, mate," Iain said.

"Yeah, I think that's our best bet. Maybe the weather will calm down too."

Roy had been replaced on the radio by Don Henley, who was singing "The Boys of Summer." Rain continued to hammer the cab's windows, the wipers on full, making them squeak and groan even more.

"Jesus, have we got a mouse trapped under the wiper blades?" Iain asked.

"Sounds bloody awful, doesn't it?"

"I'll get them changed as soon as we get back. We got a long haul next."

"Where? I haven't seen our schedule for the next few days."

"Clyde."

"*Clyde?*" Rigs blurted. "What the hell are we picking up there?"

"Drums of fuel. Drop zone is Bideford."

"That's going to be some job. We'd better make sure this pile of scrap is in fine nick," Rigs said.

"I wouldn't worry about it. With all the work we got going on, we'll soon have enough to buy two new trucks and can scrap this bloody thing."

"Sweet." Rigs put his fist out for a bump off Iain, and his mate slammed his knuckles with force.

"Look, up there," Iain said, indicating with a point of a finger. "Isn't that a pit stop we could use?"

Rigs squinted at the blur and ripple of a red light up the road. It was either a petrol station, Road Chef, or a service station. Rigs hoped for the latter, as he wanted to be off the road until the rain eased. His longing for home had ceased now that Iain was awake.

"Nice. It's a Motto service station, mate."

"Great. My throat's as dry as an Arab's dap."

"Dap? They don't wear daps," Iain said, smiling.

"Sandal, then. Happy?"

"Better. Best get over to the left lane."

"How's it looking behind? I can't see shit out the wing mirror," Rigs said, flipping the indicator downward.

"Go on. The guy behind is flashing you to go."

"How sweet of him."

Rigs maneuvered the rig to the left-hand lane and up the offramp, pulling slowly into the Motto parking area designed for lorries and coaches. He killed the engine, which grumbled to a stop. The bonnet hissed and spat as rain splashed the heated metal.

"Well," Iain said, not taking his eyes off the windscreen, "who's getting the coffee?"

"I'll go. Don't worry your pretty little features about it."

Iain produced a twenty-pound note out of his pocket. "Get us something to munch on, too. Sarnies, sausage rolls—you know, the same old heart-stopping shite. I think we're going to be here a while."

* * *

By the time Rigs got back into the lorry with a bagful of goodies and two coffees, he was soaked to the skin. Beads of water trickled down his face and trembled off the end of his nose. "Jesus H. Christ!"

"Raining, is it?" Iain asked as droplets fell from Rigs's unkempt beard and long hair.

Rigs shot Iain a sarcastic glare as he handed one of the coffees to him.

"I wouldn't get your panties in a bunch with me just yet, mate. I have bad news."

"Great. What is it now?"

"The fuzz have closed off most of the main roads and motorways this side of Birmingham. We either find another route home, or we're stuck here until they reopen them. Your call, mate."

"Shit. Right, okay, this is what we'll do then: we bunk down here for a couple of hours, finish our drinks and food, maybe get a bit of shuteye, then move on."

"What if the roads are still closed by then?"

"Then we get the Tom-Tom out. She'll find us a route around the major roads and get us home. Don't worry. It's not as if we're in any sort of hurry or danger, right?"

"If that's how you want to play it, that's fine by me," Iain said.

Both men sat there sipping their coffees while listening to the radio.

The torrential downpour continued.

CHAPTER TWO

HE WATCHED THE LONE FIGURE APPROACH his pub on his CCTV screen, which was rigged up behind the bar. The silhouette drifted across the deserted car park with urgency. Even though the picture was grainy, steam rising off the approaching shape was visible.

He'd concluded it was a man making his way to the bar door, due to the sheer bulk of the person's frame.

Could be trouble, he thought, bending down and eyeing the steel bat suspended on hooks under the counter. Carved into the bloodied steel was the name Mary. He winked and clucked his mouth at the clubbing instrument. "Hey there, lovely."

The door chimed and footsteps pounded toward him. "Pint!" the newcomer said, slamming the counter. An empty glass farther down the bar jumped and rattled to a stop.

Porky straightened up and faced his customer. Beads of sweat broke on his forehead due to the exertion, and his gut pushed against the pumps. "Hello, sir. Hell of a morning to be out." He smiled his yellow-toothed grin. The other half of his dental work was either chipped, scuffed, or damaged by decay and plaque. "Pint o' what will it be? We have fine ales from Shrewsbury, Nottingham, Sheffield—"

"Give me anything," the man spat, his face cheerless.

Porky glanced at the stranger's hand. Underneath his big, gnarled mitt was a crisp, ten-pound note.

He tentatively reached for a glass, not taking his eyes off the weird customer. He placed the container under the Ancient Breed Beer tap. "York's finest, this one. Yes, sir," Porky said, trying to make conversation as he drew the pint. "You from around these parts?" He placed the glassful of dirty brown liquid in front of the man, who had a scar running down the side of his face.

"No," he said, all the while leering at Porky.

"Business?"

"Yeah. I'm with the crew working on the motorway."

"Cutting in the new road?"

"Yeah."

"I see. Right, that'll be three of your English pounds," Porky said, indicating the pint of ale.

The man took his hand off the tenner. "Open early, ain't ya?"

The question took Porky by surprise. "Uh, well, yeah. Getting ready for our big night, friend."

"And what night might that be, *friend*?"

Porky flushed, irritated by the man's tone and inquisitive looks. He gave his best smile, then pointed at a poster on a wall opposite them. "Info is over there. Why don't you join us, maybe earn you'self some serious money?"

Grant looked over at the poster, which was yellow with cigarette smoke. One of its corners was peeling from the wall.

Porky's Annual Pool Tournament
Entry fee: £50
Prize: £2,000!!!
- Open to all -

For Rules and More Information,
Please See Bar Staff

"Two-grand prize?" the man asked.

"Yes, sir, two—"

"It's Grant. The name's Grant." The man snorted into his beer, then muttered, "Two grand, my arse."

"Genuine. It's the truth, Grant. Every penny goes to the winner."

"How many are you expecting to turn up?" Grant scanned the deserted pub. "Hardly roaring with trade here, is it, Tubs?"

Porky ignored the insult, having been called worse by better men. "Our annual pool tournament is a crowd drawer. Always has been."

"And you play this *lavish* competition on that piece of shit?" Grant asked, nodding at the disheveled pool table situated a bit deeper into the sitting area. A vintage jukebox hugged the wall by its side.

"No, sir," Porky said, shaking his head and sniggering. "That's the everyday one. The tournament table is in the lounge area."

Grant took a hearty swallow of his Ancient Breed and wiped his mouth on the cuff of his donkey jacket. "Tastes damn fine, does that. York ale, you say?"

Porky nodded, a glowing beam on his face. "Glad you like it. It's the pride pint of my pub."

"Any chance I can see this table of yours? After another glass of this ale, of course."

Porky looked at the clock mounted on the wall behind him, noting it was almost eleven a.m. "I can show you the table, sure, but I'm not so sure about that second pint. I mean, I shouldn't have served you that one. It's not technically opening time."

"But your door was open."

"Yeah, I was just in the process of locking it again. I've been taking empty barrels out."

"I see. Guess I got lucky."

"You did," Porky said. "What are you doing out so early on a Saturday morning?"

"Just clocked off. Some of us boys were behind with our work, so we stayed on. All good now though."

"In this weather?"

"Oh, aye. We have tents to protect us as we work."

Porky admired hard labor and shrugged. "I guess one more won't harm, seeing as I'm showing you the table." He took the glass off Grant and placed it back under the tap.

"How long have you been running this place?"

Porky rubbed his chin with his spare hand and closed his eyes in concentration. His mouth moved rapidly with his calculations. "Must be close to twenty-five years now, I'd say."

Grant whistled. "Hell of a long time. Bet you've had some right bozos in here over the years."

"Ha! Yes, you could say that," Porky said, snorting out a laugh. "But we deal with the troublemakers. They never come back."

"Oh?"

Porky placed the pint in front of Grant, accidentally sloshing a little over the rim. "We see them on their way, is what I mean," he said, snapping his green braces, which covered a food- and ale-spattered white shirt. One of the middle buttons was missing, exposing a doughy portion of his gut.

"I see." Grant took a long gulp of Breed. "Ah," he gasped, putting the glass back down. "'Ell of a nice pint, this."

"Glad you like it. Maybe you can try one of my famous Porky Pies this evening?" Porky said, beaming ever so angelic.

"Homemade pies?"

"Oh, yes. The very finest." Porky touched the tips of his right hand to his lips and kissed them.

"Tempting. The ale is fine too, mind." Grant worked his lip. "I don't know . . ."

"Maybe this will convince you," Porky said, bending and reaching beneath the counter. He retrieved a decrepit chest and set the grubby box on the bar top, grunting and sweating with the effort.

"Did you get that from Long John Silver or summat?"

Porky didn't answer, instead working on the padlock with a small key he kept around his neck, a portion of his tongue protruding from his mouth. "Damn thing is starting to rust," he uttered softly. "Must get it replaced."

"What ya got in there, the family jewels?" Grant mocked.

Porky finally opened the lock. He undid the clasps either side of the box, lifted the lid, and spun it around.

Grant's eyes almost fell out of his head at the sight of the money, which was placed in neat rows of crisp fifty-pound notes. He licked away a thin mustache of froth. "My God, you really do have that cash prize. I thought you were shitting me, Tubs."

Again, Porky let the comment slip and slammed the chest lid shut. "That's your eyeful copped, sir."

"What's the catch? Nobody salts that kind of money away just to hand it out."

"There is no catch, sir."

"You're telling me that your customers enter, play one another until there is only one left, and then walk away with the lot?"

"Well, yes, but only if that winner can then beat the Champ—our house champion. He's very good, too. Never lost a game."

Grant snorted. "So there *is* a catch. I bet that money has never been won in all the years you've been running the game, huh?"

"No, sir. Never."

Grant shook his head. "What a fucking swizz. Who's the Champ—Ronnie O'Sullivan?"

"Er, no, my son is, actually." Porky huffed as he replaced the box under the counter.

"Show me the table," Grant said, almost threateningly.

A right fucking drunk cunt, this one, and he's hardly finished his second glass, Porky thought, burning with regret of having entertained the lush before opening. But he wasn't about to be intimidated. *Besides, I've got my bestie, Mary, close at hand, along with other backup . . .* "Right, okay. But very quickly. Then you *must* leave." Porky bustled away as fast as his legs would carry him.

"Yeah, okay," Grant said, getting up and following.

Porky entered his lounge and inhaled through his nose in adoration. It had taken years to afford everything within it, and he kept it cleaner than anything else in the pub. The red velvet seating and plush tables smacked of wealth. A cue rack clung to one wall where a giant clock ticked the morning away. The pool table itself was unblemished, the baize fresh as always—as it should be, as he had brushed it that morning. A massive lamp hung above it on the ceiling, from which polished fans also dangled. Mirrors surrounded the playing field on every wall. *Ancient Breed Beer Co.* was etched into their thick glass, along with the pub's name: *The Rack and Cue*.

He spun and faced Grant, offering a lopsided smile. "Well?"

The man nodded, glancing about. "Nice room."

"Right. Now please, Grant, I'm afraid you're going to have to leave. I must prepare for tonight's event."

Grant strolled to the rack, took down one of the cues, unscrewed the butt, and returned to Porky. He was much taller than Porky had initially thought.

Grant's face twisted with sudden rage and he grabbed Porky by the front of his shirt, pressing the stick into his neck. "Now this is how it's going to go down, fat man: you're going to give me that box in the bar, along with the key."

Porky wriggled like a virgin, "What? You can't—"

"Yes, I can. Now hand over the key, or I'm going to smash your cunting skull in with this cue." He snarled. "I'm fucking warning—"

Someone grabbed Grant's shoulder, spun him around, and yanked the cue harshly from his hand.

"Big mistake," Porky said, smoothing his shirt back into place.

"Jesus Christ!" Grant bellowed, staring into the eyes of a gigantic woman clad in bondage clothing. A gimp mask, complete with zipper across the mouth, covered her face. "Who—"

The woman hoisted him off his feet and slammed him down onto a table. Grant bellowed a high-pitched scream as the S&M freak hammered his face and skull with the cue. Blood spattered the walls and tables, slowly seeping and soaking into the carpet.

The smacking sounds turned wet and sloppy after the twentieth or thirtieth welt, and Grant's head started to resemble a mound of mashed potato. His body twitched and flopped as the woman continued to beat at his obliterated face.

"Enough, Baby," Porky said.

The woman stopped lashing Grant and stood straight. Her chest heaved.

"Take him to Doc."

Baby scooped Grant off the table, throwing him over her shoulder like a sack of spuds. The wall of a woman carried the carcass to the cellar entrance and threw it down the steps. It tobogganed the wooden hill with unruly speed.

"It would seem the party has started early," Porky said, laughing hysterically and slapping his thigh.

CHAPTER THREE

"MANDY. MANDY, LOVE. WAKE UP," Grace called as she shook her friend in the sleeping bag by her side. "I think the rain may have stopped now."

Grace floundered out of her bag and got to her bare knees—being naked around her best friend didn't bother her. She crawled to the tent flaps, pulled the zipper down, and peeled one side back. "Glorious," she scoffed as the rain poured down. "Any more of this, and we're going to get washed away."

Mandy groaned, stirring. "Turn the lights out, will ya? It's too bright and way too early."

"Too *early*?" Grace laughed. "It's gone midday, you lazy cow."

Mandy propped up on her elbows and peered out the tent. "That's some shitty weather out there, missy."

Grace laughed. "Have you seen the state of your hair? You look like a scarecrow, woman. Shock's not the word for that crow's nest."

Mandy gave Grace the finger while pulling a sour face. "Says the girl sitting in open view with her bangers hanging out. Yeah, awesome look, Grace."

"Pfft, please. You love it, dirty bitch. Always knew you wanted a piece of this," Grace quipped.

"You wish." Mandy peeled herself out of her sleeping bag, stretched, and joined her mate at the open flap of the tent. They hugged each other and stared at the water slanting down through the trees. "What's the plan?"

"Well, if we stay here any longer, our tent is going to sink." Grace broke the hug and pointed. "Over there. It's getting boggy."

"Not such a hot idea, bedding down on marshland, chick."

"It's not like we knew this last night, is it?"

"True. We were walking around blind in a storm. If we hadn't have decided just to bunk down when we had, God knows what would have happened. It was so dark out here," Mandy said.

"Guess we best pack up and haul arse then, now that we know we're on wet ground." Grace scanned the jumble that was their gear inside the tent. "Any more of that soup left?" she asked, stepping away to dig through their rucksacks and coats in search of their flasks.

"There should be." Mandy began rooting through her belongings too. "Ah, there you are," she said, picking up a tobacco tin buried under her sleeping bag. She removed a fag, popped it into her mouth, and sparked it, taking a deep drag of Golden Virginia. She blew the smoke out through the opening in the tent. "That's some good shit right there. Want a puff?"

"No, thanks." Grace found one of the thermoses tucked under dirty clothes. "Ah-ha! I've got one of them. Feels reasonably full, too."

"Save me some, you greedy wench," Mandy said, taking another drag on her cigarette.

"Of course." Grace unscrewed the lid to the flask and poured a nice hearty beaker full of broth. "Here you go," she said, passing it to Mandy.

"Oh, you're a dear."

Grace admired her friend's beauty as she passed the cup to her. Her figure was full, much fuller than her own. Mandy's breasts were ample for her frame. Her brown hair was rich in color, which brought out the best in her lightly tanned skin. Her pupils were a mix of green splashed with grey. She could have any fella she wanted, but she was too busy enjoying the single lifestyle. "Girls just want to have fun," she'd always say, mimicking the Cindy Lauper song. Grace smiled at the thought.

"Something amusing about my nakedness?"

"Yeah, you've got a hair growing out of your left nipple. If I pull on it, will the butler come running?"

Mandy looked down at her breasts. "Ooh, you little fibber. I should throw this soup over you."

"What's stopping you?"

"Hunger!"

Grace tittered, pouring another beaker of soup for herself.

The girls greedily drank their lukewarm broth as they watched the rain fall as heavily as it had the previous night. They'd been hiking along the main road when the thunder and lightning had started and had decided to go into the forest to set their tent up for the night. But before getting the tent fully erected, the rain had begun to blast down, soaking them to the skin. Once the tent was standing, they'd thrown their gear inside, stripped, and headed straight to bed.

"Guess we'll have to stick to that road we were on last night, Grace. See where it comes out. Hopefully we'll catch more traffic today. Maybe get ourselves a lift as far as Birmingham."

"That would be nice. But at the rate we're going, we may as well turn around and go home," Grace said, almost pouting. "We should have just caught the train or bus down to Gina's. We could miss next weekend's gig."

"Hey, come on—don't go all moody on me now. We aren't going to miss the gig. Besides, we both agreed it would have been too much money to catch public transport and more fun travelling like this. It's been a great laugh so far."

"Yeah, I'm sorry. You're right." Grace put her dirty beaker back in her rucksack. "Best we get moving then."

"That's the spirit," Mandy said.

* * *

By the time they finished packing up their gear, dressing, and storing the tent away, it was past one in the afternoon.

Their hiking boots squelched and slopped as they traipsed through the boggy forest, causing them to pant and puff. The patter of water as it struck leaves and foliage reverberated in the woods. After a few minutes of tireless mud-trudging, the road came into view. A car whizzed by as rain pelted the tarmac with vehemence.

The women headed in the direction which Mandy had suggested earlier until they'd travelled half a mile without another car passing by. They plodded farther still, until Grace asked to stop for a rest.

Both women took off their packs and sat on a couple of large rocks by the side of the seemingly disused road.

"Where the hell are we, Mandy, love?"

"I've no idea . . . Wait. I see something."

"What?" Grace asked, peering through the gaps in the row of trees on the opposite side of the road where Mandy's gaze was fixed.

"A building. Looks like it could be a farmhouse or something. Maybe we could give them a knock, see if they can point us in the right direction?"

"Or give us a lift to the nearest town?" Grace added.

"Yeah. Come on, let's get our lovely arses over there."

Huffing, Grace put her heavy rucksack back on and sloped after Mandy, who sprinted toward the trees. "Wait up, Mands! I have little legs." But by the time she reached the windbreak, Mandy had disappeared.

"Where the hell did she get to?" Grace muttered as she battled her way through the bushes. Nestles and brambles clawed at her bag. "Mandy! Where are—"

"Over here."

Grace stepped through the last of the green. Mandy stood before her, staring at an exceptionally large building which loomed over them, casting a deep shadow. The old, weathered stone structure had sharp edges and dainty windows. Two massive chimneystacks poked from its roof, emitting copious amounts of smoke, which billowed into the ominous sky.

A rusted sign hung high above the main door, which was painted black. It squeaked as it swung back and forth on its decayed hinges. Its insignia was that of racked pool balls with crossed cues. The words *The Rack and Cue* were etched over the top of the faded photo.

"A pub?" Grace asked.

"It would seem like it. Let's go inside and get out of this rain." Mandy headed for the door.

Grace shivered. Something about the place seemed off. "Maybe it's not open yet. It's only early afternoon."

"No harm in trying," Mandy said, turning the doorknob before using the ancient brass knocker, which was in the shape of a beer bottle. "Cute."

"It seems we've missed the last shout," Grace said, smiling and relieved they wouldn't have to enter the pub. She wanted to take her chances on the road instead.

Mandy raised her fist to welt the wood again, but before she could rap on it, the door creaked open.

"Yes?" said a voice.

"Oh," Mandy said, slightly startled. "I—*we* were wondering if you—"

"Yes, please, do come in out of that dreadful weather," the voice said, all hearty and cheerful. "It's about opening time anyway."

"Come on, Grace." Mandy headed into the building.

By the time Grace got to the door, it was wide open, and as she entered she could now clearly see the owner of the voice: a rather rotund man.

"The name's Porky," he said. "Nice to have some customers this early in the day. Please, go on through to the bar, ladies."

They did as instructed, Mandy in the lead, Grace right behind her as the large aproned Porky took up the rear. The floor was made entirely of flagstone, and their footsteps echoed off it and rang about them. The inside smelled of stale beer masked by a flowery scent.

"Are you serving food yet?" Mandy asked once they reached the bar.

"We sure are, little lady," Porky said, smiling at Mandy and then at Grace as she made a beeline for her friend's side.

"Great!" Mandy took her rucksack off and undid her jacket.

"I thought we were just asking for a lift, Mandy," Grace whispered.

"Yeah, I know. But while we're here, we may as well take a load off and grab a bite to eat, hey? Maybe have a drink or two."

"But—"

"Oh, come on, Grace. Loosen up. Have some fun."

"Oh, fine," Grace said, wanting something to calm her nerves. "What tap do you recommend, Porky?"

"Your poison?" he asked.

"Cider."

"Same," Mandy added.

"Well, in that case, I'd have to suggest a half-pint of Rotten Apple. One of Warwickshire's finest, ladies."

"Sounds scrummy," Mandy said. "But make it a full pint, please."

"Coming right up. And for you?" he asked Grace.

"Yes, the same please."

Mandy glanced about the area. "Ooh, a pool tournament!" she blurted. "I'm a dab hand with a cue!"

"With balls too, or so I've been told," Grace muttered.

"It's paying out a two-grand cash prize," Mandy said, ignoring the comment.

"You're good, you say?" Porky asked, plunking their drinks on the counter before them.

"Yes, sir. Borough champion three years running," Mandy replied.

"Oh, you *must* enter," he said.

"I plan to, especially with that kind of money floating around."

Grace said nothing, knowing how good her friend was at the game. The thought of bagging two grand was nice.

"Splendid!" Porky said, a huge grin developing on his sweaty red face.

CHAPTER FOUR

"Bloody motherfucking pigs," Charlie raged, thumping the steering wheel of his car. "Fucking telling me I have to detour just because of a bit of rain. Fuck's sake!"

He blew his horn aggressively at the bus in front of him, which was crawling along the carriageway at five miles per hour. "Bloody move it! Some of us have meetings to get to!" Charlie yelled, rattling the steering wheel as he looked at the clock embedded in the dashboard. It was 3:05 p.m. *I'll never make it there for four. Never. Fuck*! He gave the wheel another good rattle on its plinth.

The bus came to a complete standstill.

It took all his energy not to punch the driver's side window out. "Damn it, *move*!" he shouted, his nose almost to the windshield as he thrust his body towards it.

He glanced to his right. A woman sat in her car staring at him and shaking her head.

"What?" He shrugged. "Got a problem?" he said, jabbing his finger into the glass.

She looked away, mouthing and shaking her head some more.

He wound his window down, allowing the cascading rain into his car. It splattered his face. "Oi! I'm fucking talking to you," he roared over the sound of rainwater, frantically waving one hand to draw her attention. But still she ignored him.

"Right, you bitch," he muttered, turning to the passenger seat where his briefcase lay. He unclasped it, lifted the lid, and drew out an apple and orange. He decided to go with the orange first. It was much softer.

Charlie lobbed the hunk of fruit at her passenger window and yelled, "I'm talking to you!"

The furious look on her face almost had Charlie in stitches. Her window rolled down and she screamed, "Are you out of your tiny mind?"

"What's the big idea, shaking your fucking head at me?"

"You're crazy!"

"Can't a man be mad without being judged by some little princess in a Jag her daddy probably bought her?"

"Princess? You cheeky bastard! I'll have you know—"

"Yak-yak-yak-yak," Charlie said, pulling a face and mimicking a mouth with his hand. "I know a stuck-up princess when I see one."

"For God's sake, grow up, man. How old are you? Call yourself a businessman?"

"Ah, dye your fucking roots, ya cunt," he shouted as he started rolling his window up. Before he could fully close it, she began another rant, but he paid her no heed—the bus had started moving. He put his car into gear and followed close behind. Her Jag fell three, four, six, ten cars behind before he came to another standstill.

This is ludicrous. I'm not going to get anywhere if it's only ten feet of tarmac I cover every ten fucking minutes.

He crept forward another couple of car lengths before halting again. The rain seemed to be coming down harder and the wind whipped up, rocking his little Ford Fiesta.

On the roadside to his left, a sign flashed "Delays Due to Accidents."

Charlie turned the radio on to see if he could get any traffic reports. He fiddled with the tracking button, searching for a station, *any* station. The weather seemed to be causing a lot of problems, as every channel he tuned into crackled and spat static.

Finally, a voice broke through his speakers: ". . . the heavy rain, which will continue throughout the week and into next, has caused many floods in most parts of the country . . ."

"Great! Typical. I have a long drive to Newcastle for a meeting, and I get stuck in the worst storm the likes of which us Brits have never seen before," Charlie muttered, his anger dissipating.

". . . and the police have closed many of the main roads, such as large sections of the motorways between Birmingham, Derby, Leicester, Leeds, and Newcastle. It is advised people cancel all long trips across the country until further notice . . ."

The radio crackled violently and the station was lost. Charlie huffed, turning it off.

Next exit, I'll get off. No point trying to go any farther, he thought, resigned to the fact that he probably wouldn't make his meeting. *Best I give John a ring first chance I get, tell him what kind of hell I'm stuck in.*

The traffic ambled on slowly and steadily for another three miles before an exit finally came into view. Charlie swapped from the right to left lane and took the clear junction, which led him to a roundabout. He veered onto the third exit and drove down another dual carriageway. A few miles later, he maneuvered onto yet another junction, thinking it would direct him back the way he'd come.

It didn't.

"What the hell?" he said as he steered his Fiesta down an old, broken carriageway. Tree branches jutted out over the road. Potholes shook the car, forcing Charlie to take his foot off the accelerator and brake slightly. The pelting rain covered his windscreen, cutting his visibility in half.

"Fuck!" he yelped as something scraped underneath his car, followed by a loud crack. The Ford skidded, bounded off the crash barrier, and plowed through a hedge. A portion of the windshield caved in, showering Charlie's lap with glass.

Something bogged the car's tires down, bringing it to a complete halt. Charlie was thrown against his seat with such force that his head snapped back and rebounded off the headrest. Everything went dark.

Rain spattered his face. He groaned, his eyes rolling like marbles.

The first thing he did was search for his phone, which should have been on the seat beside him. "Where the hell . . . ? Ah, got you," Charlie said, finding the device under his case. While wiping specks of blood from his nose and forehead, he checked the screen, expecting it to be either smashed or out of charge. It was neither, but there was no signal. "Fucking typical," he said, undoing his belt and getting out of the vehicle.

His shirt and trousers soaked through as he stood in the downpour inspecting the damage to his car. *Shit. Now what the hell am I going to do?* he wondered, scanning the empty, muddy field that had stopped his Fiesta. *There's got to be a home or small business somewhere close by. I'll just continue down the road a bit, see if I can find someone who can help me.*

He grabbed his sports bag off the rear seat and headed back out onto the desolate road, walking briskly. It didn't take long for his shoes to fill with water and muck as he tromped along, cursing and kicking loose stones as he went. He was in prime shape thanks to his healthy diet and workouts at the gym, which was a good thing because after a mile he still hadn't come across anyone, not even a house or car. The road was equivalent to a ghost town, with only ancient and shoddy road signs still standing. Some were peppered with buckshot.

He quickened his pace. When he rounded the next corner, hope almost lost, a massive house came into view.

"Oh, thank God!" he gasped. The sight of the place fixed him to the spot. It wasn't a house as he'd originally assumed. *Strange place for a pub*, he thought. *But then again, this road was probably thriving with traffic at one time.*

Charlie raced for the pub's entrance. His shoes squelched with every footfall and cast water over their sides. He felt like a late schoolchild, running for the bus. "Please be open, please be open . . ."

His body collapsed against the door, causing a massive clatter. "Hey! Is there anyone in there? Hello? Hello!" he shouted, pounding on the old black door.

Deadbolts clacked and he jumped back, not knowing what to expect.

"Hello, sir," a plump man said, holding the door open. "Come in, come in, and get out of that rain."

"Are you open?"

"Yes, sir."

"Out *here*?" Charlie exclaimed.

"The Rack and Cue is *always* open, sir. Now, come on in and get something warm inside you. Dry off by the fire."

The promise of food and warmth sounded heavenly to Charlie. "That's very kind of you. Thank you," he said, unable to stop his teeth from chattering.

"Bah, Porky'll hear none of it. Inside with you, now."

Charlie stepped through the entryway and into the coziness of the pub. A pair of female voices giggled and chatted somewhere inside, and glasses chinked together. Straightaway he was put at ease. "Do you have a phone, uh . . . Porky, was it?" Charlie asked, thinking the name more than fitting.

"Yes, Porky, sir. And yes, I have a phone, but I rarely get service. Did you need to call someone?"

"Yeah, roadside assistance."

"I see. That explains why you were running around in this weather," Porky said. "Go on through to the bar, I'll be right with you."

As Charlie set off to locate the other punters, the pub door closed and locks clicked at his back.

CHAPTER FIVE

THERE'S NO SIGN OF THIS STORM EASING, Rigs thought, staring out the window. He checked his watch. It was almost four in the afternoon, which meant they'd been at the service station for almost four hours.

Both men had eaten and taken naps, hoping by the time they were ready to set off again the weather would have improved. But the rain seemed to be coming down harder and faster, with thunder and lightning also kicking up. Radio stations hadn't provided any good news either: rain was forecasted throughout the night, heading into the next day. More major roads had been closed off, with the flood hotline number being repeated every ten minutes or so.

Rigs sighed. *We either stay here at the truck stop for another couple of hours, or we head off and get as close to home as possible, maybe find a cheap room for the night.* He didn't care for either option.

Rigs removed his cellphone from his pocket, scrolled down the contacts, and found Jill's number. *Nice girl. A bit lazy. The type of woman who would drive me fucking cuckoo if I were in a relationship with her*, Rigs thought. But she deserved to know what was going on.

"Hello, Jill?" he bellowed down the line as it crackled from poor reception. "It's Rigs."

Iain stirred in his seat, yawned, and stretched. "Is that Jill you're talking to by chance?" he whispered, smiling.

Rigs gave him the middle finger and continued his conversation on the phone. "Yeah, I was hoping to have been home by now, but this weather is causing havoc." He paused as she answered. "Yes, havoc. You know: chaos, mayhem, disaster." Another pause. "Yes, Jill, *mess* would work too."

Iain burst out laughing, snorted, and covered his mouth to stifle his commotion.

Rigs glared at him and almost broke into hysterics himself as Iain removed his peaked hat, which had "I Conquered the Pig Platter" stitched onto it, and repeatedly thrashed it against his knee, his face tomato red. "So yeah, God knows what time I'm going to get home. Probably after six or seven, I hope. Yeah, yeah, that's fine. Just make sure he has a bowlful of water down, along with some biscuits to gnaw on."

Iain composed himself, dropped the door to the glove box, and rummaged around inside, pulling out the Tom-Tom. He removed the cigarette lighter and plugged one end of the sat-nav into the snug slot. The digitized female voice said "Turn around when possible" as soon as he switched the device on.

"Yeah, yeah, thanks, Jill," Rigs continued on the phone. "I'll come round and give you a knock when I get in. Thanks for looking after Coal for me. Yep, bye." He ended the call.

"Drunk?" Iain asked.

"No."

"Bonged out of her brains?"

"Maybe. She did sound pretty zoned out."

"Puffing on that whacky-backy." Iain made a smoking motion with one hand and squinted his eyes. "Ya, man," he mocked.

"Very witty. Do you do any *good* impersonations?"

"Ouch! You really do know how to cut deep, biatch."

"Yeah, yeah. Just get us out of here," Rigs said.

"All right, everything's tapped in, mate. Let's hit the road—"

"Don't say it!"

"Jack," Iain finished.

Rigs rolled his eyes and turned the key in the ignition. The engine grumbled and groaned to a start, as though waking from a deep slumber. He popped the Foden into gear and pulled off.

"It's alive, *alive*! Whahahaha!" Iain steepled his hands together and drummed his fingertips. "Excellent!"

Rigs smiled. "You ever going to get a new routine?"

Iain rubbed his stubbly chin in mid-ponder. "Nah," he finally said, adjusting his hat on top of his bald head. His big grin made his huge jaw look more massive.

Powering the truck out of the service station, Rigs got them back on the motorway, all the while listening to the instructions given to him by the electronic voice.

* * *

Forty minutes down the road, they hit a traffic jam, which stretched out in front of them as far as they could see. Many drivers blared their horns and some were on their phones, no doubt chatting with loved ones, friends, bosses.

"Jesus, look at that," Iain said, pointing at an overturned van. It was lying chassis up in the undergrowth on Rigs's side. A police car, fire engine, and an ambulance were on the scene. "Poor sod must still be stuck inside the wreck."

"Yeah." Rigs noticed all the strewn glass, bits of bumper, and discarded metal which littered the motorway. "Hope he's okay."

"Me too."

"Hey, you remember that time up in Scotland, last May?"

"When we had all that snow?" Iain asked.

"That's it. You jackknifed this baby right across the road, remember?"

"Fuck, you have to mention that every time, don't you?"

"Well, I did warn you. Do you remember how knackered our heaters were in this baby? We almost copped it from the cold."

"Oh, yeah! There was more ice inside the cab than there was on the roads!"

"It was an inch thick, easy," Rigs said.

"And you thought you had frostbite," Iain said, chuckling.

"My toe was pretty blue, you have to admit."

"What a baby."

"This coming from someone who wouldn't get out in the rain earlier?" Rigs teased, grinning.

"Yeah, easier to send you mate, to be honest. At least you've given that mop of yours a good wash. I should have sent you on your way with a bottle of shampoo."

"There, there," Rigs said, patting his friend on the knee. "It must be hard for you, what with the baldness. After all, you can't help being follicly challenged, now can you?"

"Cheeky bastard."

"Hey, there's a junction coming up. Should I take it?"

"Yes, if it gets us out of this jam. And if not, she'll find us another route anyway, mate," Iain said, blowing a kiss to the satellite navigation system.

Rigs left the motorway at the exit and followed the signposts. The Tom-Tom spoke up now and again, telling him what he already knew. But then the signs dried up, forcing him to depend solely on his electronic co-pilot to guide him.

One quiet road led to another, and another, until it appeared they were in the middle of nowhere.

"Where the hell are we?" Iain asked.

"No idea. I'm just listening to her."

"Yeah, well, I think Betsy got it—"

"Betsy?" Rigs butted in.

"Yeah. What of it??"

"I thought we'd decided her name was Ethyl, with a *Y*?"

"No. *You* decided it was Ethyl with a *Y*. I always wanted Betsy."

"Didn't you want to call her Roxie at one point, after that stripper you shagged?" Rigs asked, snorting a laugh.

"I prefer *dancer*, thank you very much."

"She did strip though, didn't she?"

"Yeah, but . . ."

"Well, there you go then," Rigs said. He sighed. "Maybe we should turn back for the main road? We're lost at this point. There's no way we'll make it home on time."

Iain shook his head, that shit-eating grin returning. "Where's your sense of adventure, mate? I say we keep going, turn it into a right proper road trip. Eventually we'll get back on the right track, no?"

"Yeah, I suppose," Rigs mumbled.

As the scenery zipped past, he thought about giving Jill another call. She would need to watch

Coal another night. And he wouldn't be taking his boots off to lounge in front of the telly as soon as he'd hoped to either.

CHAPTER SIX

Doc started with the man's head, snapping his jaw to loosen the mouth. Next he set to work on his teeth.

Sometimes he found gold fillings, which he kept in a special jar for safekeeping. They too could be sold through their usual channel, along with the organs and meat. But that was Porky's job—he was the butcher. Doc's duty was to strip the body of organs, and Baby's was to cut the shell into sections in preparation for Porky to carve.

Gutting the innards was a necessity but yanking every tooth out of the victim's mouth was not. Doc just liked doing it for fun. He liked to imagine how much pain the poor bastards would be in if they were still alive to feel each bone being ripped from their gums. It fed his sadistic side and quieted the demons, even if only briefly.

Once done with the man's chewing implements, Doc clamped his tongue with a pair of pliers and ripped it from the cavity. It severed from the back of the throat with a sickening yet satisfying squelch. He then scooped and plucked the eyeballs from their sockets and snipped the cords.

After placing the tongue and eyeballs into a metal tray caked in blood, Doc retrieved a small bone saw from the wall and returned to his workbench. He began to cut through the man's throat with slow, laborious movements. When sweat started to sting his eyes, he stopped and mopped his brow.

Once composed, Doc continued sawing at the neck until his blade met block on the other side. The head rolled free and landed on the floor beside the table. Doc bent, grabbed it by a tuft of hair, and dumped it into a bucket next to him.

He replaced the saw and took a sharp knife from out of a block. Raising the steel high above his head, he brought it down hard and fast, plunging it into the stump. He drew the serrated edge down as far as he could. Sweat dripped from his forehead, but Doc didn't stop this time. The task was arduous enough without having to restart.

With the blade down the chest far enough, he tugged it free. Placing his hands either side of the slit, Doc split the chest and guts apart, then removed the lungs, heart, liver, and everything else he could get his greasy little mitts on.

Doc glanced at the blood-spattered clock, then recalled its rusted hands hadn't moved in over a year—they'd been welded to the spot by all the splashes of crimson and gore. He peeled back the cuff of his scrubs and spied the timepiece on his wrist. *Almost four o'clock*, he noted. He didn't want to waste much more time on this specimen, which was now almost useless.

Happy with the work he'd so far performed, he rolled the much lighter body over onto its stomach and pried open the small of the back. He tore the spinal cord and kidneys out, then cut off the penis and testicles, which he slipped into a jar for pickling.

Finally, Doc pulled off every nail on the man's fingers and toes. Once finished, he dragged the carcass off the table and onto the floor. It landed with a wet slap.

He jerked the hose from his sink, sprayed the work area down with dirty water, and began scrubbing the table with a large sponge. He wiped from one end to the other, causing a tidal wave of blood-soaked liquid to spill over the edge. With the basement floor being at a slight slant, the polluted water was free to run to the corner of the room and slip down the drain.

Satisfied, Doc picked up all his tools and placed them back on their hooks. He strode to the base of the stairs. "Baby! Come on down here, girl. I'm finished."

Seconds later, her massive frame filled the doorway at the top, her shoulders touching both sides of the jamb. With very little fat on her, Baby's body cut an attractive appearance. Her chest heaved as she slowly and heavily made her way down the steps. The sound of her hollow footfalls rebounded off the cellar walls.

As Baby passed Doc, who wasn't that much shorter or bulkier, Baby stroked his face with one hand and brushed his privates with the other. Doc let out an "ugh" and bucked slightly.

Baby wrested the body from off the floor and threw it over her shoulder. She then squatted and picked up the bucket containing the head.

The beastly woman meandered down a concealed hallway within the cellar. She passed through a steel shutter in an outer room and slammed her door closed.

"Thanks, Baby," he muttered.

He set about cleaning his area some more and prepping it for the evening ahead, trying to keep his mind off what Baby was doing in the room opposite.

* * *

The Boas powered their bikes down the motorway with total absentmindedness. They didn't give a fuck that it pissed down. They couldn't give a toss if the road surface was slippery. They wanted home, even if it meant ripping the highway up at one hundred miles per hour in wet conditions with a fatal crash possible.

They were Hell's Angels. They were the fucking Boas, one of the fifteen most notorious outlaw crews in the UK. Death on the road went with the territory.

That's just the way it goes, Diesel thought. The bandana he had wrapped around his mouth and nose was sodden, offering little to no resistance against the biting cold elements. *Better to die on the road with your bike on top of you than in a ditch with a few bullets in the back of your skull.*

He wondered when a fucking whorehouse or tavern would come into view. He needed his fill of pussy and booze. He and the boys had been on the road since early that morning. The ride up to their Manchester charter had been a difficult one, what with the rain and roads closing left, right, and center. The arduous and tiresome trek had been all for three bundles of handguns. The Boas desperately needed the hardware, as they had their backs against the wall with their most fearsome rivals: Hell's Highwaymen.

Born out of Ipswich, the Highwaymen had taken a liking to Manchester and were making it their job to hustle the Boas out of town. But it was never going to happen, as a small outfit by the name of Wild Scum had allied with the Boas over the years, and for a small-time bunch, they packed some serious heat and muscle.

A drug deal between the Boas and Wild Scum was going down tonight, just outside of Chinatown, Manchester. News of this had reached the

Highwaymen, and the Boas suspected an ambush. Hence, the rush for more weaponry.

In a little over three hours, the Manchester police were going to be knee deep in dead bikers and civilians. Hot lead and hatred were going to rip that city apart. The streets and roads were going to run red with death.

I can't wait, Diesel thought, riding down the deserted motorway. *This is going to be fun!*

However, he wanted a rest beforehand. They hadn't passed a car or lively building in miles, and his patience for some attention and drink was starting to wear thin.

"Hey, Diesel!" the man at his side yelled.

Diesel glanced at Slicks, a Boa if he'd ever seen one. Half his mouth was missing natural teeth and was filled instead with fake ivory and gold. He also sported a huge ZZ Top beard, which made him look like a mean-assed son of a bitch. He wore no tee, just his cut. Whether it snowed or hailed he never wore anything under it either. The man had a head the size of a melon, which sprouted long, dreadlocked hair. "Yeah?" he yelled back, so Slicks could hear him over the roar of the six motorbike engines.

"Over there. I think she's a pub."

Diesel followed the man's nod and noted a large building in the distance. Its roof edged above the trees and sported two impressive chimneystacks, which were pumping out black smoke.

Something about the place gave him the willies right away. Like it was looming over them. Almost threatening.

He knew danger when he saw it.

"Aye, I see it," Diesel shouted. "And?"

"*And?* Are you fucking shittin' me, dude? You've been itching to stop all the way home. We need a fucking rest, man. We can't make it all the way back without a pit stop, amigo."

Now that Slicks had pointed the place out, Diesel couldn't take his eyes off the building. But even though it gave him the heebie-jeebies, he had to admit he was busting a bollock for a stop to recharge his batteries. A rest was a rest, and he and the crew were due one, even if it did turn out to be the Munsters' fucking weekend cottage. "Yeah, I guess so," he replied. "Right, we'll stop. Let everyone know."

He watched in his side mirror as Slicks slipped back behind him. The man nestled his bike in between the other four Boas. Hoots and hollers damn near drowned out their roaring engines.

Together they all maneuvered off the highway. The road to the pub was a boneyard for yesteryear, the surface all buckled and beaten. Most of the way along it, weeds and trees pushed their way through the tarmac.

Once they stopped in the car park, it looked even more menacing. The building appeared more like a fortress than a pub. It was monstrous, not just big, subjugating the surrounding area with its mass. The stonework looked harsh, with sharp jutting corners. Three floors made up the building's height, with windows everywhere. Some of the glass had been cemented over, which suggested disuse and abandonment. The slate roof looked worn and well used, but the chimneystacks puffed away unconcerned.

A single light burned in one of the upper windows, and Diesel thought he saw a face peep out at them.

They drank the place in as the light of day started burning out. Many fields comprised the adjacent land. Some had corroded barns standing in them and others had shells for buildings.

Diesel noticed a swaying sign. *The Rack and Cue?* He snorted a laugh. *Doesn't sound as creepy as it looks.*

"Maybe they'll have a few spare rooms, Diesel?" Slicks said.

Diesel turned on his sergeant at arms with a scowl. "What the hell for, dude?"

"For bunking down. We can't go any farther in this weather. It'd be suicide, bro."

"This coming from a brother who never, *ever* wears a fucking tee? You're fucking nuts, Slicks."

"Nuts and sensible all at once."

Diesel chuckled. "Well, I'm not so keen on hunkering down, dude. I ain't liking this place," he admitted.

"Don't be a fucking pussy, bro. It's just a fucking building," Slicks said, dismounting his bike. His gut was big but solid, and, for a tubby guy, he could move.

"What do you reckon, Roadblock?" Diesel said to the prospector of the bunch.

"Seems okay to me." Roadblock's voice was as deep as a ravine and twice as thick. His nickname was apt: at six-six and with a frame of over two hundred pounds, the man was mountain-sized. He constantly blamed his bulk on his family, as they hailed from Samoa. He would often say he ate too much as it was the Samoan in him, he was aggressive because it was the Samoan in him, he was overly friendly because . . . The list was endless.

He had bones through his nose and tribal tattoos all over his face. He was as scary to look at as he was big and bulging. How he got on his bike was beyond Diesel. The guy hadn't been with the Boas but maybe two months and was labelled a prospect because he was a beginner, but it wouldn't take him long to earn his colors.

"Cool. And what about you three?" Diesel said, addressing two more prospects and an old hand by the name of Gutbust who'd been shot more times than he cared to remember. Gutbust often joked that he shit and pissed lead every time he went to the toilet. He was a small man, the smallest in this posse, anyway. His hair was long and lank, and tattoos covered most of his body. He also looked painfully thin and was useless in a fight. But he was a shit-hot scout and navigator.

"Looks fine to me. I can't see why we're standing out here in the pissin' rain when we could be warming our arses inside that place though," Gutbust said.

"I fucking second that. Come on, puss." Slicks pushed past Diesel.

"After you, dogshit," Diesel retorted as Slicks pulled his sodden jeans up his arse to cover his offending, pimple-covered cheeks. He turned to Gutbust. "When we get in there, I want you to check the place out, dude. If we do end up staying here, I want to know what type of fucking shithole we're dossing at. *Comprende*?"

"Got it, cap," Gutbust said, nodding.

"What about you monkeys?" Diesel said to the newbies of the bunch.

"Of course. We've got your back, captain," they said, almost in unison.

Diesel nodded and caught up to Slicks.

"What the fuck has got you so spooked, dude?" Slicks asked.

"We just got to be careful. Who the fuck keeps a shithole like this open in the middle of nowhere? There's fuck-all here, bro. Even the cows have fucked off from the fields."

Slicks looked at the surrounding farmlands and smirked. "You've seen too many horror movies, mate."

"I'd call it street-smart," Diesel said. "We could be walking into another gang's hive. Who's to say this ain't a cookhouse? A crank farm? A fucking pimp house? The Flying Skulls have a crew stationed around this area, and you know how much of a cutthroat bunch they are. I'm glad you're carrying, Slicks, because all I've got is a hunting knife down my boot. We need to watch our arses when we get in there."

"What about Gutbust and the prospects?" Slicks asked. "Are they packin'?"

"I hope so."

The Boas gathered at the front door.

"I'll go in first," Gutbust said, "see if I can—"

A young female opened the door to the Rack and Cue. "Ooh, more people," she slurred. Alcohol had clearly started to fog her mind. She beckoned them. "Come in and dry off. My name's Mandy."

Diesel pushed to the front of the group. "Diesel," he said. "This is my crew."

"Hi, Diesel. Hi, crew," she said, waving back at them. She let slip a small giggle, which enticed a burp to follow. She set off without another word.

The bikers followed her into the pub single file, with Diesel right behind her. His eyes were glued to her perfect arse and he desperately wanted to give it a good, hard smack.

She stole a glance over her shoulder and caught him eyeing her rump. She tittered and batted her eyelashes.

A toothy grin cropped up on Diesel's face. *Maybe I was wrong about this place after all . . .*

They entered the bar area. Another man and woman sat around a table full of empty bottles and glasses.

"This is Grace," Mandy said, stepping to the other woman and putting her arms around her. "My good friend."

"And you?" Diesel said, nodding at the suited guy who didn't look as though he belonged.

"My name's Charlie, mate," he said, offering a hand to Diesel, who shook it with an iron grip. "My car took a spill just down the road. I headed here for help. Fat load of good that did me. The hardwired phone isn't working, and neither is my cell."

"And you two?" Diesel asked Mandy. "What brings you pair to a place like this?"

"We were camping in the area and got caught in this awful rain. And, just like Charlie, we stumbled on this pub."

"Cozy," Diesel said, fixing his gaze on the roaring fire. "Slicks, grab that table over by the fireplace. I'll get the drinks."

"We're staying?" Slicks asked.

Diesel beamed. "Damn right we are. The party's just getting started, my friend."

CHAPTER SEVEN

IN THE DARKNESS OF THE CELLAR, the floorboards above her creaked and groaned. She looked up, and sawdust lightly sprinkled her bondage fatigues. Laughter and chatter brightened her eyes, causing her to smile beneath the mask she wore.

The bare bulb she stood under swayed softly due to being splashed by a gush of blood, which dripped and spattered the floor with each movement. It also dotted the workbench she was using to dissect their latest victim.

Bluebottles clung to the only window inside the underground space, buzzing, their fat bodies covering every inch of dirt-stained glass. Maggots rolled off chunks of carcasses, which lay scattered about the room and hung from hooks suspended from the ceiling.

The stench which manifested from the walls of the old pub would make most people gag and vomit. But not Baby. She adored the smell. Lapped it up.

Lowering her gaze, she eyed the broken body before her, the one Doc had prepped. The man had come in earlier and threatened Porky. There had been no choice other than to take him down.

The memory of bludgeoning the man's face repeatedly with the butt of a cue made Baby wet. She'd wanted to continue slamming his face until nothing but liquid remained, but Porky had made her stop. *And Porky must be obeyed,* she acknowledged, feeling her moist pussy dry somewhat.

She studied the decapitated body. The neck. The roughness of where Doc's saw had cut through the throat and severed the head. A light breeze blew from the drains in the room and Baby's skin prickled with gooseflesh under her tight PVC suit. Her nipples stiffened as she wound her fingers around the exposed cords jutting from the man's stump.

She retracted her fingers and stuck her leather-clad digits into her mouth, sucking them until every droplet of gore was removed from the PVC, the black material shiny and spot-free again. Every move she made forced the leather suit to squeak and squeal. It felt good against her flesh. Cool.

Savoring the flavor in her mouth, Baby traced her fingers down the sides of her face, to her jawline. She groaned at her own feeble touch. She shifted her hand to her breast, molding the impressive tit and clasping the nipple between forefinger and thumb the best she could in the slippery clothing. She got her free hand moving, which helped ply and play the fabric along with her tits.

Finished with her top half, Baby moved her hands down her body and lingered around her abdominal area. She caressed her flat stomach and rubbed her curvy sides. Then one hand found the damp area between her legs. The feel of the faux leather pressed against her wetness made her shiver.

Baby bit her lower lip and rode it out, until the heat took over. Now she wished she hadn't killed the fucker who lay dead on her table. Sometimes, Porky let her play with the meat while it was alive and kickin', but this kill had not been part of their plan. They needed to get rid of this body as soon as possible, which meant there was no time for partying.

Baby let out a small yelp of pleasure and stopped rubbing herself. She turned her attention back to the body, arranging it so it was spread-eagled on her metallic worktable. She then stepped to her wall of tools, hand brushing the blood-stained teeth of her chainsaw. Her mind flooded with fond memories of using the wood-slicing instrument on past victims. *Oh, how they'd screamed*, she thought. A tremor of excitement passed through her, but she managed to control herself. She couldn't use the robust tool now. The people upstairs would hear its motor revving and sawing.

She moved on to stroke the handle of her rusted scythe. The thing hadn't been used since her daddy hacked the hedges at the back of the pub moons ago. The corroded blade would not cut through hot butter, let alone bone and sinew. The thing only served as a token to the memory of her dad these days.

Baby's hand slipped from the scythe and brushed a grinder, but that would be no good either. It was loud, like the chainsaw. Cumbersome, too.

She sighed and eyed the array of knives and daggers she'd collected over the years. Her favorite among them was the Hitler Youth Knife. The weapon had been stripped from one of the German youths in the Great War by her great granddad. The black-as-coal handle was smooth, with a swastika embedded in the center of it. She only used that particular steel on special occasions. Unfortunately, this wasn't one of them.

Beyond the impressive line-up of steel hung a cleaver. She clenched and unclenched the tacky handle repeatedly, then hefted it off its hook on the wall. It felt good in her hand. Heavy. Threatening. And far less noisy than the other instruments she preferred to use.

Baby turned about-face and thwacked the butcher's instrument deep into the thigh of the body. Blood squirted the midriff of her outfit, reminding her of male ejaculation and how easy it was to please a hard cock.

Leaving the cleaver buried in the leg, she wheeled around again to her arsenal. Pliers, tweezers, bolt cutters, snips, gardening forks, shears, hammers, skewers, and all kinds of nasty, body-wrecking weapons lined her wall. The fourteen-inch beast which hung alone caught her eye though. It was separated from the rest because of its sheer superiority. Even over the chainsaw, it was much more dominant, powerful. It commanded her like a masterful dominatrix would. Called to her. Wanted her.

Baby unhooked the impressive machete, which she kept in top-notch condition by sharpening and polishing it every night even if it hadn't been used that day or recently. It was her pride and joy.

She spun to the body once again and brought the machete down, severing the hand at the wrist. Without taking a breath, she attacked again, this time chopping through the elbow in one clean blow. She then hacked the rest of the limb off at the shoulder before moving to the other side of the body. Once both arms had been cut from the torso and sectioned, Baby used a tiny pair of shears with a wide mouth to snip the fingers from the hands. After that, she placed the diced bits onto a massive tray.

Feeling moist again, she lifted one of the dead man's legs into the air so his toes were in line with her eyes, then proceeded to slice them off. She placed them on the tray with the other dismembered pieces and went to work on the other set of piggies. After severing both feet, Baby hacked through the knees, adding them to the meat platter.

Picking up the massive metal tray, which felt light to her, Baby strode into the room opposite. Nothing occupied the space apart from a dumbwaiter. She placed the prized meat in the center of the makeshift lift, gave the bell a ring, and sent the first load up to Porky.

The lift clamored to a halt.

The intercom squawked at her side. "Baby, where's the rest of this fucker?"

"On its way," she said, her voice soft, words clipped to perfection.

"Good. That's very good, girl," he said. "I'll have this lot chopped, bagged, and sealed, ready for shipment tomorrow. Champ can take it up to west country in the morning."

Baby stalked back into her room, gathered up the torso, and returned to the dumbwaiter. She stuffed the meat inside it, slammed the door shut, rung the bell, and sent the remainder of the body skyward, all the while grinning and touching herself.

* * *

Porky beamed at the steel tray filled with various body parts ranging from toes to elbows. He removed it from the tiny space, closed the door, and sent the lift back down to Baby, who, as always, had done a fine job chopping the corpse into manageable amounts.

He carried the platter of flesh to his stainless-steel table, which had been immaculately polished to a military gleam that morning. Porky spied his unblemished reflection in the surface. "Cleanliness is next to godliness," he uttered, placing the load down. "Can't be making my famous Porky Pie in filth-ridden conditions, now can I?"

Next, he set a deep pan filled with water onto a ring of the stove and cranked it on. Besides the cooking implement, a large freezer, and some spice racks, there wasn't much else inside the room. The walls were stark white. A hint of sanitizer lay heavy in the air. When Porky returned to his pristine table, his white wellies made horrendous squeaking noises on the scrubbed tiles, paying tribute to his scouring efforts.

Before he could unload the tray, the bell rang again. He rushed to the dumbwaiter and was welcomed by the sticky torso. He removed it and set it onto the table next to the rest of the body parts as fast as he could.

As he started picking through the fingers and toes, a burst of laughter from the bar caught his ear. He smiled. The pub hadn't been busy at this hour of the day in years.

The water on the stove bubbled and gurgled with heat, so he added the fingers and toes to the large cooking pot. Almost upon submersion, the skin on the digits melted from bone. Porky sniffed the trail of steam rising from the boiling concoction, filling his lungs with the aroma. He grabbed some spices off his rack and sprinkled the contents from three jars into the pot.

"Ah, yes," he said, inhaling anew. "What a delicious smell. I'll have some pies on sale before I know it." Another burst of laughter erupted from the bar. *Right on time too. With this weather and the drinks flowing, they'll be here until the end*, he thought, gaffing at his little inside joke. *Yes, the pub is filling up nicely. This could be the best harvest yet.*

Taking the hefty meat cleaver and butcher knife from the shelf under the table, Porky set about slicing the meat into cutlets for bagging. The price for human meat through their channel was insane. The organs, of course, went for much, much more. It was how they survived these days. What with the road closed and most of their regulars dead, it was hard keeping the old place going, and calling last orders on the Rack and Cue was not something Porky wanted to entertain. He'd come close to selling the joint a few times over the years, but his promise to his dear brother had been enough to sway him.

He could almost hear his brother's voice over the noise of his cleaver chopping through the flesh and bone on his table. Tears welled in the corners of his eyes.

Richard "Skinner" Baby had loved the place, though not near as much as he had loved his little girl, Baby. "Promise me, Pork," Richard had croaked. "Promise me you'll never sell the old place. Whatever it takes, you keep the Cue going, little brother. Doc and Champ will help run it, along with Baby when she's of age. You have to pass it on to her. I'll just be sitting it out . . ."

The disease had set in roughly ten months prior to that, Porky recalled, and those had been the last words out of the condemned man's mouth. Porky remembered, too, how Baby had folded to the loss and become withdrawn for months on end. How she'd started wearing masks to hide her face.

Yes, those were tough times, he thought.

Porky stopped to wipe the loose tears from his cheeks and eyes and pushed the memories aside. He bagged the meat he had already chopped and stored it in the freezers. After that, he went to the bubbling pot and gave it a stir. The meat was boiling nicely.

Back at the table, he gathered the stripped bones and took them to the back door which led to the rear of the pub. The garden was closed off by high walls on either side. The yard had once been used as a beer garden but was now the home of Hugo and Former Lee, two massive Doberman pinschers. They gnawed through bones like babies munched through rusks.

Both dogs whined, bounced, and leapt as Porky advanced with food.

"Down, boys. Down!" he commanded. "Got some lovely treats here for ya, lads." He threw the bones and the dogs ran for them. "There'll be more where those came from, soon as I can carve through the rest of it." He smiled as the mutts tore through their meal.

Once inside and chopping meat again, Porky let his mind slip back to his brother. Richard had kept a neat and tidy pub which boasted an excellent range of ales and foods, and it had been free of corruption. However, the year Richard became ill, the main road to the pub closed. A new motorway was built. Trade dried up. The rooms upstairs which had once housed guests and weary travelers lay empty. Funds withered, and soon they were dipping into their savings to keep the place afloat. This spurred the family into action.

Ideas of dart and card tournaments, karaoke, curry nights, and pie-eating contests attracted little or no attention at all. What income they made from such mediocre nights went back into the pot, but their debt quickly swallowed it. Then Baby came up with the idea of holding a pool tournament to end all tournaments. She suggested they muster all the money they could—savings, earnings, personal funds—and put it into a kitty. The winner would walk away with the lot, but only if they could beat Porky's son, the Champ.

However, the sales from food and drink still wouldn't have been enough to keep them afloat even if the tournament brought a large audience. Porky had done some research and stumbled on an article on how people were selling human organs on the black market and making thousands from it. It had been easy enough to find a buyer from there. He had propositioned his family, told them how they could set the pub up in such a way that they could butcher the losers one by one without the rest being any wiser. They had agreed without a second thought.

Porky smiled, recalling how happy they'd been at the turnout of the first Porky Pool Tournament. More than fifteen have-a-go pool players turned up. None walked out of the Cue with the cash . . . or their life.

When the night had finally been done and dusted, nobody had suspected a thing. The pub had been cleaned of all traces of their activity and nothing could lead back to them. Not that the police ever ventured out there anyway.

After that initial success, the pool competition kicked on and was now in its eighth year. They didn't advertise the tournament; they didn't want to draw too much attention. Besides, there was no need to promote or market it, as the money they made had kept them from sinking completely.

Hey, it may be dirty money, Porky thought, pushing the memories aside and focusing instead on his pies, *but it's making us rich, rich, rich*! He laughed until his gut hurt.

By the time he finished cutting and packing the haul, the meat inside the scalding pot had turned to mush. He disposed of any waste by tossing it to the dogs, then returned to the stove, cranked the knob to Off, scooped the meat out of the pot, and put it into a deep glass bowl. He pulled the bones from the tender fingers and toes with little effort, then mashed the contents to a complete pulp.

As he placed the pâté into crusts he'd prepared earlier that day, voices in the adjoining room stilled his hands. Some didn't sound like the patrons he'd already opened the door for. How had they gotten inside?

Standing there in shock, Porky almost pissed himself when the bell on the bar dinged in a frantic manner.

"Shop?" yelled a strange voice. "*Shop?!*"

Porky shuffled from the kitchen and entered the bar. A smile grew across his face when he sighted bikers in his pub—six of them in total. They looked wet, thirsty, and weary.

My, my, what a crowd we'll have this evening, Porky thought, almost unable to suppress his cackles.

CHAPTER EIGHT

Danny sat in the passenger seat of the expensive Ford Transit van, desperately trying to see where the Boas had vanished to. *How can this be? We were right on their fucking tail!*

Well, not immediately on their tail. They'd hung back a mile or so. But still . . . It was a straight road. No on- or off-ramps. No turns. No diversions. No shortcuts to the main motorway.

"Where the fuck have they gone?" Danny barked. "This isn't the fucking Bermuda Triangle. This is the fucking Midlands, for Christ's sake."

"Calm down, Danny. We'll find them," Clive said.

"Don't tell *me* to calm down, Clive. We balls this up and the captain will have our bollocks in a vice."

"No way. We've been working this case too long for him to pull the plug," Clive said. "Besides—"

"Besides *nothing*," Danny spat back. "If we don't come up with something this time, he'll not only pull the plug on the operation, he'll take our badges too."

"You think he's on *their* payroll, don't you, Sarge?"

The cold from outside seemed to seep in, causing a chill to stir the air.

"Have I ever said that?" Danny snapped, banging his bear-like fist on the dash. Clive didn't flinch, and Danny supposed he was used to his intemperance and anger. They'd been partners ever since they left the police academy many years ago. He knew Clive would take a bullet and a beating for him.

"You didn't have to say anything, mate. The silence was enough."

Danny harrumphed. "Why don't you do something constructive, like find out where the biker filth went? How about that, instead of filling your head with bullshit."

"I am!"

"Good. Because I haven't dragged myself all the way from the Cardiff nick just for some boy scout mission into the woods. I want convictions this time. I want Jason 'Diesel' Summer doing hard fucking time. Life, if I get my way."

"You really think he'd give up Dutch and the rest of the boys?"

"I don't care. I'll take as many of them down as I can. The photos we took of them with Grizzly in Manchester's a good start. We know they were concealing and trading illegal firearms back there."

"But did we get any of it?"

"We reeled off snap upon snap of them all together. We must have caught something."

"You know it's going to take hard evidence to put these guys away, Danny. The captain isn't going to act on it if it's not."

Rage peeked from behind Danny's pupils. "He'll have to act on it this time," he said, almost choking as he frantically shot the words out of his mouth. "I'll go above the old cunt's head if I have to."

"Here we go again," Clive said, doing a little huff-laugh.

"What? Don't think I'll have the nuts to do it?" Danny paused. "Well?" he pushed, but Clive didn't rise to the bait.

"Hey," Bobby yelled like an excited child on Christmas morning, poking his head between his two colleagues from the back seat. "I see their bikes. Look!"

It was difficult to see anything. The rain was coming down harder than Danny had ever seen, turning the early afternoon into a black and colorless one. It was so dark, it felt like ten in the evening.

"What the hell are you doing away from your equipment, Bobby? For fuck's sake, man! Get back on your console. We—"

"I can't pick anything up on it, Sarge," Bobby whined.

"Then what the hell have you been doing back there?" Danny snapped, turning to glare at him.

Bobby's apple-cheeked face had turned a dark shade of red, his glasses misting over. "I . . . I—"

"Cut it out, Danny," Clive chirped in. "Stop messing with his head."

"And who the hell rattled your cage?" Danny said, glowering. "Pull the van over here. Get in that lay-by. *Here*!"

"That's not a lay-by, Danny," Clive insisted. "That's just where the road has been pushed back against the hedge. It has probably disintegrated over the years with the weather and poor upkeep."

"Who the fuck are you now? Michael Fish?" Danny said, a half-smile on his face.

Clive huffed and pulled the van to one side. The tires slid in the muck but the vehicle eventually came to a stop. As the rain continued to come down in sheets and pelt the now stationary van, Danny and Clive both looked out the driver's side window— just in time to catch a glimpse of the six outlaws entering a shady-looking pub.

"What the hell is that place?" Danny wanted to know.

"It looks like a pub," Clive said.

Danny spotted a sign. "The Rack and Cue. Looks like a right shithole. I wouldn't be surprised if those fucking Boas are up to no good in there. It's probably another drop zone."

"Maybe. But wouldn't they have dropped in there on the way up?" Clive said.

"Yep, it's a pub," Bobby piped in. "Built in the early 1800s."

"Hey Poindexter, put a sock in it."

"I was just saying, Danny," Bobby said, his tone sulky.

"I have no idea why they wouldn't have stopped here on the way up, Clive. Maybe the greasy fucks know we are on to them?"

"That's a possibility," Clive agreed, nodding. "What do you want to do? Stakeout?"

Danny peered at the ramshackle establishment. "No, we're going in."

"Are you out of your mind?" Clive asked, raising his voice. "They could be armed to the teeth in there. It could be a Boa den, fortress, or crank factory. Hell, it could even be a whorehouse or all the above. We—"

"We can't what, Clive? Get our dicks out and show them who's fucking boss? Yes, we can. I'll have the fucking place shut down and every one of those sons of bitches behind bars," Danny said.

"You always did have a way with words," Clive said, shaking his head.

"Right. Okay, we'll stake the building for a bit. See who comes and goes," Danny said. "If the place appears to be what it is, then we'll *think* about going in."

"Just three guys looking for a pint of beer?" Bobby said.

"They may sniff us out, you know, Sarge," Clive said, ignoring Bobby. "Those bastards have a good nose for coppers."

"I know. You're right. We're just going to have to try and box clever. Go in there all rowdy. Throw them off guard."

"Push them into doing something stupid?" Bobby tried again.

"Yeah," Danny said, his steely gaze never leaving the building. "But first we sit and wait and see what happens."

"Well, no point in wasting the petrol or battery then." With that, Clive turned off the lights and killed the engine, cutting off the heater and radio inside the van. He nuzzled into his seat.

Silence followed. Time stretched in front of them.

Bobby set about fiddling with his equipment in the back, occasionally tutting or muttering aloud.

Danny retrieved some trashy Sunday newspaper from the glove compartment and turned to the third page. He glued his eyes to the young brunette bombshell, shifting in his seat to get cozy.

* * *

The sound of rain bounding off the roof of the van was deafening but calming. Clive had always been soothed by stormy weather, even as a child. It had never scared or worried him in the slightest.

He felt his eyes close as he tuned in on the hammering rhythm. *What the hell am I doing out here? I should be at home with my feet up, not being dragged halfway across cow country. Jan was right: I should have given this shit up two years ago. Instead, I let myself get roped back into it by Danny.*

But he could never break the partnership or turn his back on Danny. Clive understood how badly he wanted to bust these fucks, maybe go out on a high himself. It was either that, or Danny would be found dead in a ditch somewhere riddled with Boa bullets.

Clive threw that notion out of his head, fast. The thought of Danny dead was a no-no. If Danny were to die, then so would he. He would follow Danny to the very end. Bobby, on the other hand, would pack up shop and fuck off at the first sign of danger, but not before shitting a brick first.

Nope, Danny and I are in this to the end, together. Even if these biker clowns are our downfall.

He looked over at Danny and smiled as the man he had been partners with for thirty years continued ogling the page-three beauty. "You wouldn't like it if she was your daughter, mate, now would you?" Clive teased.

"Let's not start that again."

Clive smirked. "Come on, now, Danny, you know how your ex-wife felt about you looking at such images."

"That's it!" Danny gave the paper a hard shake and turned to the next page.

Clive chuckled and stared out at the rain once again. *Poor Silvia*, he thought. If any woman had suffered, it had been her. Danny had hardly ever gone home; he practically lived at the station. The man's brain was constantly tuned into the job. Clive would be surprised if the Sarge ever slept. Still, he was a great guy. Salt of the earth. No matter how big or small the favor—gardening tips to relationship problems—Clive trusted the man with his life.

"I think I'm picking something up, guys," Bobby said from behind.

"You mean your shit equipment is actually working in this godawful weather, Spock?" Danny said.

"Ease up on him, Sarge," Clive said. "He's doing his best."

"Always the voice of reason, ain't ya? You're definitely the bitch in this relationship, sugar tits." Danny blew Clive a kiss.

"Danny, I'm serious. Listen, will you?" Bobby said with a raised voice, which surprised Clive.

Danny lifted one eyebrow and craned in his seat to face Bobby.

"I managed to get close enough to Diesel to plant a bug on him. I've been trying to pick the signal up since we left Manchester, but the weather's been interfering with it."

"But you never left the van!" Danny said.

"I did," Bobby said.

"What, when you took a piss?"

Bobby smiled.

"You sneaky bastard," Danny said with a chuckle.

"Listen," Bobby said.

Inside the van, the three men listened intently on what was being said inside the supposed pub.

"I can hardly hear it," Danny complained.

"Shh!" Bobby scolded. "They're talking about the deal in Manchester. About the gun exchange."

"Are you recording?" Clive asked.

Bobby nodded.

"Good," Danny said. "These fuckers are going down this time. They ain't slipping away again."

"Now they're talking about the Manchester Boas going to war tonight with a rival gang. Or something along those lines."

"Well?" Danny urged.

"I . . . I'm losing the signal."

"Oh, for fuck's sake!" Danny yelled and thumped his door.

"Look, this gear isn't exactly top-of-the-range stuff, Sarge," Bobby said, his chubby face burning bright again, glasses misting once more.

Clive blinked rapidly as something caught his attention. "Danny, there's someone watching us . . . I think we've been made."

"What? Where?"

"There," Clive said, pointing. "There was someone standing in that window on the second floor."

"There's nobody there, Clive. Don't you go falling apart on me like Bobby's two-bit radio here, pal."

"I'm telling you—"

"Shit. I see them," Danny said.

As Clive joined Danny in gawking through the driver's side window, he noticed the curtains part on the second-floor window. A large figure stood looking down at their van.

"Let's move," Clive said, going for the key in the ignition.

"Fuck that," Danny said. "Are you carrying?"

"Always."

"Bobby, you stay here and keep your ear open. The first sign of any trouble in there, you get your fucking arse out of here."

"Where are *we* going?" Clive asked, already dreading the response.

"In there," Danny said, nodding at the Cue. "We're going to find out just what type of Boa funhouse that place is."

CHAPTER NINE

Danny and Clive disappeared into the building after the front door opened to their loud knocks. The person who let them in lingered in the entranceway and Bobby ducked out of view.

Five minutes later, Bobby poked his head up. He peeked out the driver's side window. To his amusement, nobody was standing watch any longer.

They never spotted me! he thought triumphantly, pushing his glasses back up his nose. *Good.* He stood and went to his equipment. *Now I need to try and keep track on what's going on in there.*

He pulled his stool from under the desk, which held a crackling radio and headset, a snub-nosed .38 Smith & Wesson, empty coffee cups, rumpled paperwork, walkie-talkies, and an assortment of pens, pencils, and sweet wrappers. He sat his plump arse down and put the headset on, fiddling with the dials before him, trying to pick up a signal.

"Come on, come on," Bobby mouthed, fine-tuning the dials and knobs. "Easy does it. Easy, easy." Sweat dribbled down his forehead and his tongue protruded as he fiddled with the frequency. A smile tore across his face as Danny's and Clive's voices filled his ears. The bugs he'd fitted to the inside of their lapels were working, but they still weren't coming in clear enough to be decipherable. "Almost got you . . ."

A sharp thump to the side of the van made him jump and his fingers slipped. The large radio dial rotated madly, the signal lost.

"Fuck!" he yelled, snatching the headset from off his head and slamming it on the desk. "What the actual hell?" He leapt from his seat, causing the stool to slide backward and collapse. It hit the floor behind him. He stood there listening but could hear nothing aside from rain welting the sides, roof, front, and rear of the van.

Gooseflesh clawed its way up his arms and back. *What the hell was that? Did I imagine . . . ?*

The damage to the side of the van in front of him was evident. He ran his fingertips over the humped dent. "Danny? Clive? This is *not* fucking fun—"

A second crash to the opposite side of the van made him spin on his heels. Another dimple appeared in the van's bodywork. As he gaped at the fresh wound, a third, fourth, and fifth appeared alongside the second, stitching a line of indentations all along that side.

What the fuck is going on out there? It can't be Danny and Clive messing around. They wouldn't cause—

A loud crack and shattering glass cut his musings short. He spun to the front of the van in time to see the passenger wing mirror disintegrate. Fragments of mirror mingled with rain as they were hurled along the road. Bits of plastic and wiring followed. Then, the thunderous bang of a popping tire resounded over the pounding rain, and the passenger's side of the van sagged to one side.

"Oh, shit," Bobby muttered. "Somebody doesn't want us to leave."

He pushed his glasses up his nose with one hand, his other instinctively reaching for the baseball bat propped against his com desk. The thick, steel shaft of the slugger felt tacky from the blood of many a poor bastard Danny had smacked a confession out of in the back of this very van over the years.

Bobby grasped it tightly with both hands and brought it close to his chest. "Whoever's out there, you best fuck off. This is a police operation you are interfering with. You *will* be prosecuted for obstruct—"

The van rocked violently, making Bobby drop the bat. He snatched up the .38 and gazed into the one good wing mirror but couldn't see anyone outside. He drew the hammer back on the snub-nosed gun and drew a breath, facing the back doors. He had to go out there, scared or not.

"I'm warning you, I'm armed!" Bobby yelled at the top of his tiny voice.

The rocking ceased.

Bobby smiled. Lowering his gun, he shuffled toward the rear door. He pinched his bladder tight and placed his ear against the metal, trying to block out the sound of rain. Footfalls squelched in the muck and splashed in water. Somebody was out there.

He gulped and pulled the handle, releasing the lock. Bobby eased the door outward and leveled his gun, ready to get a clean shot off. "You're getting it now, bastard." He pushed the door open wide. "Freeze!"

But no one was there. All he could see was the slanting rain. It bounded off the road and hissed as it left behind its watery mark.

Bobby's body sagged as he dropped his guard. He brought the gun back to his face and relaxed his stance.

An engine grumbled in the near distance and a single, solitary light approached. It disappeared here and there as it maneuvered bends and dips in the road.

What now? And where the hell is the fucker who was messing with the van?

Bobby jumped to the ground and poked his head round both sides. Nobody was there. *What is going on around here?*

The grumbling sound became louder. Closer. Bobby could now see what was approaching: a motorbike.

Shit! Thinking the biker another Boa, Bobby turned to scramble back into the van but slipped, his footing lost on the wet sill. He fell backward and onto the road. His shirt and trousers soaked through immediately, and his glasses jumped off his face as the gun sprang from his grip. He rolled in the muck, cursing, blindly searching for his lost items.

The roar of the engine became deafening as the bike rolled to a stop in front of Bobby. Through slanted vision, he saw a blurry boot lower the kickstand. The steel hog tilted to one side, the engine killed. A fag flicked from gloved fingers.

"Looking for this, cop?" a voice spat. It was too soft, too gentle to belong to an outlaw.

A gun hammer clicked into place as something more fragile was shoved at his face.

Bobby groped for his glasses and slowly put them on. Finally able to focus, he huffed out a laugh and his hands dropped to his sides, his palms slapping the legs of his soggy trousers. "Huh, I might have known it was you, Jack. You're never too far behind your boy Diesel, are you?"

The big man got off his bike and stalked forward. He didn't lower the gun, instead keeping it pointed at Bobby's chest. "You fucking *pigs* think you got it all worked out, don't you? I've been tailing you pricks since we left Cardiff."

Bobby's mouth sagged. Sarge was right. These arseholes were getting inside information from someone. "Which fuck in my department is snitching?"

Jack laughed, nose to nose with Bobby. He was heavily scarred and tattooed. Ink covered his face, neck, shoulders, and arms. A patch covered one of his eyes. He was a lieutenant in Dutch's army and had been for many years.

He pressed the cold muzzle of the .38 to Bobby's throat. "You honestly think I'd tell a piece of shit like you something like that?" He spat in Bobby's face, who almost threw up from the impact of the green-yellow phlegm. It reeked of tobacco and whisky.

"What are you going to do?" Bobby said, all the while smiling. "Shoot me?"

A robust elbow hammered the side of Bobby's jaw, which sent him sprawling once again. Some of his knocked-out teeth bounced off the van and rattled to a halt in the mire.

"*Shoot* you? I'm going to soften you up first, my boy," Jack said, firing a steel-toed boot into Bobby's ribs. A fierce crack ensued.

"Argh, fuck," Bobby cried in pain as his hand instinctively went to his injured side. "Just fucking kill me, if that's what—"

A powerful fist smacked Bobby in the already wounded jaw. This time, it broke. The blow flattened him to the ground, preventing him from crawling away.

* * *

Jack lowered to one knee and wrenched Bobby's head back by the hair. He then repeatedly and savagely bounded the man's head off the van's bumper, until a massive split raced across his forehead.

Jack shoved Bobby's face into the sludge and stood once again. He stamped on the injured man's back with glee. "I'm going to bust your fucking spine, little man. Put you in a fucking wheelchair. Make you a fucking cabbage!" he roared over the rain. The saturated bandana atop his head clung to his skull.

Jack stepped back and held his sides, catching his breath. Pounding filth like this fucker gave him nothing but joy, but it also winded him these days. *The smoking probably doesn't help, mind.* "I guess pummeling aresholes like you comes at a price, Bobby. And when I'm finished bouncing your head off this road, me and my boys are going to rip Danny and Clive apart. We're going to redecorate the countryside in their blood, guts, and brains."

He lit a cigarette as he stood over the fallen man, then booted him three times in the face. Bobby's left eye socket collapsed. His screams bubbled and frothed as blood flowed freely from his mouth.

Jack watched the fat man squirm on the ground. "That's right, dickhead. You dig around in the filth, little piggy," he said, oinking and squealing like a hog. Though he didn't want to waste one, he bent and stubbed his burning fag on Bobby's cheek, then kicked in his other eye.

"My eyes, my fucking eyes!" Bobby cried out. "Help! Help me! Danny! Clive! Hel—"

Jack struck Bobby's side once again, cracking more ribs. One splintered and poked out of Bobby's flesh, peeking through his shirt. The poor bastard didn't know whether to grab a destroyed eye or clutch his ruptured side.

"Ha-ha! Suffer, you filthy fuck," Jack said. He lit another cigarette, but this time he enjoyed the tobacco, taking long, hard drags of the Mayfair. "Maybe I'll shoot your knees out next, Bobby. What do you think? Or stomp your back until I hear that big ol' thick backbone crack? Choices, choices."

"Danny!" Bobby yelled, his cry pitiful but loud. Tears burst from the battered man. "Help!"

"Shut. The fuck. Up!" Jack snarled, ferociously kicking Bobby in the mouth until he was certain he'd knocked all of his teeth out. "Now, where was I? Oh, yeah: choices." Jack leaned gingerly against his bike, inhaling his nicotine poison while running through the different ways he could maim Bobby. The fat fuck deserved it. All coppers did.

Bobby somehow got to hands and knees and crawled around the side of the van.

Jack chuckled at the lame attempt to escape. "Where do you think you're going, butty boy? Leaving so soon? Party pooper!"

He stalked after his prey with a spring in his step, following Bobby's mud trail. He drew the .38 from the waistband of his jeans and clicked the hammer home. "Ain't nothing like the smell of gun oil and pistol smoke," Jack quipped, sighting the blubbering man. He unsurprisingly hadn't gotten far and had collapsed again, flailing in watery sludge.

He placed the muzzle to the back of Bobby's right knee and squeezed the trigger. The hammer slammed down and the bullet smashed its way into Bobby's flesh.

Jack didn't shilly-shally. He shot Bobby's other knee, then clubbed the man repeatedly about the head with the stock of the .38. He beat Bobby into a semi-conscious state before stopping to catch his breath. "Nothing better than making a fucking pig suffer," he said, and again spat on Bobby. "Now to wreck all that shit in your van. No doubt you and your boys have some good shit on tape of the little deal that went down in Manchester, yeah?"

Bobby lay motionless on the floor.

"You won't go *running* out on me, will you, Bobby? We'll still have time for more fun." Jack laughed, stepped to the rear of the police van, and pulled the doors open simultaneously.

"What the fuck?" The cigarette which had been pinched tight between his teeth sagged and fell from his mouth. It hit his boots and spun off, plopping on the wet ground. The cherry fizzled out.

Towering above him was a woman clad in black leather. Only her glowing eyes were visible, as a zippered gimp mask covered her face. The only indication to it being a female was the jutting tits.

"Well, well, what do we have here?" Jack said, the shock in his tone replaced by excitement. "You're a big one, ain't ya, beaut?" He started to clamber into the back of the van but paused as a flicker of electricity caught his eye. The inside was destroyed, all the communication equipment totally mangled. The wrecked console hissed and hiccupped smoke and blue sparks.

"Jesus," he muttered. "Why would you . . . ?"

The huge woman walked toward him, the steel bat raised high above her head.

"Fuck!" he said, raising the .38.

* * *

Before the man managed to level the gun, Baby smacked him across the side of the face with the bat. His shot went wide and shattered the windshield behind her. Even though her blow was hard and rocked him, the man didn't go down.

"You fucking bitch," he spat. Blood and bits of tooth surfed out of his mouth on crimson saliva. "Now you're going to fucking get it."

She smashed the bat down on his wrist, busting it in multiple places. The man finally went to ground. Baby capitalized, pulverizing the biker about the head, back, sides, and face. Bones cracked. Blood drained out of punctures.

Once the bat became dented and useless, Baby went to the rear of the van and picked up her Nazi knife. She gripped the haft, blade pointed downward, rounded on the man once again, and buried the knife in his privates.

Baby ripped open his scrotum and dug his balls out of his split sack. His whimpering and crying gave her great pleasure as she placed both testicles in her mouth and savagely chewed them up.

She ended him by sticking her knife in his throat and ripping his gullet out. His gargling crescendo was loud and soggy as he struggled for his life on the floor. This prompted Baby to then stab at his heart in quick succession.

Standing, she swallowed her mouthful and stalked around the van to the fallen policeman, who had managed to crawl off into the distance. It didn't take her long to catch up to him.

Baby slashed at his back, her swipes uncalculated but brutal. She toyed with him, eventually becoming bored. Straddling the cop, she yanked his head back and began sawing through his scalp. Once it was free, she pressed the tip of her knife to his throat and eased the steel in, right up to its hilt.

She pulled it back out quickly, delighted in the short, sharp gush of blood which squirted free. She wanted to rub her cunt but knew she had to clean her mess before someone passed by.

Baby started with the bike. She replaced its kickstand before pushing it over to the side of the road. A mass amount of foliage decorated this section of motorway, so she rolled it into the thicket.

The greenery devoured the metal beast, which satisfied her.

She returned to the dead biker, grabbed him by either side of his open denim jacket, and hoisted him off the floor and onto her shoulder like a sack of coal. She then carried him over to the rear entrance of the pub. Once there, she used the single metal door to gain entrance to the garden of the Cue.

She heaved the carcass onto the cobbled flooring. "Away, dogs. Away! He's mine," she yelled at them, growling. This sent the mutts back into their wooden home. She smiled and returned to the carnage.

After scooping up the ruined policeman, Baby threw his remains on top of the other. She opened the big double doors and went to retrieve the van. She started the engine and drove it over to the Cue, parking it in the garden—such vehicles always came in handy.

She looked out onto the road and smiled. The area was spotless. *Nobody will be any the wiser*, she thought as she closed, bolted, and wrapped chains around the heavy double doors leading onto their property.

"Oh, Baby! What have you gone and done this time?" Porky said from the back door. He shook his head and smiled. "What am I going to do with you? Look at the state of you! Blood all down you. Get in here." He pointed at the stacked bodies. "And bring them with you."

CHAPTER TEN

Rigs's brow scrunched in concentration. "What the hell?" he mumbled. A massive building loomed ahead of them, set just off the road. It was a fortress-like structure with trees and shrubbery flanking it. A few empty fields lay beyond.

Iain followed his gaze. "Ooh, it's a pub!" he said, all chirpy and wide-eyed.

"It can't be. This road looks as though it's unused, and we haven't seen anyone pass by in what, an hour or so?"

"Maybe. But the place looks open to me. That's a light on in one of the windows, innit? It's like a bloody beacon in this bleak weather."

True enough, Rigs thought, spying the glow. *It must have one hell of a local trade—doesn't appear to be anything else around here. How does the place even survive?*

"Pull over, mate. I could do with slaking my thirst with a pint of something long and cool," Iain said.

"All right," Rigs said, resigned to their short trip turning into an overnighter. A pint sounded like a good reprieve from his frustration.

He pulled into and halted in the building's car park, noting the motorbikes nearby, the dilapidated state of the establishment. It was indeed a pub, called the Rack and Cue if the sign was up to date, but it didn't appear inviting.

A large silhouette on the side of the building drew his attention. "Did you see that?" He pointed. "Over there."

"Huh? What are you going on about now? You were just asking me about Wales versus France."

"I'm sure I saw someone milling around. A *big* fucking someone, too."

"What? Are you nuts?" Iain said, scoffing. "Who would be crazy enough to be running around in this weather?"

Rigs shook his head. "You're probably right. Maybe I've been driving for too long."

"I think maybe you've been watching too many shit horror films, matey. Making you screw-bally." Iain tapped one side of his head with a finger. "You've got a bit of brain melt on the go, boyo."

"I think you should take over the driving when we get back on the road."

"I think I should, too."

"And just what is that supposed to mean?"

"Well, this place is hardly the Ritz—more like the *pits*!"

Rigs smiled. "Regular comedian on this trip, ain't ya? All that sleep, see. It's woken your brain from its five-year slumber," he retorted, his gaze never leaving the building. The place looked archaic. Surely it wasn't open for business? But the glow from inside suggested otherwise.

"So I am funny after all, hey? Well, who would have guessed it. You always used to say to me, and I quote, 'If wit was shit—'"

"You'd be constipated. Yeah, I know. And I stand by that," Rigs said, still entranced by the old place. The Rack and Cue would have been a beauty in its time. A good old cider-drinking pub for the farmers, who at one time had probably plowed and cut hay in the surrounding fields. Now those fields lay overgrown, the road itself just a busted trail with weeds and grass growing through the cracks, splits, and fractures in the decaying tar.

Crows lined its slate rooftop, which Rigs imagined had once been thatched in its heyday. Loads of them, in fact. Rigs couldn't get over how many there were—and at such an hour in the day. It was like a scene from Alfred Hitchcock's *Birds*. "Freaky," he muttered.

"What now?" Iain asked. "Did the Headless Horseman just go galloping through that graveyard over yonder?"

"There's a fucking graveyard?" Rigs tore his focus away from the pub, feverishly searching the surrounding area. But not much was visible, as the light faded with each passing minute and the rain continued to pelt.

"Jesus, I was just kidding, mate. What's up with you?"

"I told you, too many hours on the road," he said, giving off an unconvincing titter.

"Well, then, let's go inside," Iain said. His gut growled in agreement. "I'm Hank Marvin!"

"You're always starving! Doesn't your mama feed you at night?" Rigs joked, a genuine smile spreading across his face this time.

Iain rolled his eyes. "Hardy-fucking-har-har. Kill the engine, Rigs. You're burning fuel, and you know this thing'll drink us dry like the big old dirty slut she is."

Reluctantly, Rigs turned the truck off. It grumbled and rumbled to an antagonized stop. The engine hissed, gurgled, and spat, the rain hitting the bonnet helping its cooling process along.

"Noisy bitch, isn't she?" Iain said.

Rigs didn't hear him, again hypnotized by the building. Something about it had him on edge, but why? He'd been in and around much older places throughout the years. *Those birds. It's those fucking birds.* An old rhyme danced its merry way through his head: *Sing a song of sixpence, a pocket full of rye. Four and twenty blackbirds, baked in a pie . . .* "What does it mean?" he said aloud.

"What, old Betsy being a noisy bitch? Probably means she's on her way out, the clapped old whore she is."

"Yeah, you're probably right," Rigs said, not bothering to concern his best mate with his loopy thoughts. "Right, shall we?"

"Yes, please. The board over there boasts to have some of the finest ales this side of the black hole."

Rigs glanced at Iain and couldn't help but join him in laughing. His big grin and jokes were infectious.

Iain removed his hat and ran his hands over his bald, prickly head. Beads of sweat had gathered under the thick, cotton material of the headgear.

"You need to wash that bloody thing. It stinks."

"Yeah, maybe. But it's my good luck charm. The only thing I've ever won."

Rigs lowered his gaze at this, his smile faltering. "Come on, the first one's on me."

"You're actually getting a round in? Mr. Frugal himself? *This*, I have to see." Iain opened his door and jumped out into the rain. Seemingly unfazed by it, he casually strolled from the truck toward the pub entrance. The muscles in his shoulders shifted like balls of granite. He wasn't the tallest of men, but he had a bulky, muscular frame, with a bit of extra luggage around the gut to make up for it. His forearms were as thick as two-by-fours. "All those years over at the timber yard, see," Iain would say. "Made me strong. Just like Popeye, but without the spinach." This was usually followed by Popeye's famous "ugg-guh-guh-guh-guh" laugh.

Nobody fucked with him. Not even the bigger guys. He'd been known as "the Bull" in his last place of work. An apt name it was, too. Not only was he built like one, but he possessed the rage and temper of a bull too.

Rigs climbed out of the truck and hunched over in a vain attempt to remain as dry as possible.

"Hey, Miss Daisy! Are you planning on coming, or are you just going to stand there looking like a wet teabag all day, dear?"

"Hold your shit together, man. I'm coming." Rigs trotted down the car park to his friend, who was already at the pub's front door.

"I wonder if this place has rooms open for the night?" Iain said once Rigs caught up to him. "We could have a few jars, then bunk down here. Either that, or use the truck."

"Yeah, I don't think we're making it home tonight," Rigs admitted. "It wouldn't be the first time for us to sleep it off in the truck either."

"Nope. But I'm not sure I could put up with a night of your rancid arse. Especially in such close quarters."

Rigs's mouth dropped open. "You cheeky mother—"

The door burst open and a fat man in a dirty apron bellowed, "Ah, good evening, gentlemen. Won't you come in out of the rain?"

The two drenched truckers turned and looked at him, then shrugged and went inside.

"The more the merrier," the fat man said as the door closed at their backs. Deadbolts clacked. "I apologize if it seems I'm locking you in, gentlemen. The bloody wind has been causing hell with the doors: blowing them open and shut, open and shut. It's caused a nasty gash in the wall behind the door. It's making a right mess."

Would you even notice? Rigs wondered, inspecting the dirty, mold-covered walls.

The man eased past them as they huddled in the entranceway. "I'm just about to take my famous pies out of the oven. Surely you gentlemen will stay for a pint and a bite?"

Sing a song of sixpence, a pocket full of rye. Four and twenty blackbirds, baked in a pie . . . Were the birds gathered on the roof mourning their feathered comrades? Rigs wondered. He nodded as Iain's stomach grumbled in agreement.

"Right this way. The name's Porky, by the way."

Rigs stifled a chuckle. *Fitting*, he thought, following Iain and Porky into the nice warm pub.

Unlike the foyer, the bar area was grand. A healthy glow from a nearby fire danced on gleaming white walls, where an array of framed pictures of local, regional, and national rugby and football teams hung. Dotted among the sports memorabilia were posters advertising ales from all over Britain and the rest of the world (London Pride, Best Bitter, and Tetley crests being the most prominently displayed), along with a witty photo of the Hoffmeister bear playing pool. On the back wall, above a massive open and roaring fire, was the famous portrait of dogs playing cards.

Huh, Rigs thought. *That picture never gets old. A true classic.*

The floor was comprised of slabs, not a bit of carpet aside from a thin shag in front of the fireplace. On the mantle above the beastly flames was a line-up of trophies and trinkets for darts, snooker, pool, football, and rugby tournaments. All local stuff, from what Rigs could gather.

The chairs and tables spaced out around the inside looked as though they had come straight out of the '70s, along with the gleaming brass pint pumps. Even the glassware, some of which lined old, crooked shelving and others which were suspended from hooks behind the bar, appeared ancient. Also affixed to the wall behind the bar were old copper pots, brassware, and stone jugs bearing the inscriptions of various cider makes and brands.

The place was a treasure trove. *Almost a time capsule*, Rigs thought, looking up at the old wooden support beams of the roof. It felt homey, and comfortable. But although the place smelled good and was polished and scrubbed to buggery, it had an old air about it. That damp, musky sort of smell. The odor of Brasso and other cleaning fluids masked it somewhat, but it hung in the air ever so faintly.

"What a place," Rigs commented. "It's a beauty."

"Why, thank you, good sir. The Cue is one of the oldest pubs in the UK—second only to Ye Olde Fighting Cocks. We weren't always known as the Rack and Cue, either."

"Oh?" Iain said.

"No, no. This old girl used to fly under the name of Ye Olde Parson."

"Parson?" Rigs inquired.

"Yes. He was a famous local parson, according to old records and local history. Seems he was some kind of miracle worker. Cured the sick and infirm. Even livestock, by all accounts."

"Hell of a guy," Iain quipped. "Is the first one on him?"

The fat landlord didn't look impressed. "So, what will it be, gents?"

"Think I'll try a pint of Black Death," Iain said, the disappointment in his joke apparent on his face.

"Ah, a fine choice, that. It's a dark and highly creamy ale from Manchester. Smoother than Guinness, softer than silk," Porky said, claiming a glass from under the counter. He poured the black liquid into the container, taking measured care in pulling the perfect pint. He filled it to the brim expertly, without so much as a droplet wasted. "And for you, sir?" he asked Rigs, placing Iain's pint in front of him.

Rigs studied all the choices before him. "I'm not sure. I'm more of a ruby-colored ale man myself."

"Then how about a taste of home?" Porky produced a pint of Dragon's Breath. "This fiery little number has a life of its own. Brewed in Pembrokeshire, this cheeky little fellow has a honey roasted walnut taste with a brown-red hue to it."

"Sounds delicious," Rigs said, having to stop himself from licking his lips. The long trip had provoked a healthy rasp within him.

"That'll be six of your English pounds please, gentlemen," Porky said, a broad smile cast along his face as he slid the pint to Rigs. "And, as an appreciation of your custom, two hot pies will be brought out to you shortly—free of charge, of course."

"Thanks!" Iain said. "That's very good of you."

"Yeah, thanks. Much appreciated," Rigs added. "It's been a long, hard trip."

"The pleasure's all mine, gents." Porky took the ten-pound note off Rigs and returned quickly with his change. "Please, go and take a seat. I'll be over with your pies shortly. And maybe you'll think about sticking around and joining in on our annual pool tournament too?"

81

"Pool tournament?" Iain asked, eyebrows raised.

"There, on the wall." Porky pointed at the advertisement. "The entrance fee is twenty pounds per person, but the cash prize is a juicy one. Go and sit, think about it," he said, beaming and heading off to the kitchen.

The truckers pulled up chairs close to the fire and read the poster.

"I don't know, man," Rigs said. "Seems like a lot of money to throw away."

"Oh, come on—it's only twenty quid! You're an excellent player."

"It's been some time since I played A and B team at Treorchy Hotel, mate. Years, even."

"But think about what we could do with all that dosh? *Think* about it. We could fix the Foden or even replace it. If this lot here is your competition, then we're laughing!" Iain said, the excitement on his face evident.

"Let me mull it over," Rigs answered, taking a hearty gulp of his pint. As he did, he looked at the other punters and noticed six south Wales Hell's Angels were in attendance. "Shit. What are they doing here?"

"Oh, fuck," Iain said, craning his neck and spotting the Boas. "Great. Well, if any of those shitheads try anything here, I'll fucking knock 'em through the wall. Dickheads like that piss me off."

"Shh!" Rigs said. "What if they hear you?"

"Fuck 'em. I'll bust their heads open. I don't care how big they are, or how many tattoos they have."

"They could be carrying guns or knives. They're batshit crazy, Iain. You don't want to mess with those guys."

"Then they best not fuck with us first. Or they'll be leaving here in a fucking hearse."

There's that nasty streak, Rigs thought. *Just like that*. Iain could be so unpredictable. "Well, they don't seem to be doing anything unruly. Just getting wasted and trying to chat those girls up. God, the one looks like a right tart," he said.

Porky intervened, placing two hot pies down in front of them. "Here you go, gents. I hope you enjoy. Would you like any sauce? Seasoning? Cutlery?"

"Brown sauce, if you have some, please?" Iain said.

"Same," Rigs said.

"As you were," Porky said, and he was off.

"What a hell of a nice guy," Iain said. He picked up his pie and took a massive bite out of one side. "Oh, this is bloody gorgeous."

Rigs shook his head.

"Not eating yours?" Iain said through a mouthful.

"I'm just awaiting the . . ." Rigs spied Porky approaching. "Thanks," he said as the landlord plonked the bottle down on the table. "Oh, and before you go, do you happen to have any rooms free? My friend and I are thinking of staying the night."

"Marvelous!" Porky exclaimed. "Yes, we have plenty of room at the inn! I'll do a cut price for you fellas: fifty pounds for the night. I'll get one of the other staff members to prepare a room for you."

"Oh, and we'll be joining in on that tournament of yours," Rigs said.

"We will?" Iain said, again with his mouth stuffed.

"Grand, just grand. Come and pay me at the bar when you're good and ready," Porky replied, beaming.

* * *

Danny sat draped over the bar, huddled together with Clive, which enabled them to speak quietly and still hear each other over the ever-increasing raucous inside the Rack and Cue.

They'd entered the pub singing at the tops of their voices as they tried playing the drunken business fools. Clive had suggested wearing the football jerseys they had in the back of the van, but Danny had advised against it. "It'll look a bit obvious. And I don't think there's any footy on today, Clive. We just go in and pretend we're passing businessmen who are on a high after sealing a major business deal."

It wasn't much of a plan, Clive had thought, but it had worked, as they slipped into the pub and up to the bar without any questioning. The Boas hadn't been interested in them either, which had been Clive's biggest worry. He thought the outlaw bikers were on to them somehow, that they knew the police were tailing them.

Like Danny, Clive didn't trust his own department. He also believed a higher-ranking officer was feeding the Boas inside information. Hell, he suspected the chief himself, maybe even the mayor of Cardiff. The Boas had a lot of wealthy, connected, and powerful people in their pockets. He had even been predisposed to thinking their ongoing operation was a ploy to get the three of them killed. But he never spoke of these fears with Danny. Oh, no. Danny wanted this badly, to take this gang down and rip them apart from the inside out. He could compromise them if he was aware of Clive's presumptions.

"Have you heard anything back?" Danny asked. He was as close in proximity as he could get to Clive without things being obvious.

"No, nothing yet."

"These microphones probably don't even fucking work," Danny said, pinching the left lapel of his jacket nonchalantly.

"Ah, give Bobby a break, Danny. You ride him too hard, too much. He's only trying his best, like the rest of us." Clive took a gulp of his Ancient Breed. He actually hoped the mics weren't working, if Bobby was about to become the topic of conversation. Not that the equipment would stop Danny from badmouthing their tech guy.

"And why should I?"

"Because he's one of the good guys."

"Maybe."

"What do you mean by that?" Clive asked, scrunching his face in puzzlement.

"It means I'm not sure I entirely trust the guy. I mean, the things he has fitted to our jackets don't even fucking work. I wouldn't be surprised if he was on *their* side," Danny said, nodding discreetly in the direction of the bikers.

"What?!" Clive said, letting his voice get a little too high. He quickly composed himself. "Don't be crazy."

"Since when did you join his fan club, Clive? Have the higher powers got to you too?"

"I cannot believe you just asked me that, Dan. After all these years of me watching out for you, covering your arse."

"I'm sorry. That was out of line, fair play," Danny said, clasping a hand to his partner's shoulder. "I know you'd never turn on me or the job or the badge, whatever the fuck it stands for these days."

"It's okay, mate. Just settle down. Bobby's a good guy. He's been with us for years now, and he wouldn't double-cross us. No way."

"Maybe you're right." Danny drained the last of his pint. "Barkeep!" he called. "Two fresh ones over here, if you would. The boy here and I have some celebrating to do." Danny put his arm around his friend and pulled him close. "Won a big deal today, didn't we, boy?"

"We sure did! Lots of money made," Clive said, participating in the yarn they were spinning.

"Great news, gentlemen. These next two shall be on the house!" the barkeep said, that massive grin all over his face once again.

"That's bloody decent of you," Danny said.

"No problem at all, gents. And the name's Porky." Porky placed two freshly pulled pints in front of Danny and Clive. "And will you fellas be taking part in the tournament this evening? There's a huge prize, you know."

"We had noticed. What's the catch?" Clive wanted to know.

"No catch, my good man. Just a good-old honest competition. A bit of fun, with a cash prize to be won."

"Fair enough. Fancy it?" Clive asked Danny.

"Yeah, why not?"

"Fantastic!" Porky said, hurrying off to serve one of the large truckers who'd walked in about a half an hour before. Since then, three others had strolled into the pub, all holding cue cases. The competition seemed to be well known in these parts, at least.

Danny turned on Clive. "What the hell, man? We don't have time to be taking part in a game of pool!" he snapped, his voice level and low.

"Oh, but we do, Danny. Besides, we're supposed to be businessmen with cash on the hip. We've just closed a big deal, remember? We need to blend in or they're going to get suspicious. If that happens, we're done."

The confusion perching on Danny's pupils cleared away. "Okay, we'll play it your way. But this is craziness," he muttered. "We don't even know if those clowns will compete."

"Oh, they're competing all right. I overheard two of the Boas speaking earlier. It would seem the two English girls and the businessman sitting with them are also competing. I heard them chatting too," Clive said, a smug look drawn on his face. His eyes twinkled.

Danny smiled knowingly and swallowed some of his beer.

"We'll keep tabs on them all night. As soon as they make a move, we'll bust their arses. They're bound to slip up, what with the drink causing loose lips and all. And when they do, we'll have it all on tape," Clive said, winking and tapping at the lapel of his jacket.

Danny grinned wider as Clive produced forty pounds and waved the notes above his head, calling for Porky.

* * *

"Let me do the fucking pigs right here," Slicks whispered harshly, peeling back his denim jacket. The massive Bowie strapped to his underarm glinted in the firelight.

"Fuck, Slicks!" Diesel said, pushing Slicks's jacket closed. "Not now. Those lousy fucks don't know we're onto them yet. Let's keep it that way."

They had settled in one corner of the pub next to the jukebox and fruit machine, which depicted Andy Capp. At first they had fucked with Charlie, Mandy, and Grace, drinking several rounds with them. But after he and his Boas had groped, tried to kiss, and gotten downright lewd with the girls, the ladies told them to piss off. (Charlie had stayed out of it, like a good little doggie.) They had respected their wishes, as Diesel hadn't wanted the fat piece of shit behind the bar tossing them out. Not that he could anyway, but he could call the pool tournament off. And that was something Diesel didn't want to miss out on.

Win or lose, they were taking that two grand out of here.

"Where the fuck is Jack, dude?" Diesel wanted to know, feeding another one-pound coin into the jukebox.

"Maybe he got lost?" Slicks offered. "Want me to go outside and have a look? Check if I can see him out there anywhere?"

"Nah, don't bother. Fucking clown, he is," Diesel said. "Have you given fatty our entry fee?"

"Of course, brother."

"Good. The sooner we can get this monkey show started, the sooner we can fuck off out of here with that two grand."

"Well, we better get rid of those fuckers first," Slicks said, indicating the cops.

"They'll keep until the end," Diesel replied, smiling. He then headed to the bar to get another round for him and the boys. His shoulder clashed with the trucker who was wearing a hat.

"Want to watch your step, butty?" the trucker said, looking at Diesel as if he were a piece of shit he'd just stepped in.

"Why don't you watch *yours*?" Diesel said, getting in the man's face.

They stood toe to toe, nose to nose. Neither gave much away in size, and neither flinched nor backed down.

The burly trucker's mate intervened. "Come on, Iain. It's not worth it."

"But Rigs, he—"

"You heard your mate, *Iain*," Diesel said, his smile mocking. "It's not worth it. You wouldn't want to get all smashed up. Me and my crew would roll all over you."

The trucker named Iain glanced over Diesel's shoulders. He guessed the rest of the Boas had turned from playing the fruit machine to glare at him. Diesel chuckled and folded his arms over his chest, daring the burly guy to try him.

Iain smiled. "Maybe you're right, butty: you and your crew could probably smash me. But one on one, I'd eat you for breakfast, lad."

Diesel's nostrils flared, his breath escaping in short bursts as rage welled within him. "You're fucking dead." Every muscle in his body tensed as he prepared to shove the trucker and demolish him. "Fucking *dead*!"

"I heard you the first time," Iain said, not backing down even as Diesel's Boas shuffled behind him. "And yet here I am still standing."

"You little motherfucking piece of—"

The sharp clanging noise of the inn's bell stunned them all into silence.

"Hey!" Porky shouted, the sudden and fierce air of authority apparent in his voice unnerving. "Any more of that nonsense and I'll turf you all out. All funds for the tournament shall be given back. You and your money will never be welcomed here again, and a permanent ban will be issued. Understood?"

Iain nodded and returned to his seat beside Rigs.

Diesel likewise nodded compliance, and his crew sulked back to their corner without a word.

He clenched his jaw and went to the bar as planned to grab their drinks. All the while he imagined all the things he'd do to Iain once they got outside.

* * *

"I think we should forget about the competition, love, and get the hell out of here while we still can," Grace said. She'd been having a bad feeling about the pub all afternoon. The drink had managed to soothe the fears, but since the Boas had arrived, and now the truckers, the place seemed even more dangerous.

"What? Why?" Mandy slurred.

"Yeah, you can't leave now," said Charlie, who had his hand on Mandy's thigh.

Grace disregarded Charlie's comment and raised her voice to overpower the hubbub of music and chatter. "It's getting rough in here. Those bikers are trouble. They also look capable of anything. Let's go, please—Porky said we can have our money back."

"Oh, come on, Grace. You were the one who suggested it in the first place!"

"It's not like Porky's going to let anything bad happen here either, is it?" Charlie piped in again.

"True," Mandy said. "Look at how he just handled that spat. Besides, I think I've got a good chance of winning the whole thing."

Grace sighed, buckling to the pressure. "Fair point, I guess. But we go straight to our room after, yeah?"

"Yeah."

"Good," Grace said, noticing Charlie's hand had slipped farther up Mandy's leg. Biting at her lip, Grace picked her drink up and tried to relax.

Smiling, Mandy too picked up her drink and took a hearty swallow.

Charlie just sat there, copping a good feel and grinning madly.

* * *

Porky cast his glare around the bar.

The truckers were settled by the fire, each drinking their beer and tucking into their third Porky Pie, which made him smile. *A great source of income for something that costs very little—ingredients-wise, that is*, he thought, uttering a slight chuckle.

The girls were looking rather friendly with the young businessman as they chatted and laughed with one another. Also, the two celebrating businessmen at the bar looked happy in their hushed conversation. That left the bikers. They seemed to be quiet now. Apart from that little scuffle with the trucker twenty minutes ago, they hadn't really caused any trouble since they arrived.

The newcomers were scattered about: one using the ratty pool table for practice, another drinking his beer and cleaning his cue at a table alone, the third wandering and reading the clippings which decorated the walls.

Overall, there was a delightful cacophony inside the bar.

Content, Porky turned and headed toward the rear of the pub. He popped the cellar door open as he passed and stuck his head in. Below, the grinding of steel cutting through bone and fluids splashing the floor echoed.

"Doc? Doc, how's it going down there?"

The sawing and hacking of flesh and bone halted. "I'm busy, Porky. What do you need?"

"Just wondering if you'd managed to finish yet? I'll be ringing the bell in about fifteen minutes or so."

"Not quite. Best I stop yapping and get my arse in gear, yeah?"

Porky chuckled. "Okay, I'll get Baby into position."

There was no reply from Doc, only the pleasant sounds of him returning to his work.

Closing the cellar door, Porky left Doc to it. He whistled a little ditty as he entered the kitchen and opened the entrance to the garden.

Baby was still outside. Suds lathered her leather suit, suggesting she had cleaned herself down. She was letting the rain wash the soap away while slowly and methodically hosing the stonework, ridding it of blood and bits of flesh. It flowed down the path and disappeared into the storm drain.

The big woman spotted him, shut the hose off, and reeled it back in.

He nodded. She knew.

"Good. I've been waiting," she said, touching a hand to her crotch.

CHAPTER ELEVEN

CLANG, CLANG, CLANG, CLANG!

Porky rang the bell with as much might as he could muster. The clock had struck seven o'clock—it was time to get proceedings underway. "Ladies and gentlemen, can I have your attention please?"

A slight ripple of chatter continued throughout the pub, but most had settled down to hear what he had to say. For the others, he clanged the bell a few more times until the place fell deathly silent.

"Thank you. First and foremost, I see there are no returning faces this year, which is a surprise. Normally we have combatants come back time and again," Porky lied, finding it difficult to keep a straight face as he delivered his well-rehearsed patter. "We'll need to know who's who for this tournament to flow, so why don't we go around quick-like and introduce ourselves? Your name will suffice—no need for personal histories."

To his surprise, they listened well, each stepping forward and stating their names (or nicknames, he suspected in many cases). He made a mental note of each one. It never hurt to know whose body parts he was shipping, or who was on the menu . . .

Once the last one in the area spoke, he continued. "Now, on to the rules. There are few, but nevertheless they *must* be adhered to, no questions asked, or you will *not* be welcomed back. This game—this tournament—is unique. Nowhere else will you get such a prize for such a small entry fee as an amateur. This competition is not well advertised or talked about because we like to keep it small, quiet. The number we have in the room now is, in fact, perfect.

"After the rules have been spoken and before the first opponents take the table, the front doors will be bolted. The shutters that grace our windows will be closed and locked, the curtains drawn. You can still buy beer and snacks, of course," Porky said, plastering his false charm onto his face. "We wouldn't—"

"Why lock us in?" Diesel interjected.

"Yeah, what's the big idea?" Danny barked.

Porky raised his hands to the air. "Settle down, settle down, please. All will be explained."

"Well, best you fucking start speaking up," Roadblock said, standing. He gently eased past Diesel and thrust a fat finger in Porky's direction. "I'll fuck your shit up if you don't."

Porky, always aware, noticed Danny, one of the celebrating businessmen, tense up and feel at the small of his back. *Hmm, he might be packing heat. Best keep an eye on that one, and his mate.* "There'll be no need for violence," he said, still raising his hands in protest. "What we have here is a slightly unorthodox tournament, to say the least."

Roadblock's shoulders slumped and his fists unballed, the chains dangling from the side of his jeans rattling. "Hmph," he uttered.

"Fair enough," Diesel said, staring right through Porky. "Don't go trying any funny shit though, fatty, or me and my boys are going to tear this fucking joint apart. It'll be a pile of smoldering brick and mortar by the time we finish."

Porky smiled, then entertained Diesel's threat with a light-hearted chuckle. He swayed toward the biker and patted the vicious outlaw on the shoulder.

* * *

Iain gawped, surprised by how massive the landlord's balls were. *Hell, damn near bigger than mine—the man has more brass in his neck than he does in his fucking beer pumps*!

Rigs snorted a laugh beside him and whispered, "Can you believe Porky, mate? What a man. He's putting that fruit in his bloody place."

"Aye, I know," Iain whispered in reply. "I still don't like it though. Shit could get ugly, fast. I wish I was carrying El Bandito right about now."

"You still have that crooked piece of lead pipe?"

"Of course."

"Are you sure you didn't nick it from my Cluedo set? I still haven't found that missing piece, you know."

"Shit, are we going to go through this again?" Iain asked, smiling. "You're a worse nag than a wife."

"You've never been married. How would you know what a nagging wife sounds like?"

"Because you sound like a girl when you get going."

"Fucking charming," Rigs replied.

The truckers quieted as Porky spoke anew.

* * *

"See?" Porky said, continuing to pat the biker and grin. "We're all friends here. I run an honest competition, that's all. I take the participants' money and the winner gets to walk away with the cash prize. Doesn't that sound good?" Porky asked Diesel, his tone walking the line of condescension. But he didn't care. This was his family's pub. No one walked in and threatened him.

No one.

Diesel nodded and nuzzled back into his pack.

"Good," Porky said, a ridiculous smile haphazardly splashed across his face. "Then I shall continue. When the main event gets underway, which will be in ten to fifteen minutes, the front doors will be barred, the windows locked and slatted, curtains drawn. We may be in the middle of nowhere, ladies and gentlemen, but we often get the police out here doing routine checks. Why? Because they know I'm out here running this place with my family."

"Family?" Grace muttered. "But I've only seen you so far."

"Yes. That's because my niece and son are too young to be working the bar. They do, however, tend to work in the kitchen and cellar, etcetera. I also have a brother who helps me run the pub, but he's away today on important business."

"I see," Grace said, though her lip-gnawing alerted Porky she knew something was amiss.

Another one to watch closely, he thought. "Anyway, as I was saying, the police make regular trips out here, and I wouldn't want them catching wind of this little tournament. If they did, they'd shut it *and* me down. The stakes are too high for that."

"Then why risk it?" Rigs chimed in.

Everyone in the pub turned to face him. Porky spied Grace and the trucker lock gazes, the girl's cheeks turning rosy as Rigs managed a cheeky smile in return. He figured he could use that apparent attraction against them later.

"The answer to that is simple," he said, cool and calm though excitement bubbled inside. "My business is not actually making a great deal these days, but by holding this little game once a year, it helps keep the wolf from the door. I'd hate to lose this old pub, as it's been in the family for generations. I took the place over after my eldest brother became . . . sick." Porky glanced at the punters and competitors. All their expressions had gone somber. He stifled a telling grin. He now had them on his side with this last bit of information.

"But you said your brother was away?" Grace said.

"Yes, my *youngest* brother. My older brother became sick . . . Now, will you all allow me to finish telling the rules, please? Are you here to win money or to get depressed?"

"I have a quick question," Mandy said, her words almost indecipherable.

Porky controlled the twitch of an eye to keep from showing his true self yet. "Yes?"

"How come our cellphones don't work in here?"

Porky smirked as most of the others snickered. "Well, we *are* in the middle of nowhere, dear. Access to Wi-Fi and the like isn't exactly easy in these parts, and this is an older building. We aren't fully updated and probably never will be. Anything else, ladies and gents?"

"No, you crack on, big man," Diesel said before anyone else could speak. "Don't let us stop ya anymore."

"Thank you, young man. Right, so for those of you who are taking part, these are the rules: Once the pub has been barred and closed for the duration, no one may leave the premises. If anyone wants to go outside to fetch anything from the car or smoke, then please do so after this, before the first bout. Once I draw your names from the hat, play will commence immediately. The loser of each match will leave the bar area and take up seating in the lounge, until the event is finished and the money has been handed to the winner.

"The winner, in turn, will be escorted out the front door or to their room upstairs, as I know a few of you are staying here for the evening. The reason for that is because, in the past, things have turned ugly," Porky fibbed. "Some people are poor sports, mind." A few mutters and titters circled the room, which encouraged him to take his lie one step further. "Yes: fighting on the floor, lobbing things at each other, breaking tables and chairs. Some have been rowdy for sure, and after we threw them out, they continued their shenanigans outside. It was madness."

Their chuckles grew louder.

Porky had them in his palms. The lies were winning them over, the oddness of the situation diminishing.

"So, as I was saying, the winner will be escorted out the door or upstairs, depending on their situation. Then he or she must go on to face the pub champion to scoop the cash," Porky said, an immense smile spreading across his face.

"Pub champion?" Roadblock asked. "What type of stunt are you trying to pull here, dickhead?"

"Please, *please!*" Porky said, his hands in the air once again as he tried to placate the masses. "The pub champion must be defeated if you wish to capture the cash prize. That's been the rule since the competition started."

"Then where is this so-called champ?" Diesel mocked.

"Upstairs, awaiting his challenge. He's my son."

"Son? How old is he?" Iain asked.

"Seventeen."

A burst of laughter erupted around the room.

"Fucking seventeen?" someone shouted. "What's his prize for winning—a glass of milk?"

"Yeah, with a side of cookies!" bellowed another.

Porky breathed a sigh of relief. This lot thought something special of themselves. They were not going to be beaten by some teenager; they were bigger, stronger, and better than some young lad. Such ignorance would be their downfall, though. "Be warned: he's very good," he said.

"How good is he?" a voice rang out. The laughter and mutters died down.

"On his worst day, he can beat the best," Porky admitted, telling the truth this time.

"Does he always win?" Rigs asked.

"No, he has lost a few times," Porky lied.

"There's some hope then," Diesel said. "Let's do this shit."

"Yes, let's," Porky said, looking at his watch. "I'll give you all a quick break to get drinks, go to the toilet, or pop outside for whatever you need. Be back in the bar in ten minutes. If you're not, well, you won't be able to compete." He glanced at each punter in turn to allow time for it to sink in. "Right, then, I'll ring the bell shortly."

* * *

"What do you think, Danny? Are you still up for playing?"

"Too fucking right I am, Clive. But I must admit, I think our chubby landlord here is up to something."

"I get that feeling, too. I'm also worried about Bobby," Clive said. "We haven't heard from him since we got inside. I find that more than a little weird. I know you think his gear is shit, but—"

"No, I have the same feeling, mate," Danny said.

Nervousness played at his features, which perturbed Clive. He'd never seen Danny worry or give a fuck about anything. This was certainly out of character, especially if he was concerned for Bobby's welfare.

"What do you want me to do, Sarge?" Clive asked. "Want me to go on outside and check on him, see if he's okay?"

"Yeah, maybe. But if you go out there, you may not get back in. Porky seems pretty anal about his rules."

"Pfft, please. I'll *find* a way in. Besides, I wouldn't mind trying to get around the back of this place, see if everything is as legit as it appears," Clive said.

"Hmm, that's not a bad idea. We might have stumbled on to something here." Danny nodded. "Okay, you slip out the front and check on Bobby. If all is well, take him with you and see if you can dig around out back. Force entry if you must. Let's find out if anything's going on behind the scenes here."

"Will do, Sarge." Clive left Danny and spotted Porky. He sidled up to the barkeep and said, "I'm popping outside for a quick smoke. Shouldn't be long."

"That's fine—you don't need my permission," the overweight man replied with a soft chuckle. "Do as you must, but remember that the doors will be locked if you're not back on time. And I wouldn't walk away from a hefty pot such as what this tournament offers so easily, especially after you've paid your entrance fee."

Clive thought he caught a brief flicker of mistrust cross the rotund man's face. It unnerved him, sent a cold stab of fear to his bladder. *Am I doing something wrong?* he felt compelled to ask but opted to remain silent. Instead, he offered a thin smile as he turned to leave. He felt Porky's eyes bore through his back, which made his gums itch, setting his hair on end.

Clive risked a glance over his shoulder and almost pissed his pants. Porky was indeed standing there leering at him, his grin lopsided.

The fat landlord winked at him before heading off to serve one of the others.

The wink felt final . . . as though he were saying goodbye.

No, that's ridiculous. I'm just being paranoid now.

Clive shrugged off his thoughts and feelings and beelined for the front entrance. He stood just through the doorway and drank in his surroundings. The sky had turned an inky black with no stars twinkling, just thick, dark clouds which continued to leak water. The rain came down in cold, cutting sheets, which forced him to turn the lapels of his jacket upward even though he was protected from the slanting droplets by the doorjamb.

He slipped a cigarette from the box inside his breast pocket, lit it, and took a few long, hard drags. The road wasn't visible from where he stood, and the lights which graced the roadside did not burn orange although the sun had set. *They probably haven't been switched on in years*, Clive thought.

Peeking out from under cover, Clive tried to spot the van but couldn't locate it in the impenetrable darkness. The squinting began to hurt his eyes, so he gave up. *I'll finish this, then stroll on over there and relieve Bobby. Poor bastard must be dying for a piss!*

A few puffs later and he ground the fag out underfoot, stepped out of the doorway, and headed over to where they had parked. As he drew closer, he realized the van wasn't there.

In confusion, he scanned the car park to ensure he wasn't mistaken. But no, it was gone. Vanished. All that remained were tire marks in the muck which had filled with water.

What the hell? Bobby wouldn't just leave us here, would he? No. No way.

He bent for a closer look and noticed the tracks led onto the road and seemed to do a U-turn. *Weird. That'd be the opposite direction if he'd taken off and left us stranded.*

He stood tall and traced the marks, crossing the road over to the rear entrance of the pub, where the tire tracks came to an abrupt halt.

Is this some type of game? Why would Bobby move the van? Clive's face scrunched into a ball of stupefaction. *Maybe I should inform—*

A loud clanging rang out inside the pub.

Shit. That's my curfew up. He shook his head. *Nah, fuck it. I told Danny I'd check the place out anyway, so he'll know why I didn't come back in for the tournament. And finding Bobby is more important than raising the alarm just yet.*

Clive studied the gate before him and huffed. It reminded him of his training days, scaling walls and buildings. Back then his arse hadn't been so fat, and hurling himself over obstacles was a far easier task. Now, whenever he landed from reasonably high jumps, his bones ached, his knee joints screamed in agony, and his back howled for days.

"Let's get this shit over with," he muttered, staring toward the top of the gate. He stepped back and ran at the obstruction. His knees clattered against it, forcing him to swallow a scream. His back twitched as he hoisted himself up and got one leg over the crown.

Puffing, Clive swung his other leg over, dropped, and landed stiffly on the other side. His knees buckled on impact, causing him to crash down on his arse. Hard. The seat of his trousers instantly soaked through. "Oh, for fuck's sake," he said, placing his hands down either side of him and scrambling back to his feet.

He stumbled forward. His body rebounded off something solid and metallic, which sent him sprawling backwards but he managed to stay upright. "What the hell?"

When his vision cleared, he noticed it was the van in front of him.

He touched the stained paneling of the rear door. Blood lingered on it, the rain having failed to wash it all away.

Oh, fuck. Oh shit. This is bad. This is really fucking bad! He grabbed for his cellphone but recalled Porky stating it would likely have no reception in this area. He also remembered Danny mentioning his phone had no bars as they'd followed the Boas closer to the pub. *Right, then I need to get back inside*, he thought, but decided to inspect the van first. Sarge would expect more than possible blood; he'd want hard evidence that something bad had happened.

Clive pulled on one of the handles. Hinges creaked over the hiss of rain as a door edged open. The stink coming from inside the van was overwhelming. It smelled as though wild animals had been defecating in there for about a week. "Bobby?" he called out thinly, fighting spew back down his throat.

Clive reached to pry open the other door. Tacky strings pulled loose with his fingers. "Ugh, Jesus Christ." He briskly wiped his hand and fully opened the other door, which was gloop free. "Bobby?" The inside was pitch black. No lights from the sky shone in through the windshield. "Bobby, are you in here? *Bobby*!" he yell-whispered.

He stood there for long moments, straining his ears over the din of rain, waiting for some kind of response from his colleague.

When no reply came, he hoisted himself up and into the van. His foot immediately slid in a pool of something soft and sticky. He shuddered, not wanting to think on it, and hobbled to the communication desk, which had been destroyed. He rummaged through the drawers and found the heavy-duty torch, which he could use for clubbing. He quickly turned it on, illuminating his surrounding area.

The entire interior of the van was disheveled, and large indentations marked the metalwork up and down the sides. *What the . . . ?* Crimson liquid also covered the walls and ceiling and had dripped into neat, congealed pools on the floor. Bits of flesh and other gore surrounded the puddles.

Maybe it's not Bobby. He shook his head as his gut lurched. *No, it can't be Bobby. It—*

Clive lost the contents of his stomach then, and vomit splashed up his trouser legs. The smell of beer and meat pie mixed with the irony odor of blood. Staggering and seeking the exit, Clive slipped on the blood and collapsed onto the com desk. His light fell on the small fishing knife Danny kept in the van. Thinking the sharp implement might come in handy, Clive scooped it off the floor and placed it in his jacket pocket, wiped the sick from his chin and chops, snatched the flashlight, and raced for the rear doors.

Out of the van and in the fresh air once again, Clive felt as though he could breathe, his chest no longer tight. It was good being out of the suffocating reek.

After drawing several deep breaths, Clive swept the bright beam about him, wondering how he could get back inside and alert Danny. He was standing in the pub's backyard, which was surprisingly big. And the pub itself appeared larger as well. He spanned the light up the side of the building, squinting against the rain. *Ah, that would be why it looks so much more sizeable.*

From the front only three floors were visible, but from behind, there were actually five. Hidden to view from the car park was a top floor and a cellar. A small window at the bottom of the brickwork gave away the lower level of the structure, and the same went for the highest floor, where two bay windows jutted out. They appeared boarded up, covered. Blankets or such sheltered the glass to the cellar as well.

Clive's suspicions of something odd happening at the Rack and Cue intensified. With or without his partner, he intended to find out what the hell was going on.

He spotted a small door which he assumed led into the rear rooms of the pub. Healthy clouds of smoke drifted down from the chimneypots above, shrouding the whole yard. It looked like some kind of graveyard scene from a Hammer Horror, he thought, but minus the tombstones.

Letting a small chuckle escape him, he shook his head and edged his way from the van to the door. It seemed like a decent gust of wind would blow it inward. He reached for the doorknob but halted as what sounded like nails scraping along the floor broke over the patter of rainfall. *What was that?*

He rotated in quick semicircles, piercing the darkness with his light.

The nerve-grating noise rebounded around the yard once again.

He aimed the beam downward, searching the nearby ground, then farther off into the distance. Nothing. But the noise was there somewhere, just out of reach and hiding in the inkiness.

Clive wheeled back to the door and turned the doorknob violently. It didn't budge. He rammed his shoulder against the frail wood, but it stayed solid, not an inch given. *You've got to be fucking kidding me!* The thing was weather-worn and looked as though rats and squirrels had been having a joyous time gnawing at the bottom of the wood, yet his effort was akin to trying to bow a steel bar.

The scraping came again, closer. A throaty growl accompanied it.

Clive spun away from the door. There still wasn't anything there with him. Only darkness. "Who's there?" he asked, trying to sound as fearless as possible.

Nothing but the wind replied.

"I have a weapon, you son of a bitch. I'm not afraid to use it!"

This didn't seem to cut any ice with the hidden enemy.

"Stay back. I'm an officer of the law, and I *will* take you down if I have to!"

The scratching came to a halt; so too did the growling.

A vicious snarl rent the sudden silence.

The scraping sound was back, and this time it was galloping straight toward him.

Clive's eyes widened. *Dogs! Shit, shit, shit!*

He turned and threw his weight against the door. The pane of glass in the center cracked. Wood splintered. He stepped back and charged, slamming all sixteen stone against the weakening timber once again. The lock broke, and the doorknob came off in his hand. The glass fell through simultaneously.

He glanced over his shoulder. He was too late.

Massive canine heads lunged out of the darkness. One bit down on his shoulder while the other clamped onto his arm. The sleeve of his jacket and shirt beneath were torn asunder. Flesh ripped from his hand. His screams were lost in the eye of the storm as the rain washed his blood, sweat, and tears away.

Even though the weight of the two dogs on him was crushing, Clive managed to stay standing with the aid of a wall. "Motherfuckers!" he screamed from behind clenched teeth. He dug his uninjured hand into his coat pocket, flipped the blade on the small knife, whipped it out, and drove it up and into the belly of the dog ravishing his shoulder.

It howled and tried to pull away, but Clive dealt a deathblow before it could, ripping the steel up through its guts. A soft splash and thuds hit the floor at his feet, likely the dog's innards. It collapsed to the ground and whimpered momentarily, until its life bid farewell.

Pushing himself off the wall, Clive crashed the spine of the remaining dog against the left wing of the van. The headlight burst, tossing shards of glass like confetti. The beast yelped but clamped down harder still on Clive's arm. "Jesus H. Christ, get the fuck off me!" he shrieked. He then brought the knife up and plunged it into the mutt's face, behind its eyeball, hoping to hit the brain.

He did; the dog went limp and fell away.

Clive kicked the still carcass at his feet. "Fuck you," he panted, falling against the body of the van, his arm and shoulder screaming in white-hot agony. His forearm didn't look nearly as bad as it felt, but his shoulder, on the other hand, was ravaged quite badly. *Fuck, fuck, fuck. All right, come on, get yourself together*, he thought, fighting fatigue. *I need to warn the others. All I need to do is get inside and to the bar. You can do this. Come on!*

Clive stumbled over to the busted door and nudged it open with the toe of his shoe, all the while favoring his injured forearm. Glass crunched beneath his feet as he entered a long dark passageway. A solitary bulb ahead of him swung lightly, fueled by a breeze coming through the shattered door. The bulb was out. Scorch marks were evident at the bottom of the thin glass.

He crept down the corridor until he came across another door. Holding his breath tightly, he twisted the knob and swung the wood inward. A kitchen lay beyond. The walls were gleaming, the floor polished and scrubbed to perfection. A few pots and pans bubbled away on the stove.

Clive's eyes fell on the impressive knife block on a counter. Placing his blood-encrusted blade down, he drew the breadknife from its slender slit. "Come to papa!"

He headed for the next door in front of him, which led to another hallway. This one was much longer, but Clive knew he was getting closer to his target. Laughter and applause eked through the walls. "Almost home and dry," he said. His body, soul, and mind found fresh valor and he pushed on.

A buzzing sound to his left stopped him. A door caught his eye. He crossed to it and opened it. Stone steps, leading downward. In the distance, the low hum of a power tool. Condensation or the like also dripped and splashed at intervals.

Clive took the first step. His heavy footfall echoed off the granite, making him wince. Slowly but gently, he moved to the next step. Sweat broke out on his forehead. Gingerly, he went down farther.

Near what he supposed was the halfway mark, Clive ducked and squinted. Shadow cloaked the room before him. A dim light burned somewhere in the vastness. He didn't dare call out. Someone was down there. And that someone was working away busily, doing God knew what.

He decided to head back to the kitchen when hands shoved roughly at his back.

He somersaulted down the rest of the unforgiving, cold staircase, crashing to a brutally painful stop at the bottom. Clive gasped in surprise and agony. One leg had snapped in the fall; a piece of bone jutted from his left knee.

He bent and grabbed his wounded leg, rolling about the floor, eyes closed as he warded off yelps and screams.

With the torment managed, he opened his eyes. Two faces hovered over him like vultures. Only their eyes were visible. One had a green mask over the mouth, much like something a doctor would wear, and the other wore a black leather mask.

"Well, well, well, what do we have here?" asked the one in green. "Fresh meat, it would seem!"

CHAPTER TWELVE

SOMETHING CRASHED IN ONE OF THE BACK ROOMS, and Porky closed the door that stood ajar behind the bar. None of the others had seemed to hear the commotion, which was a good thing. No awkward questions to answer.

He smiled, knowing the one who had gone outside—Clive, if he recalled correctly—had now been taken care of. *Welcome to my parlor, said the spider to the fly . . .*

He cleared his throat and addressed the crowd while mixing slips of paper around inside his makeshift tombola. "The first two names are . . ." Porky reached in and pulled them out. "Diesel and Roadblock."

The bikers looked at each other and laughed. "There goes one of our chances at winning this thing," Diesel said.

"Names three and four: Iain versus Tommy," Porky continued, casting his gaze in search of the two. He spotted Iain scanning his opponent, who was one of the latecomers. Tommy was unzipping his two-piece pool cue from a swanky leather case. He then proceeded to screw the two pieces together.

"Jesus, this guy's going to be taking it deadly serious, by the looks of things," Iain joked to Rigs, loud enough for Porky to overhear it.

Wait until the Champ arrives . . . "Rigs plays Christopher," Porky continued.

"Looks like I got the other one," Rigs commented within earshot, eyeing the other man who'd come in with Tommy. Christopher also seemed like a semi-pro player, as he likewise prepared his cue and playing equipment.

Porky drew the next round and tried hard to keep the excitement out of his tone. *Looks like most of the bikers are stuck eliminating each other. How ironic!* "Slicks and Gutbust." Porky paused. "Not many left in here now." He gave the remainder a good rotation with his hand. "Danny plays Shogun. Mandy versus Smith. Grace and Charlie. And the last two, who just happened to be last through the door as well: Sheila plays Barry.

"There we have our first-round lineup, ladies and gents. Play will begin in five minutes. For those who'd like a drink, snack, or toilet break, please do so now. When I ring the bell next, that will signal the start of the first match: Diesel and Roadblock."

The group dispersed. Before Porky knew it, he had two deep at the bar, with the beer and spirits flowing. His till worked overtime as he happily served his customers with calm and expertise.

Yes, this is going to be a great night for making money!

* * *

With the lineup announced, Rigs turned his attention to Grace. Her slight features and hazel-colored eyes enticed him, coaxing him over. She locked gazes and gave him an inviting smile.

"Rigs? You okay, mate? *Rigs*?" Iain called.

"Huh?" Rigs said, blinking rapidly and wrenching his focus back to his friend. "What?"

"I said, what do you make of all this?"

"All of what?"

"This. Where we are. What's going on. All of it. Do you really think Porky is going to pay out all that cash to one of us?"

"Why wouldn't he?"

"I don't know. Just sounds fishy."

"You were all up for it twenty minutes ago. What's changed?"

"I've been turning it over in my mind. Thinking about it."

"That's a dangerous thing for you to do, boyo. You'll end up blowing a gasket."

"Now I know why we're best friends. It's that sparkling personality of yours, with a side serving of tremendous humor," Iain said, a smile tugging at his lips.

"Look, we've paid our cash already. Plus, I think we stand a good chance of picking up that prize. We could buy that new truck we're always going on about, man."

"Yeah, I know. It's just . . ."

"Just what?"

"I find it a little odd, I guess."

"Only now you're finding it odd?" Rigs said, only half-joking. "Anyway, I thought *odd* would have suited your personality more, Mr. Strangeways."

"Gobble me!" Iain said.

"Not before dinner and drinks I don't, matey."

"Don't you find it weird that a pub in the armpit of nowhere would hold such a tournament though? There's nothing around here."

"Well," Rigs reasoned, "I was chatting with Porky earlier, and he told me the place is barely surviving these days. They've had to do all they can to make ends meet. So what's he got to gain from fooling us all? It's not like he can just keep our money, rob us blind. Have you seen this lot? They'd rip the fucking pub apart."

"Maybe you're right."

"Of course I am. Settle down and drink your beer. We'll be out of here in no time, with our arse pockets stuffed with cash. Mark my words."

"Talk about famous last words. Christ!" Iain said, ramming the last of his fourth pie into his mouth and washing it down with the rest of his beer.

Rigs stole a glance in Grace's direction and caught her staring back. He decided to take a risk for once. *Probably all this drink and food getting to me, but why the hell not?* "I'll, uh, get us some fresh ones," he said, collecting his and Iain's glasses off the table and making his way toward the bar. But he didn't head straight for it, instead veering off to test his luck.

He edged and skirted around the others. As he approached Grace and her friend, he applied his warmest smile. He stopped beside them and found himself privy to their conversation.

"I thought you weren't playing, Grace?"

"Isn't a girl allowed to change her mind? Besides, they were one short, so I said I'd play."

"*Can* you play?" her friend asked.

"I played a lot when I was with Paul. He taught me a few things," Grace said.

"I'll bet he did!"

Her friend noticed him and nudged Grace with an elbow. They turned to him, questioning looks on their faces.

Rigs cleared his throat, hoping he could play it down that he'd paid attention to names during their initial mass introductions. "Hi. I was wondering if you'd fancy another, err . . . Grace, isn't it?" he asked, indicating her empty glass with a nod.

"It is," she answered, blushing. "And yes, please. I'd love another, thanks."

He showed his pearly whites. "Great. What's your poison?"

"Cider, please. Rigs?"

She remembered my name too! "Yeah, Rigs. And no problem. I'll be back shortly," he told her. "Don't go anywhere." The girls giggled as he walked away.

In front of the bar, which was now reasonably quiet, he checked himself in the mirror. He could not have looked more a mess. His beard was unkempt, his hair greasy-looking. Holes marred his oil-stained shirt and flecks of grime graced his forehead. He glanced down. Grease and dirt also soiled his jeans, and his boots were scuffed and muddy.

"Sod it, a man's been to work. I'm still on duty," he said aloud and laughed.

Porky joined in on his laughter, but his gaiety diminished rapidly. "Wait. What's so funny?"

"Look at me! I'm a bloody mess."

"Well, you've been to work, lad. You're not entering a beauty pageant here."

"True, that. But I'm interested in her over there," Rigs said, nodding behind him.

"Oh, I see," Porky said, beaming. "Let's fill those glasses of yours. And put your money away. These are on the house."

Rigs looked at the man dumbfounded. "Are you sure? I thought this place was—"

"Struggling, yes. But I'll make more than enough tonight to get by." He finished pouring, and Rigs was shocked to find he'd refilled each glass with their respective preferences even though he hadn't asked. "Here, take them," the barkeep said. "My kindness will bring you all the luck you need with that little lady over there."

"Thanks, man!"

"Oh, and the very best of British luck in the game," Porky said, winking.

"Cheers" was Rigs's parting word.

He wound his way through the crowd once again until he reached Grace. He offered her the drink. "Here you are, Grace. Give me a minute, I'm just going to take this one to my mate," he said, motioning at Iain with a series of nods.

"Thanks," she said, her smile growing wider. "And no problem, you do what you must. I'll stay put, no worries."

Rigs let rip with a snorted laugh. He couldn't get over how hard his heart was beating. *How old am I—fucking fifteen, for fuck's sake?* "Okay, great. I won't be long."

He rushed to Iain, chuckling with nervousness all the while. *What the hell is wrong with me? I'm acting like a prepubescent teenager!*

"What's going on with you and that meek little thing?" Iain asked. "Buying her drinks, too? Right Casanova on the quiet, ain't ya?"

"Meek?"

"Aye. Look at her—like butter wouldn't melt, my friend. You may want to watch that one. A tiger between the sheets probably," Iain said, imitating growling sounds.

"Pack it in. I suppose you like her friend?"

"Damn right. She looks filthy, not to mention wild. I've been watching her."

"Watching her? What are you, some kind of pervert? Want me to find you a bush to hide in?"

"How droll."

"Listen, I'm going back over there, okay?"

"Yeah, yeah, you crack on. But get me her mate's phone number!" Iain called after Rigs, who hurried back through the crowd.

* * *

Clang, clang, clang, clang, clang!

"Let play commence!" Porky yelled over the noise in the pub, tapping his foot until everyone settled down. "Now, if you'd all be so kind as to follow me into the next room, ladies and gentlemen, we can get the games underway."

In a single line, they followed Porky into the lounge area, where a prestigious-looking pool table was set up and ready to go. Most of the room was basked in darkness, with the only light beaming from the oversized lamp above the baize. It cast their shadows on the wall as they stood and absorbed the space. Benches lined the walls. Tables and chairs were scant. Porky ushered them all inside and shut the door behind them.

"Please take a seat, bar the first two players. Every game will be schooled by myself. I tolerate no cheating. The slightest hint of foul play will be met with harsh circumstances. You'll be disqualified, simple as that. I also ask for total silence from those who are not playing at the time, and to give all the respect you yourself would wish for when competing. Good luck, and may the best player win," Porky said.

The Boas gathered by each other. Iain sat alone, while Rigs continued to chat with Grace. Charlie and Mandy sat with them, and the others took up distanced seats around the lounge.

Diesel and Roadblock grabbed cues from the holder on the wall.

Porky tossed a coin and Roadblock called it correctly.

"May the best man win," Porky said.

Diesel racked and Roadblock let loose a powerful break. The striped and solid balls clattered as they collided and bounded off the cushions and each other. Three of the balls—two stripes and a solid—found pockets.

"Stripes," Roadblock announced, chalking his cue. He leaned over the table to take another shot and again his aim was true—another striped ball disappeared off the playing field. Then another. And another. He slammed the sixth and seventh stripes home expertly, leaving himself snookered behind a cluster of solids. All he needed was the eight-ball to win the match. However, he missed, turning play over to Diesel.

"Well, fuck me!" Diesel said, smiling. "Didn't know you had such cue skills, Block. I best get fucking potting or I'm heading for an early shower."

A titter erupted from the crowd.

Porky cleared his throat. "Silence, please."

The audience hushed instantly.

* * *

Diesel picked up the chalk from off the table and slowly rubbed the blue dust over the tip of his cue. He eyed the balls as he made a decision on his first move. "Are we playing two shots carry?"

Porky shook his head. "No, lad. If you pot then miss, that ends your turn."

"Bollocks," Diesel said, more to himself. He could see Roadblock grinning like a mad fool out of the corner of his eye. "Right, okay." He bent and bridged his fingers, placing the cue on his crooked digits. He took a slow, lingering shot. The white ball glided across the table like a swan crossing an undisturbed lake. It connected with a solid which was hanging over the center bag. It dropped in.

He chalked his cue as he stalked the table, circling it like a bird of prey readying itself for the swoop. Then he bent again and glided the white ball down the cushion, putting another solid home before clearing another three in quick succession. Not a shot missed.

However, his last solid was snug against the eight-ball, leaving him only one possible shot. Diesel played the dirtiest snooker he could by tucking the white ball right up behind his. "Get out of that one, Houdini!" Diesel guffawed as the smirk dropped from Roadblock's face.

"That's just fucked up, dude," the huge Samoan said.

"You can't go getting one over on your patched superior, brother," Diesel said, picking up his beer and swallowing more than half of it. Some of the brown liquid drizzled out of the glass, missing his lips completely and splashing the front of his chest and cut.

Roadblock's mouth moved as he seemed to calculate his shot, his eyes darting across the baize. Content, he bent to make his move. He bounded the cue ball off two cushions but missed the black hunk of phenolic resin by an inch. "Fuck!" he despaired, his arms going slack as he looked skyward.

"Ball in hand for Diesel," Porky chirped.

"Ooh, yeah!" Diesel said, poking his tongue out like a poor man's Gene Simmons. "You're going down, boy bach."

"Shit!" Roadblock hollered, throwing his cue aside. The rest of the Boas laughed in the background.

"Please do *not* throw the cues about the place," Porky said.

This brought a hard stare from Roadblock, who looked as though he could eat the large landlord for breakfast and still be hungry.

Diesel glared at his soldier, hoping he would understand the unspoken command to keep his cool. He then lined up his shot and sent his last solid home, followed by the eight-ball.

"Diesel makes it through to round two," Porky announced. "Roadblock, would you be so kind as to exit through that door to your left and wait in the room beyond? I'd be most grateful, thank you. The bar in there is open. I'll be along shortly."

The Samoan stomped away and disappeared through the door without further fuss. *Good. He best calm the fuck down*, Diesel thought. *He'll blow the whole thing if he doesn't follow orders.*

"Next two players: Tommy and Iain," Porky stated. "Would both men please come forward?"

Diesel returned to his Boas, unable to wipe the grin from his face.

"Nice one," Slicks said as he low-fived him. "You smoked him, man."

"Easy as." Diesel turned to his prospects. "Make sure that copper loses, Shogun. And you've got a girl, Smith—too fucking easy. But we need some wins. We need as many chances to take that pot as possible. Not that it really matters though." He turned to stare at the lardass of a landlord as the next players stepped to the table. "We're walking out of here with that cash win, lose, or draw. That fat fuck and the rest of these fucking retards won't stop us."

Slicks snorted a laugh. "You got that right, brother."

* * *

"The best of luck, mate," Iain told Tommy, thrusting his hand out in offer to shake. The man gave Iain a contemptuous look. "I'm not a piece of shit, you know? Just because my hands and clothes are filthy doesn't mean I'm a bad person, mun."

Tommy scoffed and turned his back on the offered hand. He began rubbing his cue vigorously. "Peasant," he muttered under his breath.

"Is this a Welsh thing?" Iain said, flabbergasted. "Get off your fucking high horse before I knock you off it, *boy*!"

"Now, now, gentlemen," Porky said. "Do your fighting on the table."

Tommy outsized Iain in height and weight, but definitely not in brawn. "Lucky, butty. Next time, I'll break your fucking jaw," Iain slurred, the booze working its way through his system. His usual fun-loving, banter-wielding self was slowly fading away. It was time to stop his ale intake. If not, the slightest of things could derail him further, and it wouldn't be a pretty sight. His run-in with Diesel earlier was still pissing him off, breeding under his skin.

Tommy blinked a few times, eyes wide. "No. I—I didn't mean anything by—"

"Keep your trap shut and save your sorries, or I'm likely to ram this white ball down your throat."

Tommy's face fell ashen.

"Come on, you fucking shirt-lifters," Slicks yelled. "Either belt the fuck out of one another or get playing."

Iain turned, ready to unleash his drunken rage, but Porky intervened. "Yes, Slicks is right. Either forfeit and take it outside or get playing. This is your final warning."

Iain stewed for a moment, leering at his opponent. A spark of rationality flickered inside, and he said, "Yeah, fine. Let's get this game going."

"Shake hands. Show sportsmanship," Porky chided.

Tommy stepped around the table tentatively and offered his hand gingerly, which Iain met with a vice-like grip. Bones clicked. "The best of luck," Iain said, finding it difficult to keep the sarcasm from his voice.

"Yes, you too," Tommy offered weakly, color draining from his chops.

Porky tossed the coin. "Call," he told Tommy.

"Um, h-heads."

Porky caught the piece. "Tails it is. What will it be, Iain?"

"You can break," Iain told Tommy, who nodded.

Tommy smashed the racked, brightly colored pyramid apart. The balls hurtled toward the cushions and each other. Most of them made a complete circuit of the table without one finding a pocket. After the storm, calm ensued, leaving an open playing field for Iain.

"Nice break," Iain said. He supposed it sounded sarcastic, but he hadn't meant it that way. He truly was happy with the way the pack of balls had split. Five out of the seven stripes hung over pockets, whereas only two solids did. The rest of them were hard against the cushions. "Stripes," Iain called.

He stooped and took his shot. The striped ball hanging over the bag dropped home with ease. The second, third, and fourth also found their way into pockets. After he slotted the fifth in, Iain stopped to chalk his cue. One of the two remaining was an easy shot. If he gave himself a fair leave, he'd have a decent shot on the last ball too.

The sixth ball rattled into the pocket but was burped back out with vehemence. It rolled back up the table and nestled against the cushion.

Tommy let out a huge sigh.

"Tommy's shot," Porky announced.

Iain looked on in dismay. He should have run the table, no problems.

"Hard luck," Tommy said, before hinging at the hips to take his first shot.

What should have been an easy opening pot for Tommy turned into a waking nightmare. Not only did he miss the pocket completely, but he sent a solid spinning around the table like a tornado. It slammed both of Iain's remaining balls as well as the black ball over open goals before coming to a rest in the center of the baize.

Grinning, Iain cleared what he had left to win the match, and then watched in amusement as Tommy broke his own cue over his knee. The manchild stormed for the same exit Roadblock had taken before Porky could direct him.

"Whoops!" Iain said, addressing the crowd. A roar of titters ensued as Iain stumbled drunkenly about the place. "Stop his drink!" he bellowed, much to the crowd's delight.

"Winner: Iain!" Porky declared. "Now, can we have the next two to the table, please?"

Iain hung his cue back in the rack and stumbled over to Rigs and Grace.

"Nice one, mate," Rigs said. "Let's hope I can join you in the next round."

"You'll be fine, man. Take it to the fucker." He swayed and his stomach lurched a bit. "Shit, I think I need to sit down. I was seeing thirty balls on that table."

Rigs chuckled and clapped a hand on his back. "Rest, dude. I'll be back in a jiffy."

CHAPTER THIRTEEN

AFTER STOMPING OUT OF THE POOL ROOM in a blazing mood, Tommy stood in a new corridor, lost. He'd thought by going through the door like the biker had, he'd be back in the bar area.

Where the bloody hell am I? he wondered, his anger still at peak.

The passageway was cast in shadow. Halfway down, a swinging bare bulb hung from the ceiling. *I don't remember coming through here earlier*, Tommy thought, his rage losing some of its warmth. *Maybe it leads to a different room, a different bar. Porky mentioned something about a bar being open for us. I know he did, damn it.*

He turned to the door he'd walked through, thinking he'd enter the billiards room and ask the tubby landlord which way he was supposed to go. But, to his bemusement, no matter how much pushing, shoving, and pulling he tried, the door would not budge.

"For fuck's sake." He hammered his fist on it. "Hey! Your door is jammed! Porky!" After a dozen blows, he noticed they weren't sounding hollow or strong. They were muffled, as though the door was padded. He couldn't hear any of the clatter and noise from the other side either. "Fucking retards . . . Well, this is taking the piss."

Faced with no other option, Tommy walked the long path in front of him. "Can't believe I was beaten by a sheep-shagging trucker. I'll kick his fucking arse if I see him outside," he muttered aloud, still stewing over his loss.

He passed under the bulb and spotted a door at the end of the walkway. *That must be the room Porky was telling us about*, Tommy thought, the bravado returning to his swagger. When he reached it, he noticed the surrounding floor was wet but couldn't make out what it was due to the poor lighting.

A muffled, tedious, and continuous drone whined from behind the barrier.

What in God's name is that? Sounds like a wet vibrator at full blast! Tommy put his ear to the cool wood and listened. It sounded like a laden bomber flying low.

He put his hand to the door handle, but it was tacky. As he retracted, strings of goo stretched from his fingertips, as though the handle had been drooling.

He backed away slowly and quietly. Something didn't feel right. Where was the biker?

The whirring, buzzing sound stopped. A *thud, thud, thud* grew closer and louder by the second, until it sounded as though it was right behind the door.

"Oh, fuck," Tommy gasped. His bladder puckered. He wanted to turn and run, to scream the fucking place down. But that was silly. Childish.

The door flung open and slammed against the wall, knocking chunks of brick and plaster free. Tommy recoiled, jumping backward. He lost his footing and his flailing arms hit the bulb above him, sending it into a frenzied swinging-whirling motion. He hit the floor arse first.

A huge, masked figure stood in the doorway, a meat-pulverizing hammer in its hand.

Tommy's eyes welled as he shuffled backwards like a crab. The skin of his palms tore and peeled as he scuttled.

The figure emerged, the hammer now held high. The blunt head dripped blood and gore. Remnants of hair clung to the robust weapon.

"Oh, Jesus!" Tommy squealed like a pig with a cut throat. "I have children, for the love of God. Please!"

The person brought the hammer down so hard and fast that Tommy didn't see it coming through his teary eyes. The bulky metal head shattered his left knee in devastating fashion, blowing it apart with callous effort.

Tommy half screamed, half cried as he clutched his destroyed joint, his bladder finally releasing.

Before he could pass out from the agonizing pain which tore up his leg, the attacker hammered his other knee to splintered dust.

He blubbered and pleaded, his bottom lip trembling like a toddler's. Drool hung from his chin, beads of it dripping and forming a pool on his chest.

The third blow crushed his privates, causing darkness to descend on him. He almost choked to death on his own vomit but his attacker saved him, rolling him onto his side. Had he not been in so much agony, he'd have thanked them. His mind cracked and he giggled at such absurdity.

As he fought off unconsciousness, a gloved hand grabbed a tuft of his hair and dragged his crumpled body through the door where the huge figure had appeared. Once he was inside the room, the door slammed shut.

"Where . . . are—am I . . . we?" Tommy garbled, crying again. The pain wracking his body was beyond comprehension.

Three swift, powerful blows to his jaw sent a few teeth flying loose.

"Argh, you bastard!" Tommy shouted, crimson leaking from his busted mouth. "I'll fucking kill you. Cunt!"

A boot to the ribs hushed him.

"They're coming through to us too fast," a male voice complained. "I haven't even finished cutting up that fat islander yet."

Tommy managed to tilt his head and caught sight of the big biker, the first of the tournament losers. The man's legs had been sawn off and cut into quarters. The pieces reminded Tommy of tree stumps, ready to be halved by an axe.

"Oh, God," he said, pushing the hurt from his mind, fear turning to abject anger once more. "You cunts have fucked up! The rest of those bikers will rip your fucking hick arses to shreds when they find out what you've—"

* * *

Baby raised her booted foot and stamped on the man's face, breaking more teeth along with his nose, jaw, and cheekbones. His eyes swelled instantly under the attack. Tired of listening to him, she grabbed a roll of duct tape from close by and wrapped it around his head, taping his mouth shut. Then she bound his wrists and ankles too.

She patted the top of his head when she was finished and joined Doc, who loomed over the dead biker. A screwdriver was poking out of the corpse's mouth. It had pierced through the back of his throat, where she had swirled it around as much as she could in his punctured brain stem, killing him instantly. *He fell like a damn tree*, Baby recalled, letting a giggle escape her.

"Baby, this is no time for laughing, girl! We need to get this one chopped up. There's no time for fun and games this evening. Not at this rate," Doc said, business as usual. He picked up a ten-inch knife and stabbed it into the dead biker's bare chest, ripping it all the way down to his abdomen.

The taped man struggled, kicked, and wriggled to be free of his restraints, to no avail. Baby returned to him, clamped a hand to his head, and forced him to watch as Doc dug all the organs out of their cavities. Blood popped and squirted up his already blood-drenched scrubs, soaking his once-green mask in gore.

Doc put every organ from the front of the man into steel containers until his husk was empty. He then sawed off the man's arms and head, before turning him over and ripping the back open. It was poetry in motion, the way in which he stripped, hacked, and emptied the body. He was clearly skilled at it, and rightfully so, Baby supposed—he'd sacked a load of carcasses over the years. The expression on his face whispered of a million stories, but not a story truer than that of how much he enjoyed it.

Baby felt the taped man's body lurch and convulse. Vomit eked through creases in his impromptu gag and he shook his head back and forth, face redder and redder by the second. The veins in his neck stood out. She laughed, relishing him helplessly fighting on and clinging to life.

"*Baby*! For God's sake, what's all that bloody noise, girl?" Doc slammed his snips down and wheeled on her. On seeing the pair, the makeshift doctor blurted out a few harsh sniggers. "Oh, yes, I see what's so funny now," he said. "Well, Baby, do you think we should allow this pig to breathe?"

She shook her head slowly, the idea of further torture and humiliation making her wet again.

"Very well. Death by asphyxiation it is!" Doc proclaimed.

The taped man gargled and bubbled. Baby released her hold on him and he dropped dead at her feet, body twitching until he lay still. She reached down and fondled his busted privates, wishing she were nude and alone with the corpse.

"What perfect timing!" Doc said. "How thoughtful of the dear fellow. Get him up here, Baby."

She frowned behind her mask, not done playing yet. But, like Porky, Doc must be obeyed. She scooped the dead man off the floor and threw him onto the same table the biker had been on.

"Lovely," Doc said as he set about his work. "Get back out into the corridor, girl. There should be another along in a minute."

CHAPTER FOURTEEN

Rigs couldn't stop sweating. He wished he could, because it was getting into his eyes and causing them to sting. The match was well into its twentieth minute and looking to go much longer. He'd never been engaged in such a lengthy billiards bout before. Not that he could remember, anyway.

He had started well, considering he'd had the break. Chris had potted, resulting in him then being hampered behind the black, forcing him to take a hard safety shot after that—one which hadn't gone to plan. He'd left Rigs with a shot to nothing, which he'd taken well. Having potted himself out of trouble, he'd gone on to miss the next, setting Chris up for another punt.

And that's pretty much how it had gone shot for shot so far: pot, snooker, pot, snooker . . . Now they were left with two balls each plus the black, which was tight against the bottom right-hand pocket's knuckle—an easy pot for the bloke who got there first.

Chris took his shot, managing to sink one of his remaining two. The white finished behind his last. Chris slammed his final solid home and winked at Rigs as the white nestled at the rear of the eight-ball.

"Cocky motherfucker," Rigs said under his breath. His dream of buying a new truck for the business dissipated as Chris aimed, shot, and sank the black ball. *Damn it. Well, at least Iain is still—*

"Yes!" Chris yelled, but it was a short-lived victory, as the white ball raced across the table and dropped into the middle pocket, instantly handing the win to Rigs.

Rigs laughed as Chris's face twisted into a portrait of rage, horror, and misery. "You semi-pro guys really don't like losing, do you?" he said, returning the cocky wink.

Chris threw his cue to one side, snatched up his jacket, and stalked off. "I'm fucking out of here!" he said, his bottom lip drooping. His tantrum resembled that of a four-year-old having a shit-fit in a supermarket.

"Not that door, sir," Porky said, a grin tugging at the corners of his lips. "That one over there."

"Get that smile off your face before I knock it off!" Chris told Porky.

"Please, sir, don't threaten me with violence."

"Yeah?" The crybaby stomped up to the landlord. "And what the fuck are you going to do about it, fats—*ooo!*" Chris suddenly squealed in agony, as Porky gripped him by his testicles.

Titters escaped the crowd, and Rigs watched on with twisted glee.

"What I run here is tradition, sir. I told you at the start that any nonsense would be met by harsh treatment." Porky squeezed harder. "Now, I'm giving you one last warning."

"Please, let go!" Chris pleaded. "I'm going to be sick!"

"Best shut up and listen then, sir. You can either walk out of here with or without your balls attached. Which would you prefer?"

"Attached. Attached!" Chris squeaked.

"Good," Porky said, releasing his privates. "Now get out of here. I'm starting to lose my patience."

Rigs's mouth hung open in shock. He'd taken the landlord to be a placid man, not someone who could be violent or stand up for himself in such a manner. He was unsure whether he liked it or not. Did Porky have a hidden persona? Was there someone much darker lurking behind his mask? Was the nicey-nice act a façade?

I'll need to keep an eye on him . . .

Chris scuttled through the crowd, holding his balls and jacket. "You fucking prick," he said over his shoulder. Then he tripped over Diesel's boot.

"Yeah, I did that on purpose," Diesel stated. He bent, nose to nose with the downed man. "I believe he kindly asked you to fuck off." He slapped Chris hard, leaving a red mark on his cheek, and dragged him off the floor, placing a solid knee to his gut. "*I* don't ask so nicely."

Chris doubled over, the air whooshing out of him. Diesel slammed him against the wall and buried his forehead in Chris's face, instantly puffing his eye. Then, with a brutal grip, he escorted the man to the exit by the scruff, opened it, and threw Chris through it. "Get. Fucking. Out!" he screamed, slamming the door shut.

"Who's playing next?" he said, turning to face the stunned crowd.

"Was that really called for, big man?" Iain hollered. "Try that with me and I'll bust your skull apart."

"What the fuck did you say?"

"Wash the spuds out of your ears, dickhead. I'm not repeating myself."

"You got some fucking nuts on you, talking to me like that in front of my crew."

"Then bring it, lady. I ain't got all evening, you know," Iain said, draining the last of his beer.

"Oh, I'll bring it, granddad. You just wait until we get out of here."

Rigs stepped between the warring men. "Settle down, settle down. We're here to play, not fight."

"Since when did you become a fucking diplomat?" Iain asked.

"Since you couldn't keep your half-cut gob shut." Rigs grabbed Iain by the shoulder and turned him around, speaking quietly enough to not be overheard. "Cool it, mate. You ain't sure what those crazy fuckers are capable of. They could have us buried in a fucking gravel pit by sunrise. Please, just try and keep calm. Stay focused. There's a lot of money at stake here, and we just got a step closer."

"Okay, okay, you're right," Iain said, walking off and giving Mandy's arse a hard crack. "Fancy a drink?"

Her expression was a picture, and Rigs thought he was going to keel over from laughter. But her face of thunder turned to that of calmness and serenity. She gave him a cheeky smile and winked. "Aye, go on then."

This seemed to annoy Charlie, as Rigs had seen him trying to crack that safe all evening. "You snooze, you lose," Rigs said under his breath. Leaving Iain to it with Mandy, he crossed to Grace. "Who have you got?"

"Charlie," she said, giggling. "I think he's scared he's going to lose to a girl. Nice win, by the way."

Rigs blushed. "Cheers. Let's hope we don't have to play each other, hey? I sure wouldn't want to embarrass you."

"With your cue skills, you're only likely to shame yourself, mister!" She bumped her rump against his.

He smiled, even though she caused some of his beer to slosh over the rim of his glass and spatter his dirty work jeans. The alcoholic stains were lost among the oil patches and grime. "Where are you heading, anyway?"

"We're meeting friends at Cardiff."

"Oh?"

"Yeah. We're off to see Whitesnake at the Motorpoint Arena next Saturday," she said, playfulness dancing in her eyes.

"Slicks and Gutbust, you're up," Porky announced.

Rigs ignored the tournament, too entranced by Grace. "Are you a Welsh girl? I don't detect any dialect."

The sound of the balls breaking threw a hush over the room, and she answered in a whisper, "I was born in Wales, Caerphilly, but my parents moved back to the north, as that's where my dad's from. I have a brother in Swansea, but that's about it. You?"

He matched her quiet tone. "Valleys lad, born and bred. Iain, too."

"You guys work together?"

"Yeah. We have our own hauling firm. Well, one lorry and a ton of passion. We ain't Eddie Stobbart, but we do well."

Grace giggled. "Sorry, the Stobbart comment got me. I swear I'm not making fun of your endeavors."

"Don't be silly. We rip the shit out of ourselves constantly."

"Oh. Well, good, because I can toss in with the best of them. Have you known Iain long?"

"All my life. We're brothers more than friends. We'd do anything for each other. I'd take a bullet for him," Rigs said. "I love him. In a platonic way, of course."

The sound of potting balls deadened all other noise in the room but Rigs still managed to catch that golden giggle of Grace's, which he absorbed into a deep part of his heart. He hardly knew the girl, but she was hypnotizing.

"I see. Mandy and me are a bit the same. I've probably not known her as long as you've known Iain, but we're very tight. I'd pretty much do anything for her, too."

"It's good to know you've got someone like that at your back, ain't it?"

"Most definitely. I'd have it no other way."

He swallowed hard, uncertain if he were about to cross a line. *Fuck it. It's time I live on the edge for once.* "Do you guys need a lift the rest of the way?" Heat scorched his face. "I . . . You know, I just thought it . . . Um, you know—"

Grace smile and put her hand on his forearm. "We'd love to. Well, *I'd* love to. Can't really speak for Mandy, but I'm sure she'd be grateful for a lift."

"No problem. I mean, we're heading that way anyway, so you may as well tag along. You ain't got a couple of spare tickets for the gig, have you? I ain't seen Whitesnake in years," he joked, not expecting it to go any further.

"As it happens, I *do* have a spare ticket."

Rigs's smile faded, his heartbeat quickening. "I wouldn't want to impose myself or anything, of course."

"No, seriously, you should come. Iain, too."

"I thought you only had one extra ticket?"

"Bah, we'll soon get another. There's bound to be people selling them outside. Unless, of course, you don't want to."

"No, no," he said, beaming. "We'd love to come. Iain's also a bit of a rock freak, so he'd love that. Thanks."

"My pleasure," she said, winking at him.

"It'll be—"

A commotion at the pool table interrupted their delightful conversation, as another player had lost their chance at getting the money.

"Ah, balls!" Gutbust said, punching Slicks in the arm.

"Best go join Roadblock in the Losers Lounge!"

"Fuck you, man," Gutbust said, smiling all the while. He picked his beer up and left without a fuss.

"Danny and Shogun," Porky announced, "to the table, please."

"What were you going to say?" Grace asked, bringing Rigs's attention back to her.

"Well, shit, I can't remember."

"That'd be old age."

"Gee, thanks."

She laughed. "I'm guessing you were about to say something about the gig?"

"Yeah, that's right. I was just going to say it should be a laugh."

"That it will." Grace took a sip from her drink and her eyes widened. She pointed at a nearby table. "Oh shit, looks like trouble."

Rigs craned his neck for a peek. Danny and Shogun had hold of the other's tops and were yelling in each other's faces. Porky and some of the other bikers were trying to pry them apart.

"I demand a fucking re-rack," Shogun yelled, his spittle flying into Danny's face.

"No fucking way, scumbag. It's not my fault you took a fucking wonky break-off shot."

"I'm going to rip your motherfucking eyeballs out, cunt!"

Danny clamped his teeth on the bridge of the biker's nose. Rigs grimaced as cartilage crunched. The Boa, apparently unfazed, planted his knee firmly in Danny's crotch.

"Aw, you dirty bastard!" Danny said, coming back with a head-butt.

Porky grabbed Shogun by the arm before the biker could counterattack again and escorted him to the exit. "Get the hell out of here!" he told the bloodied man. "I'm sick of you sore losers!"

After throwing Shogun out, Porky turned on the rest of them, puffing hard and glowing red. "I bloody well mean it," he said, stamping his foot. "No more of this nonsense. In all my years of running this prestigious tournament, never have I witnessed such childish behavior. Never!"

The whole room fell silent.

"Well?" he asked, a glint in his eyes nearing derangement. "Are we all going to start acting like grown-ups?"

"Yes," Diesel said. "We get you. *Fuck*! It's just a bit of healthy competition."

Porky walked right up to the Boas' leader. "It ain't healthy when it's wrecking my pub."

Rigs sniggered. It was like the man was being told off by his mother. All that was missing was the slap around the head.

"Okay, okay, we're sorry. Right, guys?" Diesel said, turning to his remaining gang members, who all nodded in unison.

"Good, then let's crack on," Porky said, calling Mandy and Smith forward for the next round.

"Go get 'em," Iain told Mandy as she walked off and picked up a cue stick. "And I'm calling it now: me and you, final game."

"Hey, shouldn't that be you and me?" Rigs chimed in.

"Sorry, mate, but she's better looking than you."

"Charming. Well, as long as you win and bring that lovely cash home with you, then that's fine by me."

"You got it, amigo."

"I reckon it'll be you and me anyway," Grace said, again bumping her rump against Rigs's.

"I think that too, Grace. I just don't want to go saying that to Iain and hurting his feelings. He's like a big Jesse at times," he said, winking.

"I heard that," Iain stated.

"Good, at least we know now not to buy you a hearing aid out of the winnings."

"Oh, funny. You're killing me over here." Iain held onto and jiggled his gut.

They all laughed and focused on the game unfolding on the baize. Mandy circled the table like a bird of prey, potting everything in sight like a pro and wrapping the game up within minutes of breaking. *She hardly broke a sweat*, Rigs thought as the black disappeared down a middle pocket.

"Mandy wins!" Porky announced, and Smith calmly picked his drink up and walked out the door.

"Another one for Loser Lounge," Diesel said. "Not many of us left now. I can almost feel the grands in my hands."

"Next, Grace versus Charlie," Porky called.

"The best of British luck," Rigs told Grace.

She gave him a peck on the cheek. "Thanks."

Rigs wanted desperately to draw her into his arms, kiss her, feel her body pressed tight against his. "My pleasure" was all he managed to say though. *She smells amazing*, he thought as she sashayed to the pool table. *Cracking arse, too.*

Rigs wandered over to Iain, who now had his arm around Mandy's waist. "I'm fancying our chances, mate, what with both of us through to the next round."

"Don't go counting your chickens just yet, my little chickadee," Mandy proclaimed. Iain laughed.

"Oh, is that right?" Rigs asked, smiling.

"Uh-huh." She took a gulp from her bottle of lager. "Gracey and I are taking you *all* to the cleaners."

"We'll see about that," Rigs mumbled. He knew Mandy was good, but he'd played and beaten some tough players in his time.

The crowd watched in awe as the game between Grace and Charlie went to the wire. It came down to a dogged fight over the black ball, with both players missing their chance to pot the elusive number eight three times. Finally, Grace potted it by running it the length of a cushion. Had she missed, it would have meant certain victory for Charlie.

"Winner: Grace!" Porky confirmed. Mandy, Rigs, and Iain all whooped and clapped for her.

Charlie pushed past a few of the others and walked up to Mandy with a scowl on his face. "I guess you've made your choice?" he said, eyeing Iain up and down. "Classy."

Iain stared at him intently. "Want a nightcap?"

"Pfft! Moron," Charlie said, leaving through the door the others had used before Iain could retaliate.

"What a douche," Rigs said. He addressed Grace and gave her a hug. "Well done."

"Thanks, beaut," she said, squeezing his bum.

* * *

Sheila won the last game and Porky called an end to play.

"All right, ladies and gentlemen," he announced, "we have our remaining eight. The draw for the quarterfinal will take place in twenty minutes. Now's the time to get a drink or use the loo. Time also to bask in your first-round win. Please return when the bell rings."

CHAPTER FIFTEEN

CLANG, CLANG, CLANG, CLANG!

"Everyone, your attention please," Porky called. "It's time to begin round two." The low whispers and conversations tapered into silence as the last eight standing joined him. "I shall now draw the names." He stuck his hand into the tombola and pulled out two slips. "First up: Diesel and Mandy."

Mandy scowled at the outlaw as he put his fingers to his mouth and mocked oral sex. "You pig."

"Ooh, a feisty one!" he said, giving Iain's arm a nudge. "You lucky devil."

Iain said nothing, which shocked Rigs. His mate had drunk enough to be in one of his rowdier moods but was holding his composure well.

"Names three and four: Grace and Sheila," Porky continued.

"Should be an easy one for you," Rigs commented to Grace out of everyone else's earshot. "She was poor in the first round against that fella she played."

Porky produced two more name slips. "Iain versus Slicks. That leaves Rigs against Danny. That completes our lineup, ladies and gentlemen. Would the first two take up cues and join me here at the table, please?"

Grace, Sheila, Iain, Slicks, Rigs, and Danny dispersed, making room around the pool table for Diesel and Mandy to commence play.

"End of the line for that slimy biker," Iain said under his breath to Rigs. "I'd love to ring his fucking neck, aye!"

"Ah, let it go, man. He ain't worth it."

"He's right, Iain," Grace chimed in. "And, as you pointed out, he ain't going to be around much longer. My girl is going to kick his arse."

But a powerhouse of a display by Diesel shocked them all into silence, as the biker potted seven of his balls in a row after breaking. If it weren't for the eight-ball rattling in the jaws of a middle bag and staying there, the game would have been over within a minute or two.

"Holy shit," Rigs said. "He's done her in!"

"No, no . . . Not yet, he hasn't," Grace said, fixated on the green woolen material adorning the billiard top.

"Come on, love," Iain called in support. "Do your thing."

"Hey, now," Porky said. "No calling out or making noise while players are at the table."

"Sorry." Iain winked at Mandy, who had a stern expression on her face.

"Come on, bitch. My cue playing arm is going stiff," Diesel ribbed.

"You mean your *wanking* arm, dickhead?" she bit back, making him laugh.

"I love that rage of yours, my lovely."

She gave him the finger, making him laugh harder.

"Take your fucking shot!" he barked.

"No rushing you opponent," Porky chirped.

"Well, she's taking the piss here, man—walking round and round, doing that stupid studying-the-table shit."

Mandy exploded into action, immediately potting one, then a second, third, fourth, fifth, and sixth before her prowess collapsed like a house of cards. The seventh rattled in the jaws, with the white going close to a side cushion. "Shit! Fuck and piss!" she yelled, raking her hair out of her eyes, which had covered her face in her frenzy.

"Crap," Iain muttered.

"He'll probably fuck the black up," Rigs said.

"Go on, boy, fucking do her!" Slicks hollered, saluting his lieutenant with his beer.

"I sure will," Diesel said, leaning over to take aim. In a cocky maneuver, he closed his eyes and struck the white ball. It slowly rolled across the table and gently connected with the eight-ball, which in turn tenderly rotated into the middle bag.

"Winner: Diesel!" Porky called.

"Woo-hoo! In your fucking *face*," Diesel screamed at Mandy. He blew her kisses and shooed her away with his hands. "Bye-bye!"

"What an arsehole," Mandy said, walking over to Grace and the two truckers with tears in her eyes.

"Hey," Grace said, rubbing Mandy's arms, "it's okay."

"Sorry, Grace. I really should have beaten him. I—"

"You've got nothing to be sorry about, Mandy. It's only a silly game anyway."

"But all that money we've put in . . ."

"Pfft! What, forty quid? Behave. We took a chance. Besides, I'm still in."

"I guess you're right," Mandy said.

"Hard lines," Iain told her. "At least I'm not the one who has to put you out of the competition."

"Hey!" She threw a punch at his upper arm.

"Ow!" Iain mocked while rubbing the area vigorously. He winked at her again.

Porky wobbled up to them. "I'm sorry, miss, but you'll have to join the others in the back room whilst we play the rest of the tournament."

Grace scowled. "But she—"

"No, rules are rules," Mandy said. "I'll be fine. Kick some arse, girl." She hugged Grace and left the room like the others had before her.

"It's starting to look pretty bare around these parts," Slicks mocked, his American accent dreadful.

"Good eyes, bell-end," Iain replied. "Never noticed myself."

Porky sighed roughly. "Would Grace and Sheila please come forward?"

"The best of luck, bitch," Diesel said, locking eyes with Grace and chuckling.

Rigs wanted to punch the guy until his fist hurt, but he swallowed the feelings. He didn't need his emotions spiraling out of control at such a crucial moment. He could win this thing, now that Mandy was out. He needed to get into the next round.

Porky tossed a coin, Sheila called and won, and she opted to break.

How Sheila had made it through the first round, Rigs didn't know. Her form was just plain dreadful. She could barely break the racked pack, let alone hold her cue straight. She must have known her chances would be slim. *Slim? More like fucking anorexic!* he thought, tittering aloud.

"What the hell are you laughing at now?" Iain wanted to know.

"At how shit that woman is. Look at how the back half of her cue moves from left to right as she takes her shot. Crap."

"Ha! I know. Pretty damn hilarious."

Grace eight-balled her into the baize. It was a deserved stuffing for a person who had literally no right in taking part, not even for the fun of it.

"Winner: Grace!" Porky announced.

Slicks scoffed. "Stevie Wonder could have beaten her."

Diesel screeched out a laugh while backhanding Slicks's shoulder. "Good one, man."

"Morons," Grace said.

"Iain and Slicks, please come to the table," Porky said, reading off a card which had all the players' names chalked on it.

As they shook hands, Slicks noticeably applied extra pressure, provoking a lopsided grin from the trucker.

"Is that the best you can do, granny?" Iain asked, wiping the smile off the biker's face.

"I'll fucking cue-whip the life out of you, son."

"I'd love to see you try."

"Please, gentlemen, let's try and keep this civil." Porky flipped the coin. "Call, Slicks."

"Heads."

Porky caught the metallic piece. "Tails it is. Iain?"

"Break," he said. Slicks racked and Iain split the pack tactically, hitting them softly. There was just enough impact for three balls to spin free and hit cushions either side of the table.

"What kind of womanly shot was that, pussy?" Slicks asked.

"The kind that'll screw you over, mate." Iain puckered his lips as if ready for a kiss.

"Ugh, you sick bastard," Slicks said. He aimed for a ball slightly adrift of the pack, rammed his cue into the white, and somehow missed.

"Well, that was pretty useless," Iain muttered. He made a delicate shot, splitting the balls up more but effectively handing over control of the table to the biker.

"Take a decent shot!" Slicks demanded.

"Now, now," Porky said. "I'll be the ref here, thank you. Iain has done nothing wrong. Tactical play *is* allowed."

Slicks gave Porky a hard stare, then went for another loose ball. It jarred the pocket and spat back out. "Goddamn it!"

Iain glanced the white off the pack again, which broke them apart further. Again Slicks missed his ball.

"You're leaving me shit, man! What is this—pool or chess?"

"Tennis, the last time I checked," Iain retorted. This time he went for a pot, which he nailed. The white ball screwed back, smashing the remainder full on. They whizzed around the table, with a second stripe finding a top pocket.

"Iain is stripes, Slicks solids," Porky announced.

"I wasn't even going for that!" Iain said. He laughed, dropping the chalk as he tried to dust the tip of his cue. He squatted to retrieve it and staggered, almost falling over. "Shit, too many beers, methinks," he said, glancing over at his mate.

Rigs gave him a stern look that nonverbally communicated his thoughts: *Don't fuck this up*!

Iain stood and inhaled deeply, almost like he was meditating, and nodded at Rigs. He finished chalking the tip, lined up his cue, and sank two more balls before scratching.

Slicks came in strong, potting six solids but leaving himself snookered behind one of Iain's. He tried a three-cushion escape, missing his final ball by an inch. "Bollocks!" he yelled.

Iain cleared his remaining stripes and downed the eight-ball.

"You piece of shit," Slicks raged, stomping over to Iain with his pool cue raised. He cracked the playing implement across Iain's back. The sturdy stick broke in half on impact.

Rigs jumped in and leveled Slicks with a powerful left hook. Then he was spun around and Diesel planted his forehead into his. "Aw, you son of a bitch!" He went to one knee. The burly biker stood over him. Rigs grabbed him by the bollocks and twisted. He drove his attacker back against the nearest wall but was head-butted in the face again.

As they continued to scrabble, Slicks and Iain rolled about the floor, each man delivering punch after punch to the other. Tables spilled over, knocking half-empty glasses of beer onto the expensive-looking carpet.

* * *

"Enough!" Porky shouted. With his trusty steel bat Bloody Mary at hand, he clubbed his open palm. "Pack it in. Now!"

They continued fighting, making a mess of his prized establishment.

Porky went in swinging. He clubbed Slicks in the small of his back repeatedly, not wanting to injure Iain—the trucker hadn't started it, in his eyes. After Porky got in a few good welts to Slicks's spine, the biker rolled off Iain, and Porky finally caught him in the face with Mary. The Boa lay on the floor moaning, semi-conscious.

Porky grabbed the man by his greasy hair and dragged him over to the losers' exit. "Get up and get out!"

He opened the door for the wounded man and was relieved to find Baby standing on the other side, waiting for their next victim. She grabbed Slicks by his ankles and dragged him sharply through the entrance. Once he was on her side, she beat him mercilessly.

Before the biker could bleat or whimper, Porky slammed the door closed and wheeled around. Rigs and Iain were laying into Diesel and the others were too captivated by the mayhem to have noticed Baby's relentless violence. They'd seen nothing. For that, he was grateful. "Right, you two—leave him alone."

Sweating and breathing hard, Iain and Rigs let up. Diesel held his pummeled gut as he slid down the wall which had been supporting him.

"That might teach you a lesson, lad," Porky said, pointing Mary in the fallen biker's face. "Now get up and go sit. We have a competition to finish here." He smoothed his hair back, straightened his dirty shirt, and called for Rigs and Danny to play their quarterfinal round.

* * *

By now, Danny had lost all interest in the game. During the short brawl, he'd kept wondering why he'd heard nothing off Bobby or Clive. And what the fuck was with this place? Why was it so quiet in the so-called Losers Lounge? Wouldn't the Boas especially be rowdy and making drunken noise in there? Something didn't gel.

He planned to throw the game. He needed to check this place out, find Clive, see if he had anything. *I can't make this look too obvious*, Danny thought, *but I need to get to my guys, pronto.*

Porky gave Danny the call. "Tails," he said.

"Heads it is," Porky announced. "Rigs to break."

The break was decent and Rigs potted four before Danny even knew what had happened. *This guy's good*, he thought. *Even if I wasn't going to pitch the game, I don't think I'd have won.*

When Rigs finally lost control of the table, Danny purposely missed his ball. "Damn!" he said, playing it up and whacking his leg with his fist. "I rushed that."

"Hard luck, mate," Rigs said, off potting again before he stopped talking. When he was down to his last ball, he missed, leaving it tight against a cushion. "Shite! Guess I've let you in here, Danny."

"Too right you have." Danny performed a shoddy pull on the cue and deliberately slammed the black home, handing victory straight to his opponent.

"Yes!" Rigs blurted, quickly composing himself. He offered his hand to Danny. "Sorry. Good game."

"It's okay." Danny shook Rigs's hand. "You win some, you lose some." He picked up his jacket and rushed for the door. "The best of luck to the rest of you," he said, making a fast exit.

"The semifinal will commence in twenty minutes, ladies and gentlemen," Porky said.

CHAPTER SIXTEEN

DANNY STOOD ALONE IN THE NEW CORRIDOR. Silence blanketed him. Nothing moved. Nothing creaked. He attempted to reopen the door he'd entered through but it wouldn't move, and he couldn't hear anything beyond it. *Well, this doesn't seem right.*

He hitched up his trouser leg, pulled his snub-nosed .38 from his ankle holster, and cocked it. In the quiet and narrow space, it sounded like a crack of thunder.

Danny held his gun out in front of him, edging down the passageway with his back against the wall. He didn't care if his assumptions were completely wrong and he burst in on a room full of people with whom he'd just been playing pool. He'd rather have rouged cheeks than regrets should his sudden hunch and instincts prove correct.

As he grew closer to the door at the end of the corridor, he stopped. *Did I just hear screams?* His brow furrowed. *No, can't be . . .*

A clicking sound made Danny jump back from the wall, a portion of which slid to one side, revealing a staircase beyond. *Jesus H. Christ—a secret passage? Am I stuck in a game of frigging Cluedo or something?* He wondered if this was where the screams had emanated.

He crept to the first step and tiptoed up them. The wood in the wall shut behind him, cutting off all light and sealing him in. Danny rooted around in the breast pocket of his jacket and withdrew his lighter.

He thumbed the indents on the back of it. An inscription: "From all the guys. Congrats, Sarge!" He remembered that day well. There had been a party, a celebration of his promotion complete with scotch and cake. *A good bunch of lads,* Danny thought. Sadness briefly took hold as he reminisced. Only he and Clive were left from their training group. The others had either moved on or been killed in the line of duty.

Danny shook off the memories and struck the Zippo. Once was all it took. "You've never failed me, baby," he muttered. He climbed upward, brandishing the lighter and gun. Cobwebs and dust littered the staircase. The harsh stench of rot and dampness filled his nostrils, along with the smell of shit. He coughed but didn't gag. He'd come across worse. Much, much worse.

He reached the top of the steps, rounded a corner, and found another flight of stairs. *Well, shit.* How big was this place? Three or four floors? Five? Six, even? He couldn't recall it appearing that expansive when gazing at it from the car park.

He took the first step and his foot went straight through one of the floorboards. A rat squawked. "Fuck off," he half-whispered, still attempting to keep a low profile. "Pissing rats." Halfway up, Danny slashed through spider webs with his .38 just to get by. The dust finally got to his nose, enticing a sneeze, which he stifled.

He finally reached the summit, which opened into a massive room. "Fuck," he said in awe, voice almost nonexistent. He'd never seen an attic that large and figured it must span the entire width and length of the pub. All the windows were bricked up apart from one, which had loose boards covering it. From behind those planks peeked the moon, its milky glow poking its way into the dust-covered room and lighting it naturally.

Danny heard the panel in the wall slide open below, at the foot of the bottom staircase.

Danny frantically looked about and opted to hide behind a stack of boxes which were piled to the beams. He made sure he was fully obscured, aimed his gun at the opening at the top of the second flight, and thumbed the hammer back in readiness.

Footsteps clomped closer.

Danny wiped the sweat from his brow as droplets stung his eyes.

A head popped into view, covered by some type of mask. The shoulders emerged, the chest. *Clomp, clomp, clomp*—the footfalls were heavy and lethargic. When the silhouette crested the stairs, Danny gasped at the sheer size of the person.

He prepared to call a warning shout but decided against it and lined up his sights. His index finger rested against the trigger, beginning to squeeze.

A rattle of chain and a low growl off to his side caused him to pause.

He turned toward the menacing sounds, thinking he'd never heard anyone or anything shriek as loud or hideously in his life.

A humungous beast lurched at him from the darkness.

He squeezed the trigger and bullets exploded from the chamber of the .38.

CHAPTER SEVENTEEN

CLANG, CLANG, CLANG, CLANG, CLANG, CLANG!

Porky gave the bell a few more hearty rings this time, hoping he'd muffled the rapport of gunfire. *I knew this lot would be trouble, I bloody knew it*! *I just hope Richard hasn't been discovered in the garret or we may be in for some real shit*, he thought.

He hadn't lied when he'd proclaimed his brother to be dead. He was, practically, ever since that stray had bitten him . . .

"What the hell was that?" Iain asked.

"Can't say I heard anything," Rigs said.

"Me either," Grace chipped in.

"I believe it was the bell," Porky interjected, giving it one more *clang*.

"No, I heard it too," Diesel said. His lip had swollen, and dried blood had nestled in one corner of his mouth. His nose also seemed to be slightly misshapen but not broken. He didn't appear to be in any pain as he spoke or moved about. "Sounded like a gun being fired to me."

"You'd know," Iain said. Dried blood also surrounded his mouth, and his left eye had darkened. "Hell, it's probably your lot messing about in the lounge area."

"What?" Diesel snapped. "*My* lot? What the fuck is that supposed to mean?"

"Enough!" Porky said. "Look, are we going to play or not? I'd hate to refund your entry fees when you're a few games away from winning the kitty, but if that's what you all want, it can be arranged."

A grave silence fell over the room, and Porky prayed no other sound would come from within the pub that might expose their operation.

* * *

What seemed like an age passed before Rigs decided to break the quietude. "Of course that's not what we want, Porky."

"And the rest of you?" the fat landlord said. Sweat poured down his face and his teeth ground together. He was obviously irked to no end.

The others nodded and muttered like scolded children.

"Good. Diesel and Rigs, you're up. And no more nonsense. If there's so much as a murmur of banter," he said, pointing at them with a rigid finger, "then I'm disqualifying the pair of you. Understood?"

"Yes," Rigs said.

Diesel nodded.

"Great. Rigs, it's your call."

"Heads."

Porky tossed and caught the coin. "Heads it is."

"I'll smash 'em," Rigs said, placing the white ball behind the curtain. He struck with everything he had and blasted the pack apart, sending balls everywhere. Nothing potted.

"A nice open game," Diesel said, eyeing his first move. "Stripes."

Porky nodded.

"Not what I would have gone for," Rigs muttered under his breath. Thankfully, nobody heard his statement. He was especially wary of Porky's temperament. The pub owner seemed to have reached his limit. *I better bite my tongue if I want to take the prize home.*

Diesel tapped the first target into a middle pocket. The white ball screwed back just far enough for him to be able to take out a second stripe in the same pocket. With those two down, he picked up the chalk and walked around the table dusting the tip of his cue, studying the lay of the baize.

Rigs noticed him eyeing the awkward stripe stuck against a cushion. *And that is why I would have gone for the solids. They're all open, apart from the one right by the eight-ball.*

Diesel was off again, this time clearing the other middle bag, where three of his balls loitered. After putting two of them away, he cannoned the third off a solid, which pushed Rigs's ball to the cushion.

"Shit," he huffed, not quiet enough this time around.

Diesel smiled at him in response.

Porky said nothing, though one of his eyes twitched.

Next, Diesel went for a stripe hanging over the bottom-left pocket. He executed the shot well, slamming the ball home. He then went for the one stuck to the bottom cushion, which rolled along the side and dropped into the bottom-right pocket.

With all his balls slotted home, he gave the eight-ball a hard crack. It careened around the table, missing every hole and clipping one knuckle before coming to rest against a side cushion.

"Right, okay," Rigs said, already having formed a plan of action. He took out the two solids nearest his end of the table, giving enough spin to the white on the second so it zipped down the center of the baize and landed nicely on the one Diesel had nudged into the cushion. He dropped that one into the middle bag, giving enough bottom to the cue ball to keep it rooted in the same spot after striking the object ball. With that done, Rigs potted a long, risky solid into the adjacent pocket, which put him back where he'd started. But it left him no clear shots.

Rigs tucked the white ball between the two by the black, making it impossible for his opponent to sink the eight.

Diesel didn't complain, not even after Rigs gave him a cheeky wink and a smile. He took his shot, missing the black by miles. However, he once again struck with too much force and bounced around the table. His haphazard vigor split the solids, pushing them out in the open.

"Ball in hand for Rigs," Porky announced.

Clutching his breath, Rigs placed the white behind the curtain and picked his remaining solids off. He exhaled only after the eight-ball disappeared off the table.

Oddly, Diesel didn't throw a fit like most of his Boas had. He just placed his cue down, picked up his stuff, and headed out the door with a wry little smile on his face.

"Congratulations, Rigs. You've made it to the finals!" Porky said. "Shall we find out who you'll be playing?"

"Let's," Rigs said, beaming.

* * *

"Iain, Grace, you know the procedure," Porky said. As they stepped to the table, the landlord scrutinized Iain's face. "Are you sure you're okay to play?"

Iain waved off his injuries. Although his eye was now almost completely closed from the blows he'd received off Slicks and Diesel, he remained emboldened by the beer. "Bah, just a scratch. I'm fine."

Porky shrugged, though his expression betrayed his doubts. "Right. Grace, your call."

"Tails," she said.

He caught the coin. "Tails it is. Would you like to break?"

"No, I'll let Iain do it," Grace said.

Shit. Stooping and bending put vision in his battered eye next to zero, and he'd hoped Grace would have taken the break. It was going to be difficult smacking the pyramid, let alone potting anything. But lean, aim, and break he did, potting three—two solids and a stripe—in the process. (He had to count balls remaining on the baize with his good eye to figure out which ones had gone down.)

He called stripes and managed another three clean pots before finally missing.

"Ooh, that was unlucky," Grace said, giving his arm a rub. Before he could reply, she whipped around the table like a tornado, clearing five solids and then missing on the sixth.

Iain chuckled and rubbed her arm in turn. "Ooh, that was unlucky," he mocked.

"It's not over yet."

"You're right—the fat lady hasn't started singing," he said, pointing at Rigs.

"Hey! Cheeky bastard," Rigs replied, a smile spreading wide on his face.

Iain attempted a sixth stripe again, but his eye watered anew and he again botched it. "Damn it," he said, wiping the tears off his cheek.

Grace didn't banter this time and sank her sixth and seventh with ease. However, she missed the eight-ball, giving Iain a lifeline.

But, with his eye itching and annoying him, he messed up this shot too. The white settled by the black, an easy claim for Grace, who quickly stepped up and sealed her place in the final with Rigs.

"Winner: Grace!" Porky proclaimed.

"Well done." Iain gave her a hug and a peck on the cheek, then strolled to Rigs and clamped hands with him. "You need to watch this one, mate," he told his friend. "The best of luck, bro. I'll see you after you win this thing."

Iain picked up his beer and headed for the Losers Lounge as Porky announced the final would soon commence. *Rigs has got this. Definitely.* He smiled as the door closed behind him.

CHAPTER EIGHTEEN

Iain walked the length of the corridor, the huge smile still spread across his face. *That new truck is going to be ours*, he thought. *Fucking awesome. So glad we stopped here.*

His curled lips began to straighten as he spotted the door at the end of the corridor though. Something didn't seem quite right. Not that anything seemed out of place—it was the sudden quietness, as though he was the last person on Earth, which unnerved him.

He stopped halfway down the hall, desiring to turn back, when he noticed with his uninjured eye a section of the wall had a massive split down it. On further inspection, he could see it was not a simple crack or damage, but the outline of a door. Like a secret entrance. He cocked his head to the side. *But why the hell would there be . . . ?*

Still bolstered by the drink, curiosity swayed him to put his fingers in the gap and try to slide the wood paneling. It didn't budge. He grunted and growled with effort, but to no avail. "There must be a button or some shit," he muttered. His hands fumbled across the adjacent wall, up and down and side to side. Nothing. The wood remained where it was.

"Fuck it," he said, deciding to move down the hall. Eventually he got to the door at the end. Without hesitation, he opened it, ready to hang with the other losers and imbibe some more.

He stood at the top of a short staircase. At the bottom, a dingy glow cast a room in a grungy orange hue. Rank, putrid air blasted him, and the buzz of flies droned in the background. From what little he could see, he guessed it was a sort of cellar-cum-laboratory. He found it an odd theme for the so-called Losers Lounge but shrugged it off, figuring he could work with it. *All that's missing*, Iain thought, chuckling softly, *is Norman Bates's mother!*

Cautiously, he took the steps one at a time, and more of the room came into view. Bile leapt up his throat and scorched the back of his tongue.

The floor was awash with spilled blood and other fluids. Various jars and containers rested on shelves and countertops, housing a variety of what he assumed were body parts, everything from toes to eyeballs. Tongues and scalps had been nailed to walls.

He managed to get to the last step and staggered forward toward the center of the room, mind whirling. He bumped his waist into a table . . . on which sat Mandy's dismembered head. Her eyes were blank and staring, mouth agape, face filthy. Behind her permanently scared visage hung a torso on a hook. The spike had punched a hole through the chest area. Iain couldn't tell if it was Mandy's body or someone else's—it had been disfigured and dissected beyond recognition.

He stumbled backward from her accusatory, dead gaze. "What the fucking hell is going on here?"

he choked out, heartbeat thumping wildly in his ears.

He then noticed all the Boas' cuts, blood-spattered and torn, stapled to the walls.

"Help," a voice croaked.

Iain grabbed the first thing he could reach, which happened to be a rusty wrench. He spun toward the speaker, raising his impromptu weapon high.

It was Diesel. Hooks through his shoulders suspended him off the floor.

"Holy fuck."

Diesel pointed a shaking finger at Iain. "Be . . . behind you."

Iain turned in time to see a person—a man, judging by the build—dressed in scrubs and a face mask rushing at him with a meat grinder. The would-be doctor's eyes twinkled with glee as he started the power tool. The disc on the grinder came to life, swirling at a deadly, skin-stripping pace. The noise it emitted bit into his senses, and Iain could barely hear his own screaming thoughts.

"Fucking . . . stand there?" Diesel choked out over the sound. "Take . . . the fucker down!"

As the nutter lunged at him, Iain reacted, striking out with the wrench and catching the grinder mid-swipe. The blow sent the mechanical device crashing to the floor, where it continued to whirl against the concrete, emitting a shower of sparks.

Iain wasted no time, swinging the wrench upwards like an uppercut. The tool connected under the doctor's chin, and the impact sent him reeling backward. He banged against a large, termite-infested cabinet, which crunched and teetered. Jars dispersed and burst apart, and body parts—male and female reproductive organs, tongues, ears, toes, fingers—were crushed beneath the attacker's feet.

The madman wailed as he went to ground, bleeding from multiple wounds.

The cabinet lost its tottering war. With groaning, splintering wood, it crashed on top of him. His screaming was cut short as the heavy structure slammed his throat. Some of his bones popped and snapped. He lay still under the debris, aside from a twitching limb or digit here or there.

"Take that, psycho!" Iain shouted. With a cackle and his rationality slipping away, he stepped to the cabinet, pushed it somewhat off the fallen man, and clubbed him about the head three times. The final impact caved the lunatic's head in.

"Jesus . . . Christ," Diesel said as Iain returned to him with his gore-covered wrench.

"Sorry, had to. They always fucking . . . get back up in films," Iain said, breathing hard. He watched the man's blood, piss, and brains mix with the fluid from the jars and wash down the drain in the corner of the room. "Well, he sure as hell ain't."

"Help me down, man," Diesel said, strength returned to his voice. "Please."

Iain glared up at him. "After all the shit you and the rest of your goons gave me and my mate tonight, I should leave you here."

"Get me the fuck—bollocks!" Diesel screamed, jiggling about on the hooks. Flesh tore. Blood trickled and spilled. "Come on, man. *Please*! I'd do the same for—"

"No you wouldn't," Iain said, pointing the wrench in Diesel's face. The veins in his neck throbbed. He wanted to lash out some more, hurt someone else. It was the fiery rage he kept tucked deep inside, clawing its way out like it always seemed to do. "You'd leave me to rot down here, you prick, so don't go giving me that horseshit."

"Okay, okay, I probably would have, but this is a bloody game changer!"

Iain's nostrils flared. He looked away, avoiding Mandy's cold stare, and could make out some of the other tournament losers in the room. The two semi-pro players had been diced and bagged, along with most of Diesel's crew. It appeared the nutcase doctor had been up to this shit a long time.

Or maybe it's Porky and his entire family who are in on this . . . Iain recalled the fat pub owner mentioning his niece and son worked the kitchen and cellar because they were too young to man the bar. Even Porky himself had to be part of this—such vile deeds couldn't be happening in his establishment against his knowledge, surely, regardless of his generosity and polite nature.

Iain's heartbeat quickened. *Shit. What if the pool tournament is just a cover? That means Rigs and Grace are also in danger!*

His rage subsided. Diesel was right. In other circumstances, he'd have left the scummy biker on the hook, but this was totally different. This sick operation—whatever the fuck it was—needed to be shut down for good.

"Okay, I'll let you down," Iain said, "but you have to help me take the rest of these fuckers on. It's got to be a family operation, so that includes Porky's fat arse. Deal?"

"Damn right. They killed my boys."

Iain nodded and grabbed the biker by his legs. He heaved Diesel upward to allow him to slip a shoulder free.

"Keep me like that! Don't fucking let go, or this hook will rip out of me."

"I got you, just—"

A thunderous crash filled the room. Iain jumped, and Diesel slipped in his grip. A wet, squelching sound ensued as the biker was jostled on the hook.

"*Argh!* Fucking Jesus, dude! Be fucking careful!"

Iain offered a hushed apology and shushed Diesel as the clatter continued to fill the room. His ears perked and he noticed a chute on a nearby wall—the noise was coming from within it. He pointed at it. "There. It's coming from that pipe."

"Just fucking get me down. I'm no use to you stuck up here!"

Hurriedly, Iain grabbed the man's legs tighter and lifted anew. Diesel used his loose arm to slip his shoulder free, crying in agony as the hook ripped from his flesh, taking with it a chunk of skin. He flopped over Iain's shoulder, who then placed him gently on the floor.

The clunking came to a crescendo, and the chute spat Danny into the room. His body hit the floor at an awkward angle. He was bloody and torn, a revolver clutched in one hand.

He appeared dead, but Iain rushed over regardless and plopped onto hands and knees beside his still form. Claw marks graced his face and chest—he'd literally been torn to ribbons. "Danny? Danny!" he called. After receiving no response or noting any sign of life, Iain placed a finger to the man's neck.

"Is he dead?"

Iain's shoulders drooped. "I'd say so, yeah. There's no pulse."

Diesel chuckled. "I guess he won't be taking me in after all then."

"What?" Iain couldn't believe the nerve of the guy and wondered if freeing him had been a mistake. Only a sick fuck like the would-be doctor would take pleasure in someone's death.

"He's a copper. He's been on my tail for the past forty-eight hours, trying to catch me in an illegal act."

"For fuck's sake," Iain said, reaching for the gun in the dead man's hand.

Before he could dislodge it, a hulking figure in a PVC suit and gimp mask dropped out of the chute and backhanded him off his feet.

* * *

Grace and Rigs shook hands.

"The best of luck," he said.

"It's *you* who needs the luck, matey," she teased.

"The best of luck to *both* of you," Porky interjected.

"Cheers," Rigs answered. "Would you like to call, Grace?"

"Tails," she blurted, giving Rigs a sly wink.

The coin flipped through the air and Porky caught it. "Heads it is. Rigs?"

"I'll split them."

After Grace racked, Rigs slammed the white ball. It hurtled down the baize and plowed through the pyramid, sending stripes and solids all around the table. Nothing potted. "Oh well, you win some, you lose some," he said.

Grace nominated stripes, bagging four on the bounce. She missed a tricky fifth but sent the white reasonably safe.

"Not bad," Rigs said, chuckling.

"Not bad? That was brilliant stuff."

"Yeah, for a novice." Rigs went off on a six-ball potting spree. His seventh clipped a knuckle and tucked itself behind the black ball.

"Pfft, and what do you call that?" she asked.

"*Crap*, that's what I'd call it!"

"Cheeky so-and-so," he said, chalking his cue and taking a drink of his pint.

Seriousness quickly lined her face, and she took care of her fifth and sixth ball.

His breath caught in his throat as he saw the winnings slip from his grasp, but he exhaled with relief when she too clipped a knuckle and missed her seventh.

He took his time, stalking the table, weighing his options. A snooker seemed the best choice, so he tapped the ball as lightly as he could, nestling the white behind his final solid and the black. "Figure that one out, Poirot!" he said, sniggering.

"You dirty—How the hell . . . You little shit!" she exclaimed.

Rigs grinned, then stifled a "Yes!" when she completely missed her ball.

With ball in hand, he wasted no time taking out his remaining solid and gave himself a proper, unimpeded leave. The eight-ball was pushed close to the bottom pocket, just short of the bag. He lined up his shot.

"No!" Grace moaned.

Rigs's cue stick glided forward smoothly on his steepled fingers. "Get"—the cue ball moved slow and graceful like a swan on water—"fucking"—it dropped in the pocket—"in there!" He whooped, then thumped the table with a closed hand.

"Tournament winner: Rigs! Well played, sir," Porky congratulated, sticking his hand out for Rigs to shake.

"Thanks," he said, obliging and beaming.

"Well played, Rigs," Grace said. "Guess I'll be off now."

"You still want that lift in the morning?"

"Of course. And the offer for the Whitesnake ticket still stands."

"I'd very much like that," he told her, beaming wider.

"Good. When you get done here, maybe we can have a few quiet drinks in the lounge before we head to our beds?"

He blinked but quickly wiped the shock from his face. "Sounds like a plan."

"Great. See you later."

Sadness washed over him as she made for the exit. He wanted to go with her, take her up on the drinks now rather than later. He shook his head. *Man the fuck up, for Christ's sake. You'll see her in about thirty minutes.*

"Rigs?" Porky called, breaking his thoughts. "I'll go and get the Champ. Shouldn't be more than five minutes. Would you like to get yourself a drink, maybe use the loo?"

"I'm okay for booze, but I'll use the loo. I'll be back in less than a few minutes." Rigs slapped Porky's shoulder with an open hand and chuckled. "The sooner I win, the better."

Porky smiled and left the room.

CHAPTER NINETEEN

IAIN CLIMBED BACK TO STANDING, scanning the new attacker head to foot. If the mounds on their chest were any indication, this one was female. *Porky's niece, maybe*?

He growled and ran at her, tackling her rugby-style. She took the impact of his shoulder blow and kneed him in the gut. She then chopped the back of his neck and threw him to the floor like a rag doll. Lying on his side, Iain watched her stomp over to Diesel and drag him to his feet by his hair. She slammed his face repeatedly against a wall, spun him around, and dug her thumbs into his wounds. He screamed as she twisted her digits.

Iain scrambled up, grabbed a nearby chair, and smashed it over her back. She released her grip on the biker.

As she staggered aside, Diesel held his nose, which streamed blood and snot. "You fucking bitch!" he yelled, drawing a blade from his boot. The steel measured a good eight inches, with a shaft made from fine bone. He ran at the big bitch and slashed his knife down her back. He cut through her suit. The serrated blade stripped skin, and blood splashed across his face.

She hardly flinched, and before he could get another stab or slash in, she punched him in the throat. He hit the dirt and rolled about, holding himself and cursing. As he got on all fours, she hit him in the jaw with a solid kick. He collapsed fully.

While she was distracted, Iain placed his arms around her and picked her up in a bear-hug. His biceps strained against his top and the veins in his neck protruded as he took on the role of boa constrictor. But again, she seemed little put out by the attack. She moaned and groaned as if she welcomed being manhandled. *Is she fucking getting off on this*? he wondered, applying more pressure.

She flung her head back, connecting her skull with his face once, twice, three times.

He let go. "Jesus!" Iain shouted, more annoyed with himself than injured. Before she could turn around, he punched her rapidly and repeatedly in her kidneys. "You bitch!" he screamed, brutally attacking her lower back. "Fuck you!"

Finally, this was enough to get her to drop to one knee. Not wanting to let his advantage slip, Iain punched her hard in her temple. She slumped to the floor unconscious.

"Thank God for that," Iain gasped. He stepped over to Diesel, who was coming around. "You okay, man?" He put a hand out.

"I've felt better," the fallen biker said. Diesel accepted the offer and Iain helped pull him to his feet. "Thanks."

"No problem."

"What do we do with this one in the suit?"

"Tie the bitch up," Iain said.

"It's a fucking woman?!"

"Yes. I got a face full of her fat tits. I'm pretty sure she was getting off on being beaten, too," Iain said, leering down at her.

"Fuck."

"Yeah. Crazy bitch. How about you tie her up and I'll go warn Rigs and Grace? We need to let them know what's going on, fast."

"Okay," Diesel said.

The cellar door whined open at the top of the stairs, and both men halted in place. Footsteps descended, echoing eerily.

"Shit, another one of them," Diesel said, snatching up the gun from the floor.

Iain stepped over the large unconscious woman's body and picked up the biker's knife. He brandished it before him, ready to stab away. *I'm getting out of this alive, damn it. Rigs too, along with Diesel and Grace, if she's still alive.*

Diesel thumbed the hammer of the gun back as a silhouette stepped to the cellar floor.

"No!" Iain yelled. "Don't shoot—it's Grace!"

She shrieked and cowered, shielding her face momentarily. When she put her hands down, her wide-eyed gaze traveled from the men wielding their weapons to the carnage about her. "What . . . What the fuck?"

"Christ, I could have killed you!" Diesel said.

Iain rushed to her. "Grace, I think these sick bastards—Porky's family, and probably Porky too—have been holding these pool tournaments, then killing the losers one by one." He centered himself in front of the table to prevent her from seeing her friend's dismembered head. "I'm afraid Mandy's . . ."

"What?" Disbelief shrouded her features and her lower lip trembled. "No!"

"He's right," Diesel said. "It looks like these sickos have been up to this for a long time, too."

"No, I don't—Mandy, she's—" Grace attempted to maneuver around Iain, tears running down her cheeks. "Get out of the way! Mandy can't be—" She shoved his arm and he lost balance for a second. Abject shock settled on her face, her eyes fixated on the head of her friend. "No, no, no, no, no, it can't be. It just can't be," she muttered, blubbering.

"Look, we have to warn Rigs," Iain said, placing his free hand on her shoulder to direct her attention off Mandy's gory stump.

"And then we need to get the hell out of here," Diesel added.

Iain turned to face the biker. "We will, after we get my—Shit, look out!"

Diesel wheeled around and came face to face with the leather-clad woman, who clamped her hands around his throat and squeezed. Iain spun, knife still in hand, and readied himself to charge over, but the biker managed to place the muzzle of the gun to her gut. He squeezed the trigger repeatedly. Gunfire set Iain's ears to ringing as bullets exited her back and drilled into the wall behind her. She lethargically relaxed her grip on the biker, then staggered around the room.

Iain wasn't taking any chances though. Not this time.

He stepped right up to her and ran his blade across her throat.

* * *

Rigs walked around the room, studying the photos on the wall as he waited for Porky to bring in the Champ. Most of them were black-and-white photos of the pub and people—Porky and his family, he presumed. The pictures of the establishment seemed to chronicle various stages of development throughout different decades and eras, and they were situated in a chronological order. He hadn't really noticed them before, but checking them out kept him from getting too anxious. The kit was within reach. He had to maintain steady nerves.

He stopped in front of one and bent for a closer inspection. Squinting, he noticed it was dated 1931. A new roof adorned the Rack and Cue and it appeared to be open for business. He glanced to the left, at the picture before it. The roof was different: thatched in the former photo, slated in the one before him. The name had also changed from one picture to the next, just like Porky had told them earlier.

Rigs walked a few photos along. The same person turned up time and again after the 1930s to 1940s photos. It looked to be a Boa gang member. But they didn't have a chapter in these parts that Rigs could recall. Why would a Boa be so far from home? And if they had been involved with the Rack and Cue throughout the decades, why had Porky been so standoffish with the motorcycle crew?

Rigs scrunched his brow, uttered a hasty "huh," and continued down the line of pictures. He spotted the Boa a few more times and also noticed several faces didn't reappear as time went on. He supposed they had died or been cut off, maybe even moved away.

He made it once around the room and sighed. Nothing else really caught his attention, which was dwindling by the second. He wanted to get this game done and dusted. *It's going on for midnight, for God's sake.*

He took hold of his pint and gulped some of it down. He was starting to feel heady. *I'll be lucky to pot anything if I carry on. This is* definitely *my last*, he thought, ripping a watery burp. His stomach rumbled. *I could do with a few more of those Porky Pies right about now.*

The door to his back creaked open and in walked Porky, all smiles and dimples. "Well, I hope you're ready for your final challenge?"

Forever clichéd, Rigs answered, "I was *born* ready."

Porky chuckled. "That's good. We do love optimists at the Rack and Cue."

"Well, where is he?" Rigs inquired, standing on tiptoes to peer around Porky's bulky frame. "Where's the Champ?"

"Right here. Rigs, please meet your final opponent," Porky said, performing a little bow of sorts and stepping aside.

Rigs stifled a snort as the nerdiest, geekiest, spottiest teenager he had ever had the misfortune to lay his peepers upon stepped forward. He was gangly and walked with awkwardness. He was coy, too, shying away from Rigs's big, battered, bruised, and scuffed hand when offered for a greeting shake.

"The best of luck," Rigs said.

The boy pushed his glasses up the bridge of his nose. "Y-you too."

His voice was everything Rigs had expected, and he thought the boy's spine was going to snap under the effort of uttering a single word. He half expected the kid to whip out a Superman cape or give him a Vulcan sign. But he didn't. Rigs grinned. *What a fucking weaselly, wimpy nerd. The cash is as good as mine*!

"Something amusing?" Porky asked.

"No, I just think I'm going to steamroll your Champ into the baize, Porky."

"Oh-ho-ho, many have thought that."

"I'm sure they have," Rigs quipped.

"Now, the Champ gets to call the coin as it's his turf. And, after all, he is the champ," Porky said, giggling. The way in which his jowls wobbled and his cheeks rouged reminded Rigs of a portly clown.

"Fine by me," Rigs said. "Just as long as you're not using a double-headed coin."

The fat man let out a roaring guffaw. "Oh, of course not, lad, but I must make note of that and get one made!"

Something about Porky had changed. His demeanor was different, as though he were nervous about something.

"H-heads," the Champ spoke softly.

The coin tumbled into the air and Porky snatched it. "Heads it is."

"I'll break," squeaked the boy.

"You do that," Rigs muttered, not worried if Porky overheard. It was the final game and there was no audience. He racked the balls and moved away to chalk his cue tip, a smirk on his face. The nerd would likely screw up straightaway, and he could step in to clean the table in one run.

His jaw dropped as the Champ slid his cue stick in the most fluid motion he'd ever seen and slammed the white into the pyramid. Six balls were potted: five solids and one stripe. He'd never seen a break like it. "What the hell?"

"I did warn you," said Porky, who'd shuffled closer to the door leading to the main bar. The fat landlord slipped through the jamb and out of sight.

The Champ cleared the rest of his balls along with the black in an explosive win. The game was done and dusted in less than a minute from the break.

"I . . . What the fuck just happened?" Rigs said, scratching his head. He'd been bamboozled!

A crack of gunfire erupted in the room just as the Champ shuffled around the table to shake Rigs's hand. The boy was hit square in the chest. His body propelled backward, blood spurting from his mouth. He landed on the baize with a hard crunch.

Rigs wheeled about and spotted Iain, Grace, and Diesel standing on the other side, a gun held steady in the biker's hands.

"No!" Porky screamed, running back into the room. "What have you *done*?" He raised a double-barreled shotgun and thumbed back both hammers, aiming at the Boa.

"Drop it!" Diesel yelled. "Drop it you piece of fucking shit, or I drop you!"

"Whoa, whoa!" Rigs shouted, hands held up and out to calm everyone. "What's happening?"

"Ask that fucking maniac," Iain said, nodding at Porky. "His family are a bunch of murdering, ransacking lunatics."

"What?" Rigs said. "Don't be silly!"

"He's got a cellar full of bodies down there. Organs and God knows what else are stored in jars and other containers. Probably being pickled to be eaten later," Iain said, jaw tensed.

"Fucking cannibals," Diesel added.

Rigs scoffed. "No. There's no fucking way."

"For fuck's sake, man," Iain said. "Mandy's *dead*. They cut her head off. It's down there, in that godforsaken cellar. Everyone else was cut into tiny sections—bits of them everywhere!"

"He's telling the truth," Grace chipped in, face pale and hair a mess.

"Porky, is this right?" Rigs asked.

"Why did you kill my boy? He was so young," Porky said, looking over at the youth who was spread-eagled on the table, the green woolen material atop it now a dark red.

"You reap what you sow, dickhead!" Diesel said.

"Is it true?" Rigs demanded, eyeing the fat owner. He couldn't believe it, not unless Porky confirmed it directly. The man was too kind and polite and—

"We don't *eat* them," Porky said, his consistent smile now replaced by a straight-lined grimace. "We sell the body parts, make money out of it."

"Jesus Christ," Rigs said, appalled. His mind whirled. How many more deranged psychos were loose in the pub? "Is . . ." He gulped hard, his throat suddenly dry. "Is there anyone else in the building?"

"No, it's just me, Baby, and Doc," Porky replied, the shotgun now aimed at the floor, shoulders drooping as if in defeat.

"Baby and Doc, hey?" Iain said. "How fucking cute. We'll they're dead, too."

Porky's conquered features twisted into something more akin to agony and grief. "You bastards!" he yelled, raising the shotgun and squeezing the trigger.

Diesel fired too.

The bullets from Diesel's gun drilled into the fat landlord's head and Porky's shot went down and wide, both cartridges plowing through the floor. The pub owner's face turned to instant mush. He slammed against the door he'd been standing in front of and then hit the deck.

"It's over," Grace said, running to Rigs. She put her arms around him and held him tightly.

"One question: who gets the bread?" Diesel asked.

"All you can think about is the fucking money?" Iain asked.

"We split it four ways," Rigs interjected. "I think it's only fair, don't you?"

"I can live with that," the biker said, shrugging.

* * *

After a short moment to collect themselves, Rigs snatched up Porky's shotgun and the key from around his neck and asked the others to take him to the lower floor of the building. They obliged, everyone alert in case more of the dead owner's family was in hiding. The horrors below were something Rigs had wished he hadn't insisted on seeing, but ensuring a safe escape from more lunatics would outweigh the nightmares, he supposed.

They searched every nook, behind every door, and found no one else lurking. Content that they'd taken out Porky and his family, they moved back to the original bar area where they'd met. They located the money in the box Porky had flaunted and sat to drink and count their earnings. They cut it four ways as agreed upon and then picked up to leave.

"Shouldn't we at least call the police?" Grace asked.

"No reception, remember?" Rigs said, whipping out his cellphone and indicating the lack of bars on the screen. He noticed a dejected look cross her face and shrugged. "We could try to after we get farther away, I suppose."

"I say we leave the coppers out of it," Diesel said. "I mean, we did just steal money off the dead owner, you know, and we did kill some people. We should burn this unholy place to the fucking ground, cover our tracks, and ride off. I doubt anyone would even notice."

"No, let's not do that," Rigs said, frustrated. It wouldn't be hard to fool the authorities and play oblivious, but he also didn't want anyone getting charged for murder when all they'd done was defend themselves. "For now, let's just get out of here."

"I second that," Iain said.

With their money and weapons in hand, they exited the pub. The sky was brightening, the sun starting to rise. The rain had finally stopped.

"Looks like it's going to be a beautiful day," Rigs commented.

"I can't get my head around what's happened. Mandy . . . She—" Grace choked on a sob.

"Hey, come on," Rigs said, putting his arm around her. "Is there somewhere we can drop you off?"

She nodded through the tears. "I want to get to my friend in Cardiff. Please."

"Of course," Rigs said.

Iain hustled toward the lorry. "Come on, let's get the hell out of here."

Next to their truck was Diesel's bike. The Boa was about to straddle it but paused as Iain, Grace, and Rigs neared. He held a hand to his forehead, squinting into the waning darkness.

A low grumble echoed in the distance.

"Someone's coming," Diesel said. "Sounds like a bike too."

The groan became louder and louder, approaching from the entrance to the pub's car park.

"Sounds like it to me, too," Rigs agreed. "It'll probably just pass us by."

"Come on," Grace whined. "Let's get moving."

But before they could load into the truck, a motorcycle pulled into the parking lot of the Rack and Cue. Rigs sized up the passengers, the shotgun at his side but his arms ready to heft it if needed.

The man driving was old-school; his bike was a cruiser. He didn't wear a helmet, causing his long, salt-and-pepper hair to blow wildly in the breeze. He wore shades, too, which he didn't remove upon pulling up to them. On the bike's fuel tank was the word *Boa* with a massive depiction of a constrictor encircling it, making it seem as though it were crushing the letters with its huge body.

Behind the driver was a woman. She looked younger—much, much younger than the man. Like him, she too wore shades. Unlike him, she didn't resemble a biker. She wore a loose-fitting dress, which would have cracked like a whip in the wind. She looked classy and was pale, like the driver.

Is that the man from the photos inside? Rigs wondered. The one he'd noticed time and again with Porky and his family throughout the decades? He shook his head. *It can't be—he wouldn't have aged a day.* Something in the man's shaded gaze kept him from asking too.

The driver eyed Diesel. "A brother?" he asked, his voice silky smooth.

"What business is it of yours?" Diesel said, all cocky and arrogant.

For a guy that looked like he was pushing fifty, he sure could move. Rigs wasn't even sure he saw the guy get off the bike, let alone pick Diesel up off the ground by his throat.

"Ugh . . . Fuck . . . Get off . . ." Diesel coughed and sputtered.

Iain tensed as if he were about to intervene, but Rigs put a hand to his friend's chest to stop him.

"Wise move," the newcomer said, his back to the truckers. "I've no argument with you fellas."

Diesel's face was tomato red, veins bulging on his forehead. The new biker reeled him closer. "I asked you a simple question. Try being polite—there's more than one female present here."

Diesel nodded, gagging as if unable to speak. This seemed to satisfy the newbie, who then flung Diesel one-handed across the car park.

He turned to the truckers. Not a droplet of sweat broke his brow. He spoke low and soft. "You three better get out of here before I really lose my temper."

Rigs nodded. Fear had nestled a cold spot in the pit of his gut. "No problem," he said. "We ain't looking for any trouble, mate."

They scuttled into their vehicle with Iain behind the wheel. He kicked the engine to life and slipped it into gear.

The truck was down the road and out of sight within a minute.

*　*　*

After watching the lorry disappear into the rising sun, the newcomer returned his attention to Diesel, who was struggling to catch his breath. But he made no attempt to back away as the surprisingly strong biker stepped over to him and grabbed him by his cut. His wounds from the cellar were still fresh, still causing his energy to ebb and wane. He didn't stand a fighting chance against such a brute and knew when to play submissive.

The shaded man spoke over his shoulder, directing his voice at the woman still sitting on the bike. "Toni, grab our gear, girl. We *need* to get inside. And you," he said, smirking at Diesel, "are coming with us. We're going to have a little chat."

Diesel didn't want to go back in the pub but saw no choice in the matter. Biting his tongue, he nodded.

PART II

CHAPTER TWENTY

THE MYSTERY MAN PUSHED OPEN THE DOORS to the Rack and Cue and entered like he owned the place. Diesel, holding his ribs and coughing, followed close behind.

"Man, what a shithole," Toni muttered, lugging some overnight bags at the rear of their line.

"Porky?" the man called once through the foyer. "Porky!"

"I don't think he's going to hear you, mate," Diesel said, finally managing to stand up straight.

"My name's Venom, not 'mate,' shithead."

"And my name's Diesel, not—" Diesel halted midstride, forehead scrunched. "Venom? No, that can't be . . ."

Venom turned on Diesel, who flinched away, fearing more harsh treatment. "And why is that?"

"Because you're a legend. A story. A myth. A . . ."

Slowly, Venom removed his shades. "A ghost?" he whispered. His eyes were dead white, milky. It was like looking into the eyes of a blind man: nothing moved there, no emotion or cheer evident. His leather waistcoat creaked as he moved closer to

Diesel, who was slightly smaller in stature and bulk. "Is that what you've heard? That I'm a ghost—a boogeyman?"

Diesel nodded.

Venom chuckled. "Who told you about me?" he asked, slipping his shades back on.

"You're common knowledge within the Boas."

"Am I?" Venom said, nonchalant. He cupped his lips. "Porky!" he shouted and then muttered, "For fuck's sake, where is he?"

"He's dead," Diesel said, blasé.

Venom's face contorted and twisted into shapes and spasms like no other man's could. "Dead?"

He gripped Diesel by his cut and rammed him against the bar. Bottles and glasses which had been lined up along the counter crashed to the floor and exploded on impact.

Glass crunched beneath Toni's feet as she entered the room. "Don't kill him!" she said. "He'll come in handy with the rifle." She laid the weapon on the bar.

"Good point," Venom grunted, letting go of Diesel's throat. "What happened here? Where is everyone else? Baby, Doc, Simon?"

"I—I don't know who those people are," Diesel replied, rubbing his tender neck. *Fuck, he's a strong one!*

Venom pressed his arms outward. "Baby: big tits, large woman, likes to wear a leather suit. Doc likes to masquerade as a doctor. Simon is Porky's son—scrawny little kid."

"You mean the Champ?" Diesel asked, then nodded. "He's also dead. The big lady and the doctor too. We had to kill them. It was—"

"You *had* to kill them? And you call yourself a fucking Boa?" Venom said, raising an eyebrow and digging a finger into Diesel's chest. "That patch used to mean something. The Boas did well. Looked after their community, kept trouble out, no killing—the fucking motto is 'Brains Before Bullets,' dickhead."

"It hasn't been like that for decades," Diesel protested. "Besides, these motherfuckers here at the Rack and Cue were killing people, stealing their organs, and then selling the meat. Porky said so himself."

"Bullshit!"

"I swear. Go to the cellar and look for yourself. You'll see . . . They even killed our brothers."

Venom issued Diesel a hard slap across his face. "You ain't a brother of mine. I don't care what that patch says." With nostrils flaring, he paced around the room, looking angrier with every second. He halted, shaded gaze boring straight through Diesel's skull. "Where are the bodies—Porky and his family?"

Diesel pointed toward the lounge where the pool competition had taken place, his jaw almost too sore to speak.

"Fucking show me," Venom said, gripping the back of Diesel's neck and forcing him in the direction he'd indicated. He released his hold and shoved Diesel forward.

Grimacing with pain, Diesel did as instructed.

They entered the lounge and Diesel stepped aside to let Venom take in the scene. The ghostly, legendary Boa gasped and uttered Porky's name when he spotted the fat landlord crumpled on the floor, his face covered in crimson. One of the bullets had torn through his left eye, creating a large hole.

"Simon?" Venom rushed to the youngster sprawled on the pool table. "Simon?!" Venom gave the boy's face a few gentle slaps. "He—he's still breathing."

"Oh, shit," Diesel whispered. He never would've thought the little pipsqueak would have survived.

"Stay with me, kid. Toni! Get in here with the first aid kit, quick!" Venom turned on Diesel, his massive hands covered in gore. "Did *you* shoot them?"

Diesel's heart thundered the beats out. Had his knees been closer together, they would have been knocking. If Simon didn't recall any details, he could place the blame on the truckers and the girl. They meant fuck-all to him. "No, I didn't kill either of them," he lied. "The others did, the ones you told to leave when you arrived."

"And I'm supposed to believe that, am I?" Venom asked, his expression masked by warring emotions.

"It's the truth. I didn't kill anyone, I promise."

Toni entered the room and pushed past Diesel. He scowled behind her back but kept his mouth shut as she handed the first-aid kit to Venom. The shaded Boa opened it and took out a suture needle, thread, a small pair of scissors, and pliers. He then ripped Simon's T-shirt open. Diesel stood on tiptoes to inspect the damage. A bullet had plowed into the boy's chest, but it didn't appear to be as lethal as it first looked.

Venom sighed through his nostrils. "Toni, your hands are smaller and steadier. Think you can take care of this? I need to check out the rest of the place."

"Can do," she said.

"And when you're done with him, make sure you lock all the doors and windows, and draw the curtains. Sunrise is around the corner."

"No problem," Toni said. "Be careful."

"Don't worry, I'll be fine," Venom said, kissing her softly. He then wheeled on Diesel, eyebrows knitted together. "Let's go for a walk."

* * *

Venom made Diesel lead the way. Aside from the additions they'd thrown on over the years, he was mostly familiar with the Rack and Cue, but he especially didn't want the new-age Boa making a run for it or stabbing him in the back. Not that such a feat would do any good . . .

"We all thought the Champ was dead too, you know," Diesel commented as they walked down the corridor behind the lounge. "Porky obviously wasn't so lucky, and I'm certain the others weren't either."

"The Champ? You mean Simon," Venom said.

"Yes, Simon."

"Why do you keep calling him the Champ?"

Diesel filled Venom in on why the boy had aptly been named the Champ. He also told him what had happened to the losers of the pool tournament, and what the winner had been promised. "It seemed the place had been struggling for years," Diesel said, "so they rigged this competition up and drained people of their money and organs."

"I see," Venom said, wishing he had stayed in touch with Porky and the family better for the past decade. *So much changed, and so quickly*! he thought, though he supposed that was to be expected given his lifestyle. "Porky would have been getting a pretty penny for it, too, I bet," he mused aloud.

"Yeah?"

"Yes. I know the channels and the people running them. There are huge sums of money involved."

"Maybe The Boas are in the wrong game?" Diesel quipped.

Venom wanted to give the man another hard thump for saying such a thing. "If I'd known Porky was up to this, I would have gotten him out of it. Maybe Richard is still around. I can try to save him, at least."

"Richard?"

Venom nodded even though Diesel was looking forward. "His brother. He's—"

"Porky didn't tell us a name, but he did mention his brother was pushing up daisies already."

"So that's the lie he used," Venom muttered, smirking. "I'm guessing you've yet to meet him, huh?"

"We checked. There's nobody else in this building."

"We'll see," Venom said, a sinister grin tugging at his lips.

Diesel pointed to the end of the hallway. "There. That's the cellar where they were doing their dirty work. The other bodies—Baby and Doc?—are in there."

The door stood ajar. As they neared it, a strong stench of death mingled with blood and other bodily fluids. Diesel toed the door open, Venom one step behind. Before they fully descended the stairwell, he caught sight of Doc. Most of the man's head was missing, and what remained was too mashed to identify.

Shaking his head, he finished down the steps and entered the room. The horrid scents and presence of flies and maggots did not bother him. He'd seen much worse in his life. Then he located Baby. He went to her, kneeled, removed her mask, and put a finger to her neck to check for a pulse. He had to make sure.

"She's beautiful!" Diesel gasped, standing behind him. Underneath her mask, she'd been hiding away a thicket of lush red hair. Her complexion appeared soft and free from blemishes. "Shit. Pity she had to be so fucking nuts. She could've—"

Diesel cried out as Venom punched him in the stomach. It wasn't the hardest of blows, but it was enough to put Diesel on his arse.

"Ah, what the hell, mate?" the stricken biker said. "What the fuck is your problem?"

"I told you my name isn't 'mate,' mate." Venom loomed over him, cutting a terrifying shape in the gloomy room. "And this was my family you and your friends butchered."

"Look what they've been doing!" Diesel yelled. "They've been slaughtering people for years."

"They were good people before this. They didn't have a choice. They would have had to resort to it for some reason or another—it wasn't bred into them. I know what it's like to have to make changes and adapt," Venom said, not wanting to explain any further. "Let's get out of here. I've seen enough."

"What else do you want from me?" Diesel asked, climbing to his feet. "Another fucking romantic walk? A candlelit chat? Or how about you just let me go on my way?"

"No, you can't fucking go!" Venom snapped. "You'll pay your debt for whatever part you played in killing my family, as will the truckers. But until then, I'm not letting you out of my sight."

"Come on, man. I have nothing else to give you. I don't know anything else, and I won't be telling anyone about any of this."

"You're wrong. There is something you can give me."

"Oh yeah?"

Venom nodded. "Protection."

"What are you talking about?" Diesel rubbed at his backside and neck. "I'd say you don't need anyone for that."

"I do. I need a sentry for when Toni and I are sleeping. We have people on our tail, people who want to hurt us. This is why we came here," Venom said. "For protection."

Diesel's nostrils flared and he gave Venom a cold glare. After a beat, he shrugged and shook his head.

"Well, you *are* a brother. I guess I'm obliged to help you."

"I'm not asking for your help. I'm *telling* you that you'll help. It has fuck-all to do with the MC."

"Whatever you say," Diesel said.

Venom clenched his jaw. He didn't understand the need for newer generations of Boas to be so damn defiant and disrespectful, but he really did need additional protection. *I must sleep.* "Get back up to Toni," he ordered. "I want you on the roof with the rifle."

CHAPTER TWENTY-ONE

AS DIESEL ENTERED THE BAR, he spotted Toni sitting on one of the stools. The split up the side of her dress had slipped open, revealing her long legs and perfectly sized thighs. Her skin tone was bone-white, but he found her appealing overall.

She smiled, highlighting her high cheekbones, which seemed to protrude farther given her ashen glow. Sunglasses continued to cover her eyes, and he figured they were like Venom's: white and vacuous.

"Are you going to stand there staring at my legs all day, or are you going to come over here and take this weapon off me?"

He half expected Venom to appear from nowhere and deliver a few blows for ogling his woman, but the creepy Boa had stayed in the cellar with the dead. "I wasn't staring," he said, his tone bordering on defensive. He cleared his throat. "How's the boy?" *And what the fuck has he already told you*?

"He's stopped bleeding. If he gets through today, then he's got a chance."

"Good," he lied. He decided to change the topic. "That's a sexy-looking piece of equipment you got there. A Barrett 98B .338 Lapua, twenty-inch barrel?"

"The man knows his guns," she said.

"How many mags?"

"Two."

"Tripod?" he asked.

"In the khaki satchel, along with spare rounds."

He nodded. "Good. There's a nice little spot up on that roof I can use. I saw it as I came in."

"Here," she said, handing him the gun.

He took it and placed the strap over his shoulder. "Can I get some practice shots in first?"

"I'm not sure there'll be enough time for that." She stood, pushing the stool backward with one foot and turning to face him. She picked up a chilled bottle of ale that was on the counter. "But there may be time for a drink. You in?"

"I don't drink and shoot."

She shrugged. "Please yourself." She strolled to the army holdall, pulled on the drawstrings, and opened the flaps. Inside were boxes upon boxes of ammunition. They weren't all for the rifle either, Diesel noted.

"Who are we going to war with?" he joked.

Toni didn't answer. She pushed past him and grabbed another holdall, opened it, and pulled out a submachine gun.

"Fuck," he uttered.

"Something wrong?"

"That's a Blackhawk MP5. Where did you get this kind of hardware?"

"Here and there," she said, her smile returning.

"The Boas haven't been able to get their hands on such powerful stuff. Mostly handguns: Brownings, SIG Sauers, Smith and Wessons, etcetera," he told her.

She handed it to him. "You'll probably need it. Do you have anything else you can arm yourself with?"

"I saw a snub-nosed .38 kicking around the place. I have a knife, too."

"Not bad."

"Look, I'm all for a bit of violence, whether it's retaliation, defense, or whatever. I just like knowing the cause. What are we up against here?"

She ignored him and sashayed to another bag, rifling through its contents.

He stepped close and puffed his chest out. She was much smaller than him, maybe five feet tall, her frame slight. *A midget compared to me*, Diesel thought, laying a hand on her shoulder. "Hey, I'm talking to y—"

She turned on him swiftly, gripped and twisted his arm around as far as it would go, and pushed him up against the bar.

Diesel pranced on his tiptoes. Torrid pain ripped through his arm and neck, searing his brain. He thought his elbow was going to shatter. "Fuck! Let me go!"

"Touch me again and I'll rip your arm off and beat you into oblivion with it. I'm not some timid little bit of pussy you can pet or tame," she said, a sneer contorting her pleasant features.

"You're going to fucking break—argh!" he cried.

Toni gave his limb one more twist, let go, and shoved him.

He thought he felt a rib snap as he collapsed to the floor holding his abused arm. "Bitch!"

She laughed. "That was child's play, my dear. Pray you never see my angry side. Now, pack this shit up and follow me."

Grumbling under his breath, he slung the holdall with the ammo in it over his shoulder along with the rifle, deciding to carry the other one by hand. When he had everything loaded up, she told him to trail her. He watched her arse swish beneath her dress as they walked from the bar to the back of the pub.

They went through a door Diesel had not seen before and came across a stairway which led to the second floor.

"How do you know we'll find a way onto the roof this way?"

"When I was busy locking doors and windows while you and Venom were in the cellar, I got nosey and looked around."

They climbed the stairs to the second story, where there were five rooms in total: three bedrooms, one completely empty, and a games room, which they gravitated toward for further inspection. A dusty, dirty pool table graced the middle of the space, with a jukebox stuck in one corner. A dartboard clung to a wall, and a deck of cards rested next to a domino set on one of the regular tables, which was caked in dust and cobwebs.

Brightness lit the early morning skies but it was blocked out by the heavy curtains covering the glass. The place was starting to remind him of a tomb.

"Why are we hiding like this?" he asked, walking around the games room to check out all the relics.

"I thought people like you didn't have morals. Why would you care what's going on?"

"Because I'm probably going to end up dead and I'd like to know why, if that's not too much to ask."

"You could have run," she said.

"I'd never turn my back on a brother."

"Venom's no brother of yours."

"He or you may see it like that, but as long as he has that patch, I have a moral dedication to him."

"Sweet," she said.

"You wouldn't understand."

"No, I wouldn't. So let's keep moving."

They crossed the landing and stumbled upon a second set of stairs, which they ascended. When they got to the top, they found more rooms—ten of them. Nine were fully decorated with made beds and the one at the end of the corridor was a bathroom nestled next to yet another staircase.

He went back to watching her arse as they tromped up the latest flight of steps, finding her movements hypnotizing. "How big is this place?" he asked, trying to keep her from feeling his dirty eyes scanning her.

"Not sure, but from what Venom said, there's another wing to the building. Some hidden passageways and rooms, too."

"Seriously?" Diesel shook his head.

When they got to the fourth floor, they found it to be the last. It contained only one open room at the landing with a hatch in its ceiling.

"There," she said, pointing at the small opening. "That should get you to the rooftop."

Diesel stood directly under the door and pushed. The lid sprang up and popped open. The wooden hatch dropped down slowly in his hands and he spotted a ladder beyond the entrance. He grabbed the aluminum legs and pulled them forward until the whole thing unfolded. Diesel dropped all the bags at Toni's feet, clicked the ladder into place, and climbed the rungs.

He reached the top and stood, stooping, mindful of rafters and cobwebs and the critters possibly lurking in such a place. He blinked a few times, gave his eyes a few seconds to adjust, but still couldn't see a damn thing. "Figures," he muttered.

Carefully lowering himself until he was prone on the floor, he poked his head back through the opening. "It's as black as the inside of a mine up here. Do you have a light of some kind? Torch, candle?"

"Yeah, I've got a torch," Toni said, opening one of the bags.

"I'm unsure there's a way to the roof, mind you."

She stepped up a few rungs and handed him the flashlight. "Here. Just keep looking. I know a skylight is visible from the outside."

"Well, if I come across it, I'll let you know," he said, shimmying back to his feet and clicking the torch on.

* * *

Toni surveyed the empty, short landing as Diesel's footsteps receded. It was a weird top floor. *What was this area used for?* she wondered.

"Is there anything else up there?" she asked. No answer, and she couldn't hear his movements anymore. It was possible he was out of earshot. "Diesel?" she called, bolstering her voice. "Diesel, you better not be messing around up there!"

His face suddenly reappeared at the hatch. It was ghost white. "My God, it—it's awful! I had to get some air," he said, panting.

"What are you up to?"

"I—I think this was where they stored leftovers." His cheeks puffed out and he gagged. He swallowed hard. "There are boxes of preserved . . . The fucking smell!"

"Pull yourself together. You call yourself a man?"

"Why don't you come and see for yourself, sweet-cheeks?"

"Don't call me that, fucking pussy," she muttered. "Have you found that skylight, or are you too busy pissing your trousers? We haven't got all day."

He nodded. "I think it's in the left-hand corner. I've been moving fuck-loads of boxes, containers, and jars out of the way. The place is crammed full of stuff."

"Well, pull your finger out of your nappy-covered arse! We need to get you set up as soon as possible, before we lose the light."

He smiled. "Yes, ma'am."

"Fucking idiot," she said as he disappeared again to shuffle around upstairs.

While waiting for him to clear a path, Toni decided to haul the bags up to the attic one at a time. She scrambled up the ladder with the first holdall and gazed at the room. Though completely blacked out, she could penetrate the darkness just fine—she had eyes better than a shithouse rat's. She spied Diesel in the far corner moving stuff beneath the entrance to the roof, where a pull-cord dangled from a door. It would be easy to reach once the area was cleared. Next to it was the skylight, darkened by grime and dust through the years.

Though it was slightly obscured and no light passed through it, she could feel heat from the skylight filling the room. It brought back wonderful memories: picking flowers in the fields behind her parents' house, days spent at the beach, the smell of sand and sea and food. She remembered running to the park close to their home, going for a dip at the pool there.

Then the awful memories of *that* day came back to her, the day when her time in the sun would be forever numbered. . .

She shook herself out of her reverie and said, "Don't mind me. I'm just getting the gear up here. This room will be perfect for Venom and me."

"What? Why? It's a rat-hole. Too dark for anything. Unless Venom and I can rig some—"

"It's perfect," she cut in. "The darkness is perfect for us."

"Bloody fucking freaks," he muttered.

She tossed the bag at his back.

He cried out and wheeled on her. "What the fuck was that for?"

"Have some respect, you piece of shit. You know nothing about Venom and me, so keep your filthy comments to yourself or I'll rip your nuts off and shove them down your throat."

"I'm trying to fucking help you!"

She smirked. "No, you're *going* to help us. You keep making it sound like it's a choice, but it's not." She walked to the ladder to climb down for another bag. "Now get your arse back to work. Time is ticking."

* * *

Diesel scowled as she disappeared from view. He could break her in half if he wanted to, or take one of those guns and riddle her full of bullets. Little bitch.

And he didn't care if Venom was a Boa. He'd shoot him too. Many of his brothers had been killed by another brother. It was the game they were in. *If they keep up the physical attacks, it's fucking on*, he thought, turning his attention back to the task at hand.

Ten minutes later, after Toni had lugged all the equipment up the ladder, Diesel broke the awkward silence which had surrounded them. "I'm finished. Look," he said, dropping the hatch beside the skylight. Sunlight blazed down through the entrance.

When she didn't comment or join him, he shined the torch at her. He blinked a few times, uncertain if what he was seeing was right or if the darkness and shoddy flashlight were throwing off his vision. She appeared to be shaking, almost as if she were . . . afraid? "Are you all right?" he asked.

"The sun," she replied, quivering. "I can't . . . be in it."

He laughed. "What? Are you on crack or something? It's bloody gorgeous!"

She jostled her head and offered a meek smile. "I just have a . . . reaction . . . when I'm in it. I can't be in the heat," she said, looking straight through him.

"Grab what you need, then go up and pick out a good spot. You need to be able to see what's coming for miles, both directions."

"Okay, but I wish you'd tell me what's going on."

"If it's a quiet night tonight, I'm sure Venom will fill you in. But for now, please just stand guard, okay?"

It was the first time she'd been soft with him. He liked her better this way. "No problem," he said, grabbing the bags. He spotted a large blanket on top of one of the boxes and yanked it free. It would make his waiting game a tad more comfortable, at least.

Before he began to ascend, Toni said, "Venom will be up to relieve you later this afternoon. Probably when it starts to go dark. And I'll bring food for you. I'll leave it on the top rung so you can grab it easily."

"Sounds good."

* * *

When he was out of sight, she nabbed some blankets and sheets from the clutter, spread them out over the floor, and lay down. The heat was making her giddy. She needed rest. They'd been on the road for seventy-two hours, which was starting to take its toll. This would be the first decent place they had stopped at in a long time—since leaving her home, in fact.

She closed her eyes and drifted off to the sound of Diesel's boots clomping on the slate roof above.

* * *

Diesel could see up and down the old motorway for miles. The vast openness meant nothing could hide, which suited him well.

Below and near the pub, cows had finally come out to graze. He dared a look over the side of the roof and located his and his crew's motorbikes. They looked like little black ants.

He frowned. He missed Slicks and the rest of them. *Cut to fucking bits by the nutters who ran this place . . . What a way to go.* He snorted. *And now I'm helping one of their family members, just because Venom is a brother. Fucking crazy, how the world works.*

Diesel sighed, grabbed his gear, and walked gingerly over to the farthest chimneystack. The roof there was unusual. It had a flat surface and didn't slope like the rest of it, as though it had been designed for a lookout post. *Well, I've found my spot.*

Once on the flat, Diesel dumped the bags. "Nice," he said, putting a hand to the stack and leaning on it. He drank in his surroundings, familiarizing himself with the layout. *Think I'll set the Barrett up on the bricks*, he thought, giving the chimneystack a clap with his hand.

He rooted through the closest bag, pulled out the tripod for the rifle, and set it up. He then took the gun off his back and put the butt of it snug against his shoulder, gauging the efficiency of its scope. "Perfect," he uttered. He left the weapon where it was and unloaded all the boxes of ammunition for it, setting them on the flat under the tripod legs.

Satisfied, he turned his attention to the MP5 that was tucked away in the second bag. He retrieved it and snapped the cocking mechanism back. A shell loaded into the chamber. "Great," he said, putting the gun close to hand. He then dug out the rest of the ammo for the submachine gun. As he rustled through the bag, he unearthed a pair of binoculars and set it aside. *That should do it.*

He lay his blanket down and sat on it, making sure he could still see all around him. *Right, that's great*, he thought, snatching up the binoculars and peering through them. They were in perfect working order. He adjusted them slightly and then scanned the whole area. Nothing seemed out of the ordinary. He decided he'd pull surveillance every ten minutes until relieved.

Though he was determined to find out just what he was involved in, he was happy to sit and wait. But he also knew it would be a long day.

A very, very long day.

CHAPTER TWENTY-TWO

Johnson stuck his arm out the driver's side window, clenched his fist, and brought his four-by-four to a complete stop.

The convoy of jeeps, cars, and motorbikes behind him likewise halted. They were his hired team. Some he'd worked with for years, others months, a few only weeks. They were a mixed bunch: bikers, thugs, contract killers, hunters, drug pushers, thieves, most being former military members. Not all of them could be trusted, but they knew what would happen if they should even think of crossing him.

They'd been on the road for seven months, three weeks, and four days—five, counting today. Johnson and his men had searched every outhouse, B-road, dense countryside, derelict town, and building. They'd acted on every lead and sighting from scouts the whole breadth of the country. All their hard work had amounted to nothing. The man they were looking for was a phantom of the road.

And if the stories about Venom were true, then he was a monster, too.

Johnson tended not to believe in such childish rumors. He'd hunted and killed many things, but never had someone or something been so tricky to apprehend. But he had no doubt he'd eventually nab the notorious biker. Deadlier predators had been bagged before. *The lousy petrol-head may have a knack for good disappearing tricks, but his majestic prowess* will *run out,* Johnson thought, smiling.

He pulled a black-and-white photo from the top pocket of his combat jacket (one he'd worn during and since his service days). The picture depicted the long-haired Venom. He was estimated to be in his fifties. He'd once operated a biker gang in and around the Cardiff area known as the Boas. They could have gone directly to Venom's old MC, but Johnson was pretty sure they weren't harboring the man. Besides, had they turned up at the Boas headquarters asking silly questions, the brown sticky stuff would have hit the fan.

Johnson didn't want that. He had neither the bullets nor men to waste or spare, if the stories about Venom proved true. And he truly did believe them. Johnson's backer had been very convincing and afraid, stating that Venom *was* out there. Even prison walls had ears.

But if Venom was still roaming wild, then why hadn't he gone after Johnson's payer and ended it all years ago?

No, something screwy was going on, and Johnson was going to get to the bottom of it. He was in too deep now. One way or the other, he'd find truth. And if it did turn out to be a wild goose chase, Johnson would be paying his benefactor a visit. No amount of security and bought thugs on the inside would keep the man safe.

Johnson rubbed the photo with his thumb. He had that tingly feeling at the back of his neck.

"You're nearby, my boy. I can feel you," he whispered.

"Sir?" Max asked from the passenger seat.

"Nothing, Max. Nothing. Time for a fag break. We've been driving all night without one anyway."

Johnson unfastened his seat belt, opened his door, and got out of the vehicle. He sucked in a lungful of air and exhaled. The stench of shit was rife, but he loved it—the smell of nature at work. They were close to Manchester, he figured, but he couldn't remember the last time he'd seen a road sign.

He rooted around inside his cargo trousers and removed a pack of Hamlets. Johnson took one out and lit it with his expensive Zippo. He inhaled deeply, then released a build-up of smoke through his nostrils.

"We're near our target," he told Max, who was coming around the front of the Mitsubishi four-by-four. "I can tell."

"If you say so, sir," Max said. Dawning sunlight glinted off his dark complexion, adding a bright sheen to his skin.

Johnson regarded the man for a while. He was built like a brick shithouse: muscles on muscles, neck as thick as a bull's. Max was twenty years his junior and his most valued man. They'd seen combat together in the Gulf, where Max first worked under Johnson. They'd become solid friends before Max was dismissed from the forces due to injury. After Johnson left the army and got into the contract business, Max had been the first man he'd recruited. Whatever disabilities he'd suffered had no effect on his current job.

"Tell the others to stand down," Johnson said. "We'll build a camp in those woods over there. No one has passed us all night or morning on this road, so I doubt anyone will. The vehicles should be safe out here. We can post guards and do shift swaps."

"Rolling by six p.m.?"

Johnson nodded as he exhaled plumes of smoke. "Around that, yes. Make sure everyone is ready to go by then. If I decide to move earlier, you'll be the first to know," he said, smiling at his right-hand man. "And make sure they fuel their tanks before they make camp. It's not good to let the tanks get too dry."

"Got it, sir."

Johnson nodded with appreciation as Max headed off, stuck the cigar back in his mouth, and took a few more drags, his attention drawn to the back window of his four-by-four.

Inside stirring from sleep was his second most-valued soldier, Dawn, a family woman with two daughters and a husband at home. Like Max, she had worked under Johnson during the Gulf war. She too had been injured during combat and discharged by the forces. After her dismissal, she was determined to go back to action but was refused many times. Without someone to fight, Dawn would have crawled into many bottles of gin and stayed there, finding her way into an early grave. Having worked closely with her during combat operations, Johnson felt he could trust her. He'd been more than happy to draft her.

He watched as she stretched her arms and arched her back, thrusting her tits out and giving him a good eyeful. She wasn't much to look at, but she had a gorgeous figure. The best part was that she knew he was ogling her, yet she didn't care. Rather, she indulged him. Winked at him.

His jawline tightened. He'd been married three times, with all three marriages ending in them hating and divorcing him. "You're nothing but a male whore, Carl," his third and final wife had barked at him as she'd departed with his daughter. This was the same wife who'd emptied his office safe and taken some of his hard-earned cash and most prized possessions. That was why he'd had her killed.

She'd been right though. He had womanizing ways and wouldn't apologize for it.

He smiled and opened the door for Dawn. "Care to join us, dear?"

"Thought you'd never ask," she said. Her military boots stomped the gravel as she stood. "Where are we, sir?"

"Somewhere close to Manchester, I think. We've been going all night. Figured we could set up camp for the day."

"Shouldn't we push on, sir?"

He loved her enthusiasm and appetite for action and death. "All in good time, Dawn."

"I guess these pussies need a rest, huh?" she said, smiling.

"Says the one waking from a nap!"

"Only a power hour, sir," she gaffed.

"If you say so, soldier." His gaze shifted to her nipples, which jutted from her tight combat T-shirt. "Right, catch up with Max and help him inform the others. We roll out at eighteen-hundred hours."

"Okay, sir," she said, hustling off.

Lazily getting out of the other side of the four-by-four was Johnson's third and final elite soldier, Geraint. The man's military experience had been short-lived: he'd been an insubordinate little fuck, resulting in the army being unable to control him and thus booting him. After being dishonorably discharged, the fiery Welshman fled the UK, taking jobs as a hitman in various countries around the world. He was a loose cannon and a danger . . . and the perfect addition to Johnson's group of killers.

"Rest time?" Geraint asked.

Johnson nodded, looking directly at the red-headed, big-bearded man. He was slight of frame—ninja slight. He was trained in Ninjutsu and could wield various lethal weapons associated with the deadly martial arts, some of which he carried in a holdall along with an AK-47 and an Uzi.

"Good, I want to check my stuff," he said. "Are we bunking down in those woods?"

"Yes," Johnson said, chuckling.

"What's so funny?"

"You check your stuff every stop we make, Geraint. It hasn't gone anywhere!"

"I know, I'm just touchy about my things."

Johnson shook his head and moved away from the vehicle, drinking in the hubbub of activity. His group of men and women laughed and joked with each other as they unloaded bundles, blankets, tents, and various other camping equipment. Nobody sported a gun. That was the rule: they could openly carry knives and other cutting or hacking instruments but never a gun in broad daylight, especially on the side of a road, abandoned or not.

Right, it's high time I address everyone now that they've been informed. Johnson snuffed out his cigar against the bottom of his boot and placed the half-finished smoke back inside the Hamlet box. He cleared his throat and shouted, "Ladies and gentlemen, please, if I could have a moment of your time?"

A hush fell over the gathering and the buzz of activity died out.

"Thank you," he said. "Now, as I'm sure you're all aware thanks to my associates Max and Dawn, we are to set up camp here for the day, leaving at approximately eighteen-hundred hours, give or take. We'll assign guards to stay with our vehicles while everyone else sleeps, eats, or just gets some rest. Every hour, there will be a rotation to relieve the lookouts. Max and Dawn will delegate the duties and shifts. Any questions?"

"Yeah," one of the Huns called. "When do we get paid for dragging our arses all over the country looking for someone that probably doesn't exist?"

Johnson laughed. *Fucking Huns.* They were named so after his benefactor, Attila the Hun, who had obviously adopted the moniker from the legendary conqueror he adored. And, like the old ruler, Hun and his gang of misfits were known to go on plundering sprees. They had made headlines daily for years, as they'd enjoyed wreaking havoc on the other side of Cardiff, in Boa territory—until a showdown in a local pub turned ugly one night, resulting in the deaths of many bikers. Johnson knew that was where Hun's hatred and fear for Venom had begun.

"Always about the money, hey?" he bellowed. "Well, you'll all get paid once we've found and terminated our target. And believe you me, he's out there. You Huns should know that better than anyone."

"What if we *don't* find the target?" another Hun asked. "It's been over a half a damn year."

"You shall all be compensated for your trouble regardless," Johnson said.

They seemed happy with this, chatting among themselves, nodding, smiling.

"However, I don't think this particular hunt has been in vain," he continued. "I know of a few places where he could be hiding out around here. I also believe the man has blood ties in the area. If all else fails, we go to his family and get answers that way, but I don't think it will come to that. I happen to think we are right on Venom's heels. We found evidence of him being back at the last town we came through. We just need to keep going.

"Now, if you'd all like to grab your stuff and follow me into the woods, we'll get settled. Potentially, we have a long, long night ahead of us."

CHAPTER TWENTY-THREE

JOHNSON LAY INSIDE HIS ONE-MAN TENT, thinking about how tedious this job had been. He normally had contracts done and dusted within three or four weeks. Had he been wrong in taking this mark?

He thought back to how eager he had been to accept the task, when Hun had put out the call for an exceptional hitman . . .

* * *

The noise was deafening inside the corridor he walked down with the two guards. His arrival had excited the inmates. Some probably knew him. He didn't always kill his target; sometimes his employers only wanted someone roughed up or scared or locked behind bars. He wasn't one to shy away from money, so although he liked to spill blood, the bosses got what they wanted in the end.

The caged animals threw stuff at him: bottles, paper, cups of piss, even their own turds. *Fucking sickening*, Johnson thought as he was led to Hun's cell. He allowed the missiles to bounce off him without flinching. He couldn't show any signs of annoyance even though he wanted to kill every last motherfucking one of them, preferably as they slept. They'd pounce if he displayed any cracks in his defense. And in this jungle, he'd be outnumbered and overrun in a matter of seconds if he faltered. No, it was best to hold his head high and take the literal shit on the chin.

The missiles and filthy language stopped as he got closer to Hun's domain. Outside the caged biker's concrete-and-steel box stood a man who made Johnson feel tiny. He considered himself a big man at six-foot-four and eighteen stone, but this guy was almost head and shoulders above him and had more muscles than Johnson could count. The sentry's hair flanked both sides of his face and appeared wet. He wore nothing but a biker's cut inscribed with the Huns' logo on his torso. His chest was covered in oriental art: dragons, pagodas, ghostly faces and gods. His jeans looked as though they had been painted on, his thighs like tree trunks. At his hip was a sheathed hunting knife, which was highly unorthodox.

I guess money talks, Johnson thought, smiling at the monster of a man.

When the monster smiled back, a chill rippled down Johnson's back—the man didn't have *normal* teeth. His mouth was filled with metal, which looked sharp enough to chew through cables. It was horrendous.

As Johnson tried to slip past, the bulky man grabbed him by his lapels and reeled him into his chest.

"Shark!" barked the man's master from the depths of the cell.

By this point, the guards who had been escorting Johnson had dropped back. One had drawn his baton, while the other had a stun gun at hand. *Fat lot of good they'll do on this buffalo*, Johnson thought as he was flung into the cell by the aptly named Shark.

Annoyed, Johnson spun around, ready to square off against the man, who now filled the entire entranceway.

"Enough!" barked the master once again.

Johnson faced the interior of the cell. Two more of Hun's goons stood beside a bunk bed. They were big, but not like the man-mountain barring the door—they could probably just about make up his mass if they were melded together.

Hun himself sat in the shadows. Smoke vapors rose about him as he smoked his pipe.

With a flick of his hand, the two by the bed sat and Shark sidled away from the doorway, which in turn filled the cell with light. The master came into focus. He was old, far older than Johnson had expected the biker leader to be. If he was a day under eighty-five, he would have been shocked.

"Expecting a younger man, soldier?" Hun said, smirking. "Your face says it all." The older man filled his lungs with more smoke and exhaled it. The tobacco smelled exotic. Spicy.

Silent, Johnson dug his cigars out and indicated as to whether his own vice could be granted.

"Go ahead. Guards, leave us," Hun said.

"Got the run of the place, hey?" Johnson cracked.

"Power, money, and fear have a way of getting one what he wants or needs."

"And what is it that you need, Hun?" Johnson asked, wasting no time in pushing on with business. The old man and his thugs had him slightly rattled. He didn't like confined spaces at the best of times.

"A blunt man. I like that," Hun said, then chuckled. "I'm looking for a man. A very dangerous man. One who has caused me terrible problems and keeps me in constant fear, Mr. Soldier."

"Johnson," he corrected Hun.

The other man smiled. "I want this man killed. Wiped from this world, once and for all." A mask of loathing briefly covered his face as Hun looked through Johnson and stared into space.

"Who is he? What's his importance?"

"Are such questions important to a mercenary?" Hun spat. "Needless to say, he's a cold-blooded killing machine who clearly sleeps well at night. This man has cost me a lot: my freedom, my club, my business, my woman, my friends. The list is inexhaustible."

Johnson began to relax and took a long drag on his cigar. This would be the first time he'd worked for a convicted felon. But, as he always said, if the money and target were both right, then no job was too dirty for him. After all, he was a merc, and even a merc needed to pay his bills and put food on the table.

Johnson nestled into the chair which had been placed in readiness in front of Hun, wanting to know more before he ventured forward with the mission—provided he was going to take the job. It was no big deal if he didn't because he had others lined up. "Tell me more," he said.

The older man, who still wore his MC cut, biker boots, and jeans, adjusted himself in his chair. He took a deep drag on his pipe and exhaled. "Have you ever heard of the Great Biker War of 1970? It started in The Traveler's Arms pub, Cardiff, between the Boas and the Huns. It was big news. Made every paper."

"It rings a bell," Johnson admitted. "But I would have been far too young at the time to remember it."

"I thought you may have been," Hun muttered. "The Traveler's Arms was Hun territory. Had been for many years. The pub served as the Huns' headquarters. It was run by the club, originally bought as a way of making clean money."

"I see," Johnson said.

"That night in 1970, a bar fight spilled over, got ugly. A lot of people got hurt—killed, even," Hun said. He leaned forward. A huge scar ran from his temple to his jawline, no longer obscured by the shadows within the cell. He pointed at it. "This is a reminder of that night."

"How did it start?"

"It was late evening. Eleven, maybe twelve. We had loads of members in the pub, along with a few punters. Just before closing time, in walked twenty Boas, armed to the teeth. They'd called in Nomads and some muscle from other chapters they have close to Cardiff: Newport, Swansea, Carmarthen, the Rhondda Valleys. They marched in with clubs, bats, crowbars, knives, but no guns. We later learned they wanted us out of Cardiff for good and were only there to enforce, bust the place up, break some heads, see us out. But they hadn't counted on coming up against ten to fifteen Huns."

"They were taken by surprise?"

"Yes, their leader's face had been a picture."

"This is the man you're looking for?"

Hun nodded.

"I see. Go on," Johnson said.

"Apparently, the Boas had been closing down a lot of the smaller clubs around town. I guess we were the last to be shoved out. Venom, their leader at the time, ordered us to shut down business immediately and get out of town or else there would be bloodshed. Naturally, we declined his kind offer. We were making too much money in the city to be pushed out by another gang—especially one we thought we had an alliance with."

Hun stopped for another quick puff on his pipe. "They came in making plenty of noise and I'm sure they thought that we were just going to fold. But that was never going to happen. I was behind the bar that evening, and, ever the vigilant man, I had a 410 shotgun under the counter—my uncle's old hunting favorite. It was a bolt-action, which I always kept loaded. Lucky, hey?"

A coughing fit seized the old man. He choked and gargled on mucus, waving one of his thugs away when he started to get up to help. "I'm fine," he wheezed. He indicated the pipe and winked at Johnson. "I really should give this thing up."

"Probably," Johnson said meekly. He lit another cigar.

"Drink?" Hun asked.

"What have you got?"

"Whisky."

Johnson nodded.

"Pour two," Hun told one of his helpers, who did as he was asked.

Once they each had a glass in hand, Hun continued his story. "It certainly didn't go the way the Boas had hoped. When their demands were laid before us, the Huns reacted how you'd expect any other gang to act: with violence. In the ugliest of ways. They homed in on Venom, of course, as I always taught my soldiers to go for the highest-ranking enemy first."

Soldiers? That's rich, Johnson thought. But he wasn't about to call the man out on it. He planned to walk out of the prison.

"One of my men leapt onto Venom's back and sank his teeth into the fleshy part of his neck. When he was kicked off by one of Venom's men, a massive chunk of flesh came away. I saw Venom go down. I thought he was dead."

"He *bit* him?" Johnson asked, mouth agape.

"Yes."

"It wasn't this chap's daddy, was it?" Johnson quipped, gesturing behind him at Shark, whose silhouette had fallen on them and darkened the room anew.

"My men were always told to take their enemy down by any means, especially when cornered," Hun said, apparently not seeing the funny side of it—not even so much as a flinch of a lip.

Johnson heard the cracking of knuckles behind him.

"When Venom went to ground," the old man continued, "it sparked an outrage. A fight ensued. One of the Boas even lunged at me with a cleaver. The fucker got me, too, but I blasted him with the bolt-action. The pub was smashed to bits. I'd never seen so much carnage in a small space of time. Most of my men were either killed, wounded, or maimed. The Boas took their fair share of loss, too, of course."

"Were the police involved?"

"No. The Boas fled after losing as much blood as they could stand. When the dust settled, I noticed Venom's body was gone. I thought that had been the end to the matter, but we knew the Boas would plan retaliation. So we decided to act first.

"We hit the very next night. I had been right: Venom was alive and being nursed by his wife. After forcing him to watch the rape and murder of his pregnant woman, Venom was shot, stabbed, and beaten to death. We then proceeded to work our way down the Boas' list of hierarchy. When the night was over, most of their officials and original crew were dead. We left it at that, hoping our point had been proved.

"Things settled down for a few days, but then he came back for us—for me and my remaining Huns. He came back and slaughtered everyone and everything around me. He disappeared after that and things went back to how they were. Venom's replacement agreed on peace. The Boas and the Huns would go on living and working together in Cardiff. And so it's been that way for near fifty years. But he's still out there—Venom. His revenge may have been fulfilled, but he still walks the earth."

"How in the hell can that be possible? You said he was dead. I don't know about you, but I don't believe in ghosts."

Hun took a drag on his pipe, face lined with a heaviness Johnson wasn't privy to. He exhaled and gestured at one of his men. "Show him."

One of the Huns on the bed produced a stack of photos and placed them on Johnson's lap.

"What are these?"

"Your target," Hun said.

"But the man is dead! You and your men killed him all those years ago," Johnson stressed.

"Entertain me."

Johnson flipped through the pictures. Some were black and white, some color, past and present. He blinked rapidly as image after image of this Venom character appeared through the decades. He was identical in every depiction. "He doesn't look like he's aged a day," he muttered.

The old man grunted and took a swig of whisky and smacked his lips. "I'm not a religious man, and I too don't believe in ghosts or things that go bump in the night. I'm a realistic and logical, grounded man. But I saw him cheat death, saw what he did to my men decades ago." That faraway look returned to his glossy eyes. "He's not of this world anymore, Johnson."

Johnson almost laughed at that one, but the seriousness in Hun's hard-edged features stopped him short. "What do you mean?"

"He's no longer a man. That night in the pub changed him. You see the proof for yourself, Johnson. I want him dead, once and for all."

Johnson glanced at the photos. It was a mystery, and he was hooked. He wanted to know the truth of it all. "I'm in. But if you're lying or sending me on a wild goose chase, you'll—"

"Do not threaten me, soldier man. I'll have you chopped up and fed to the dogs." Hun's nostrils flared momentarily before his gaze softened again. "I'll pay you fifty million, should you take this man out and bring me proof."

That's a large haul! Johnson swallowed the remainder of his liquor in one go. "Mission accepted. But I'll need a big team for this one," he said, trying to play it cool. "Fifty million might not be enough."

"I'll cover your expenses. I've heard you're the best."

"I am. And that is most generous." Johnson scrunched his brow. "He really fucked you up and over, didn't he?"

"Yes," Hun said. "I want retribution for everything he's taken from me."

"Right, but why not send your dogs after him?"

"I don't want a direct link. I can send some of my men along if you wish, but on a low, quiet scale."

Johnson nodded. "I'll take the help."

"Okay, I will make that happen. And I want him to suffer, Johnson. Make sure you do that."

"Oh, that's my specialty," Johnson replied, slipping one of the photos into his jacket pocket.

CHAPTER TWENTY-FOUR

JOHNSON AWOKE WITH A START, having drifted off with his memory.

Max knelt beside him, roughly shaking his shoulder. "Sir?"

Johnson coughed, rolled onto his side, and propped himself on his elbow. "Yeah, what is it?"

"It's ten minutes past five, sir. I thought maybe you'd like to freshen up before moving out."

"Shit. Right, okay," Johnson said, yawning and shaking the grogginess from him. "Rally the men and women. I'll be ready and at the jeep five minutes to six. Make sure you're behind the wheel and Dawn and Geraint are loaded into the back by then. I want us to cover the next few towns before sunrise."

"Yes, sir."

Johnson hopped into action, cleaning up and shaving and slipping into fresh clothing. He then set about taking the tent down. Once finished, he headed to his vehicle. Most of the heat was dying out of the day by now. Light was starting to fade, and the makeshift campsite was a hive of activity as others rushed about him to fill their trucks, cars, and bikes.

At the promised time, Johnson arrived at his four-by-four and clambered into the passenger seat. Max, Dawn, and Geraint were already in position inside the jeep. "That's what I like to see," he said. "Promptness."

Max cranked the engine to life. "Okay, where are we heading next?"

"We move on to the next town. He's got blood in these parts, but I don't think he would hide behind family. Not if the man truly is something born out of hell," Johnson said.

The others remained silent as Max stomped on the accelerator. The convoy was moving again and soon the next town came into sight. They would explore this one like the countless before it.

They would pick the trail up again. Johnson was sure of that.

He'd never let a target slip through his fingers.

* * *

The sun was barely peeking above the horizon, the heat burning away. Diesel finished giving the whole area another sweep with the binoculars. Still nothing.

He sighed. Not a single car, bike, or truck had passed by or entered sight since he'd taken his post. He'd been vigilant and diligent, too. Nothing had slipped his attention. When he'd needed the toilet, he'd taken a piss off the roof. Luckily he hadn't needed a shit, but that too would have been done in the same style.

His mind had run wild with questions throughout the day: Why the hell were Toni and Venom scared? What were they running from? Where the hell had Venom been all these years? And why the hell did the enigmatic man look so much younger than he should?

As dusk crept in, Diesel settled back on his blanket, prepared for a long and cold evening. He suspected he was on the roof for the night. Toni had been true to her word, leaving dinner and water in the attic for him, but he'd need sleep though. He wondered if the other two would uphold their shift responsibilities.

No sooner had he finished the thought than Toni called: "You may come down now, Diesel. Venom and I would like you to join us for something to eat. You can also get some rest. We've had ours."

Why doesn't she just come up here? he wondered. *It would be easier than shouting.* He hopped to his feet, went to the hatch, and poked his head through it. "Don't you guys sleep at night?"

She studied his upside-down face with a smirk. "Not really."

"Why?"

"In case they come for us at night."

"Oh, for fuck's sake, will you just tell me what—"

"All will be revealed to you this evening, Diesel," she said. Her voice was soft, like Venom's. "Come on down. Venom wants to see you. You may leave everything up there, as you will be back on guard tomorrow morning."

He acquiesced with a shrug of his shoulders. "Fine, okay," he said, using the ladder.

They walked through the oddly quiet rooms and down the flights of stairs.

"This place spooks the fuck out of me," he admitted.

She chuckled.

"You don't find it eerie?"

"No, not really. I've been living in ruined buildings for years."

"Freaky," he uttered. "Where's Venom?"

"I think he's been looking for his nephew."

"What? You mean there's someone *else* here?" Diesel blurted.

"Yes. This was his family, mind. The one dying on the pool table—the Champ, Simon—was his great nephew. The man in the doctor's attire was another nephew," she said.

"Oh, fuck," he muttered, shaking his head. "He's going to slaughter me, too, isn't he? I mean, once I've served my purpose."

"Relax. He's not mad at you. The men and woman you were outside with this morning, on the other hand . . ."

"I bet," he said, hoping to change the subject and maintain his lie. "Who were the others to Venom? The barman? The big lady in the gimp suit?"

"Porky was his nephew too, and the woman was his great niece."

Diesel scrunched his brow as they marched along. "But that's not possible."

"Why not?"

"Because Venom's roughly the same age as the two men are. *Were*," he replied. "What is this bullshit you're feeding me?"

"I told you, all will be revealed."

"You've already said that. I want—"

"You'll get your answers," she reassured him. "Sooner than you think."

"Wait, now. That takes care of the ones I saw or met, but then who's Venom's other nephew, the one he's searching for now?"

"It would seem he's been kept locked away somewhere."

"I see. This third nephew—I think Porky mentioned him. He said he had a dead brother. The one who helped him run the pub."

"Huh," she scoffed. "That was a cover story, I bet."

"But—"

"I told you—"

"Yes, all will be revealed," he mocked. He was getting sick of all the cloak-and-dagger shit.

"Venom's nephew was struck down tragically and became . . . disabled. Porky and his brother Doc probably had no choice but to lock the secret away. But now that everyone is dead, it's going to take a little bit of time to find the secret," she said.

"You're talking in riddles," he said, annoyance in his voice.

They entered the competition room and found Venom standing by the pool table, his head bowed.

"Venom?" Toni said, breaking away from Diesel and stepping slowly toward her pale lover.

"The boy's dead," he said, letting out a sigh.

"I'm sorry," Diesel said. "If I'd known—"

"Save it," Venom barked. "Come here. *Now*!"

Diesel halted in place.

"I'm not going to hurt you," Venom said over his shoulder.

Reluctantly, Diesel moved closer, until he stood off to the man's side.

"I want you to witness this."

"Witness what?" Diesel asked as shadows enveloped Venom. Then the darkness faded, and his gaze was instantly drawn to Venom's hands, which seemed to grow larger. Blood seeped from the mysterious biker's fingers as his nails elongated, becoming razor-sharp talons.

Diesel took a step backward. "What. The actual. Fuck?"

Venom glanced up, his face a mass of furrows. His pupils were nothing more than reptilian slits, his mouth filled with needle-like teeth. Crimson trickled out of his eye sockets and nostrils.

Diesel's breath lodged in his throat. He was incapable of screaming, of forming a single word. His heart thumped harder and harder. The color washed out of him.

His bladder emptied, forming a neat puddle under his boots.

Venom turned his attention back to the Champ. He punched his fist into the kid's gut and ripped his talons up to the youngster's throat. Blood spurted out from the body.

Now Diesel was screaming. Screaming like a four-year-old girl.

Toni shoved past Diesel, her appearance now similar to Venom's, and joined in on the ripping and tearing. The two scooped blood and organs into their mouths, their hungry slurps and noisy chewing causing Diesel's stomach to churn. Moments later, nothing remained of the Champ apart from his clothes, glasses, and scraps of flesh and dried blood.

Diesel turned and emptied what little food he had inside him onto the floor. His spew mixed with his piss.

"You wanted to know what you're involved in?" Venom spat as Diesel dry-heaved on hands and knees. "Well, now you know."

"Jesus *fuck*!" Diesel yelled, tears flooding down his cheeks. He batted the droplets from his eyelashes and got to his feet, swaying. Venom's and Toni's faces had begun to relax back to normal. "What . . . What the fuck are you?"

"I would have thought it's obvious," Toni said.

Creatures of lore pranced at the forefront of Diesel's mind. "No, it can't be. It can't. It's not possible." He shook his head. "I don't believe it. I *won't*."

"Better start fucking believing," Venom said, snarling. Gore which clung to his chin waggled as he stalked closer to him. His fingernails were back in view, the talons retracted.

"Holy fucking hell," Diesel said, afraid he'd have pissed himself again if his bladder weren't already flaccid. "How did . . . ? What happened to you?"

"I thought you said you'd heard the rumors about me. You should already know."

"I'd heard you were involved in the Great Biker War and somehow cheated death. But that was all supposedly a myth. There was never any mention about . . . this," Diesel said, choking down more vomit as he caught sight of the Champ's remains over Venom's shoulder. "Does this have something to do with why you're being followed? Why you two stay up all night and hide during the day?"

"Tell him. The boy's clearly eager to know the whole story," Toni said, wiping blood and flesh off her chin.

"Fine. Let's get it all out there then, shall we?" Venom pulled up a chair and sat before Diesel. "I was bit during that famous brawl, see? After that, well, that's when I realized something wasn't quite right with me anymore . . ."

* * *

After his wife Sue's horrifying death—and the death of his unborn child—at the hands of Hun and his henchmen, all fight had left Venom. He'd been numb to his own death after that too, so stricken was he with grief.

And then he'd awakened days later, perfectly intact, the stab and gunshot wounds and burns gone.

Enraged, he'd sought his revenge. He'd spared Hun himself so the man would forever look over his shoulder. It was only right for the piece of shit to fear the boogeyman.

Several days after paying Hun back, Venom had fled, bouncing from place to place trying to come to terms with his new identity. He had changed; that much he was aware of. He was stronger yet weaker, healthier yet malnourished. He'd left his crew behind to spare them the strange metamorphosis he was experiencing . . . and because he found them tantalizing. Savory.

He'd tried consuming normal foods, like cold meats, but that had made him ill. Next had been livestock, but this too was fruitless. He craved human flesh—human *blood*, specifically. Within a week of the run-in with the Huns, the urges overwhelmed him, and he found himself sneaking into a dwelling set off the road in a quaint town outside of Cork, Ireland. No one knew him there. He could assuage his thirst and slip out unnoticed.

Breaking into the house with his newfound strength, he'd skulked through the property, hoping to surprise his prey or ambush them as they slept. But it was Venom who was caught by surprise. The blast from the double barrel shotgun behind him was deafening. Both cartridges drilled holes through his chest and punched into the wall in front of him. The ball bearings spread; a lamp shattered, a photo frame burst into a shower of glass, and a single chair and a two-seater sofa were peppered.

Venom's blood splashed up a wall and redecorated a painting of a schooner at sea above the fireplace. Sucking in air, he tried to shake the blur from his vision before collapsing to his knees.

A shrill Irish voice came from behind. "Who are ye? What d'ye want?"

Venom rose unsteadily to his feet and spun to face the man, his torso smoking. Vapor escaped his lips, which were lightly coated with gunpowder. The pain in his ribcage was excruciating. "Fuck," he howled, his face twisting into something beyond ugly. He tumbled to one side but the wall propped him up.

"Jesus," the Irishman said. The old geezer broke the barrel of his shotgun. The twin holes emitted gray smoke as he plucked out the stale rounds and slammed in two fresh shells. He snapped the shotgun shut again. "Freeze!"

"Save the bullets," Venom said in a flat tone.

The old man thumbed the hammers down, but Venom moved in fast and low, grabbing him by his throat and lifting him off his feet. A heavy choking sound squeaked from the man's throat before his neck cracked.

After draining the poor bastard of his blood, Venom found his powers even stronger—and his wounds healed over in a matter of minutes.

And yet, the hunger didn't dissipate as he'd hoped it would. In fact, it grew stronger too.

With more understanding of his new identity and what it could do for him should he slake his thirst, he carried on in the same manner for years: trawling the world, breaking into homes and apartments, feeding. (He never killed the young though. He drew the line there.) His regimen was to stay in a town five or six days, feed twice, then move on. His chopper was a fine machine for travel, which was also easy to conceal.

Years turned into decades. He watched mankind slowly destroy itself through drugs, famine, death, disease. All the while he both avoided human interactions and yearned for companionship. He missed his old crew and Sue even more. She had been a loyal and loving wife, snatched from him prematurely. She'd meant more to him than the air he breathed. But he guessed the big man upstairs hadn't seen it that way, having cursed him for it. He was fine with taking the punishment on the chin though.

One night while seeking his next victim, Venom happened on a huge house set on its own. It was like a manor but missing its fields and open country. A For Sale sign had been drilled to a wall beside a top window which had spider-web cracks in it. The windows looked decayed and worm-infested, the brickwork worn and weather-abused. He'd felt immediately drawn to the place, hypnotized by it, and brought his bike to a screeching halt.

Spotting a window ajar on the lower floor, Venom rushed to it and scrambled inside. A single candle burned in the room he entered, held in a sconce shaped in the form of a goblin's skull. Wax had spilled into its empty eye sockets. The meek candlelight partly illuminated dust- and cobweb-covered portraits on the walls. A shag pile in the corner was a tatty brown and holey. The plaster on the ceiling was deteriorating fast, and the wallpaper had come unglued, exposing garish yellow stains. The smell inside was stale, the light cheerless and unsteady.

The sole flickering flame was a beacon as he shuffled to a staircase and climbed the steps. At the landing, he was greeted by intense snarling and a snapping of jaws. The formidable Doberman yelped to silence and lay down as his and Venom's eyes fused.

Venom stormed in the dog's direction, stepped over the beast, and turned the handle to the door the mutt had been guarding. He edged the slab of wood open. One massive mirror hung on a wall, the glass smashed to smithereens, shards scattered on the carpet. There was not a stitch of furniture elsewise. Then he spotted a woman sleeping on a disheveled mattress in the center of the room.

He threw the door fully open and entered. A board creaked under his weight. Her eyes darted open.

She sprang to her feet, her mouth wide, exposing razor-sharp teeth. Her initially angelic-looking face corkscrewed into a veil of grotesqueness. She flew at him before he could speak and backhanded him across the cheek. He crashed against what was left of the mirror, his head rebounding off the shattered object.

Before he could regain his bearings, she was on him. Her long dark hair covered his eyes, blinding him as her talons scratched his skin and tore through his T-shirt. He managed to block a few of her swipes, gripped her by the waist, and tossed her flimsy frame away.

She charged and rammed him against the wall again, sinking her teeth into his neck.

"Argh! Get off!" Venom said, yanking her head back by her hair and chopping her throat. She went to ground. Blood poured from his neck as he gripped her by the throat and pinned her down. He gasped as he recognized her pale features, the way her face contorted into something otherworldly, her talons and teeth.

They were the same, both creatures borne out of darkness, possessing the godforsaken bloodlust and godlike strength.

He released his hold as she fought for air and gazed down upon her with a strange longing. "You. Me. We're the same."

Shock washed over her visage, her face relaxing back to its normal state. "What?"

"We are creatures not of this world. I . . . understand your desires. Your torment."

"That's not possible," she spluttered. She sat upright, blinking rapidly. "I'm alone. Alone in this world." Her eyes glazed over. "Forever."

His heart fluttered as he realized they shared the same dour mindset as well. "Apparently not."

The next day, they hit the road together, moving on to the next town, then the next. Their unfortunate lives had brought them together and bound them.

Through this, their feelings for each other intensified as the days, weeks, and months continued to pass.

However, they were still not alone.

* * *

"About half a year after stumbling upon Toni, I noticed we were being tailed," Venom said. "The same faces would pop up in the same vehicles at the same time of day no matter where we were. I *know* it's Hun's doing. The fucker is rotting in a jail cell these days, but I don't doubt his influence still extends around the country, maybe farther. We don't really know how many are following us either, but we know they've closed in." He glanced aside, gnawing at his inner lip. "Probably shouldn't have come back home, but I wanted to see the family and end this once and for all."

"You should have come back to the brotherhood," Diesel said. "We'd have taken you in, looked after you, even after all these years. Dutch and Ollie—they lead us now—wouldn't have thought twice to give you shelter and protection. You're a patched member, Venom. It wouldn't have mattered about your . . . condition."

"Condition?" Venom huffed out a laugh. "That's a fucking joke. It's a *curse*. A curse for all the bad shit I've done in my life. Hell, if I didn't know any better, I'd say Hun himself fucking cursed me."

"Jesus." Diesel shook his head. The whole fucked-up situation fascinated him, and he wasn't scared any longer. "You said Hun's in prison, right? Why not just go there and take him out?"

"That would be too easy. I want that fucker to rot inside. Once this is over, I'll be sending him a message."

"Oh yeah? What kind?"

"Questions, questions, questions," Venom mocked.

"An inquisitive fellow, isn't he?" Toni chided. "Next he'll be asking for my personal history too!"

"Well?" Diesel said, a crooked smile on his face.

She giggle-sighed. "I've been like this for the better part of twenty years," she said, lowering her gaze. "I can't remember much about my past, except my family. My dad disowned me, basically, after my mother left him. I don't remember much about him, only stories she used to tell me before she was murdered." She glanced back up and held Diesel's stare. "I heard it was my father who had her killed. I searched for him for years but could never find the bastard. It . . . it was his old house Venom found me in."

"And it's where we found each other. That's all that matters," Venom said.

Diesel thought it best not to ask Toni any more questions. "What about your other nephew, Venom? The one Toni said is still here? Is he the same as both of you?"

"Oh, he's here, all right—locked away for safekeeping, no doubt. And no, he's worse," Venom said. "We need to find him before sunup."

"Why? What happens then?" Diesel wanted to know.

"I think we'll have company before sunrise, and I don't think we'll be able to take them all on without a little help."

"Okay," Diesel said, some of his steel finding its way back into his heart and gut. "Let's get it done."

"Good lad. I was beginning to think you didn't own a set of nuts," Venom said.

Diesel offered a weak smile. He supposed pissing himself and throwing up hadn't helped his image any, but he was eager to find this family member. It sounded like they would need the backup. *Even if he happens to be more terrifying than this lot.*

"Right, let's go hunting," Venom said. He nodded at Diesel. "Grab a torch, you'll probably need it."

Diesel bustled about to gather a flashlight and joined Venom at the exit all the pool tournament losers had gone through.

Toni and Venom shared a quick peck before she turned and winked at Diesel. "Look after yourself, beaut," she told him. "We wouldn't want those rugged good looks of yours spoiled, now would we?"

She laughed as he and Venom headed through the door.

As they trekked down the hallway beyond, Diesel felt a thrill of excitement fill him. He'd always liked adventures as a child—the danger, the chills, the unknown. Venom and Toni's appearance may have thrown him off-kilter to begin with, but now he was immersed in it.

He was starting to regret having killed Porky and the others.

"If you and those fucking truckers hadn't killed my kin, especially Baby, then we'd be safe. I came here expecting a haven, not a fucking abattoir," Venom said.

"I told you—"

"I know you claim you didn't kill anyone. But it's still my family, no matter what."

"Agreed," Diesel said. "I'm willing to do anything to repay whatever debt you feel I owe you, brother."

"How noble."

Diesel let it go. He wasn't about to argue with a man who could tear him limb from limb. He was just going to have to prove to Venom that the patch meant everything to him.

They moved along the corridor which led to the dead and their pickled remnants.

"There's nothing down here, you know," Diesel commented, breaking the awkward silence. "Just that room where they carved the dead."

"You're probably right. But there must be something here: a door, another room we've overlooked. They've added secret passageways and rooms over the decades—the pub has gotten much larger since I was last here. And I've searched every other nook of this place, so I figured our best bet would be to search where they were doing their . . . more clandestine work."

"And there's nothing on the upper floors?" Diesel offered.

"That's just one section you've seen. There's another part to it."

"How fucking big is—"

A creaking floorboard above them sent a snaking chill down Diesel's back. They halted mid-stride.

Venom looked up and smiled. "So you're up *there*," he whispered at the ceiling. "Come on." He placed his hands on the wall in front of them. "Take the other side. Look for a switch or button. There's got to be an entrance around here somewhere."

Diesel jumped into action. They palmed the walls on their respective sides until, minutes later, Venom shouted in triumph. Something clicked behind Diesel and the hallway filled with the groans of grating metal. He turned in time to see a section of the wall slide to one side, revealing a stairway that led upwards. Footprints marred the dusty steps.

"Someone's been up there recently," Venom pointed out. "Right, up we go. Stay behind me though. Richard will kill you on sight."

Creepy, Diesel thought.

He obliged and stepped aside, following Venom as he ascended the staircase. Cobwebs slapped his face and mouth, causing him to spit and cough. The boards below him creaked and protested his weight as he went.

When they reached the top, Venom said, "You may need your flashlight now."

"Don't you want it?"

Venom shook his head. "My vision in darkness is sharper than in daylight, no worries."

Diesel shrugged and flicked his torch on as Venom approached a doorway across the landing.

"Richard, are you in here?" the ghostly Boa called into the black room beyond. "Richard, it's me, Venom. Your uncle."

As he followed Venom into the gloom, he had to bite his breath down. The single beam of light fluttered as Diesel failed to keep his arm from shaking.

"I'm not going to harm you, Richard," Venom continued, his soft voice echoing tenfold in the still, quiet room. "Please show yourself. I need your help."

"I really don't think there's anyone up here," Diesel muttered.

"Shh!"

A large silhouette appeared in the murkiness behind Venom as the biker turned on his heels. Diesel would have yelled had his throat not been so dry and tight. And when the beast moved forward into the beam of the flashlight, Diesel stepped back, tripped, landed on his arse, and scooted backwards as fast as he could.

The hairy hulk outweighed and outsized Venom in every way. Twice the height of any normal man, Richard had to bend slightly to keep his head from touching the rafters. The floor below him bowed with the effort of fighting gravity and his mass. His back, chest, arms, and legs rippled with muscle; shackles, chains, and cuffs graced his wrists and ankles. He was naked bar a few rags which clung to him. The length of his claws matched his sizable teeth, and saliva dripped from his wet chin.

Diesel cringed as Venom reached his hand out and smiled at Richard. He figured the undying man would be ripped to shreds, and then he and Toni would be left alone to fend off both this giant *thing* and those who were tailing Venom.

He blinked in confusion as the beast likewise reached out and clasped Venom's hand.

"It's good to be home," Venom said, staring into his nephew's eyes. "I've missed you."

He threw his arms around the colossal man and they embraced in a heartfelt hug.

CHAPTER TWENTY-FIVE

Teeth rattled free from the bitch's jaw as Johnson delivered yet another powerful blow to her face. More blood splashed out, coating his soaked gloves anew. He was pleasantly surprised at how tough she was. For a woman, she was really holding her own.

He circled her, clicking his tongue against the roof of his mouth. Johnson was getting tired. Tired and pissed off. They'd been on the road for hours, passing through more than five towns since their stop in the woods, and the trail he thought he'd been following turned cold. He had finally decided to play the ace he had up his sleeve and directed the convoy to Slough. He hoped visiting the family would help weed out Venom's whereabouts, or at least give them something more to go on.

The woman he now had tied to a chair was a distant relative of Venom's. She might not even know about him, but it was a risk Johnson was willing to take. They had nothing else to go on.

"You better start talking, Gail, or my associate here," he said, pointing at Max, "will bite your fingers and toes off. You wouldn't want that, would you?"

She picked her lolling head up and smiled. "I've already told you, I know nothing," she slurred, her blonde hair stained red from flecks of blood. Her once pretty face was now cut, puffy, and black and blue.

"Are you sure, Gail?"

She laughed. "Yes."

"Maybe we should start extracting the nails from your toes and fingers? See if that loosens you up a bit?"

Gail leered at her captors. Vomit graced her chin and the front of her pajama top, which had a Snow White emblem on it. A pool of blood gathered around her feet. Some had splashed her furniture, but it mixed well with the chocolate color scheme and the dead, splayed-open cats lying on the living room rug. She'd shown no emotion when Max and two more of Johnson's goons had killed her pets.

"I can assure you, Gail, you will be begging for your life at the end of this ordeal."

She spat at his feet. "Fuck you, dickhead. I'm not telling you anything."

"But Gail, what have you got to gain by protecting this man?"

"He'll do far worse things to me than you could ever do."

Johnson shook his head. "Okay, we'll play it the hard way." He clicked his fingers.

Max opened the toolbox on top of Gail's coffee table. Inside was an array of sharp, blunt, and serrated tools.

"Pliers, please," Johnson said to Max, who obliged and handed him the extracting implement. "Now, I should think this is going to hurt. But it'll be fun for me."

She shook her head frantically, her eyes bulging.

Johnson removed one of her slippers. "I'll start with your piggies. But before I begin, are you sure there's nothing you want to tell me?"

She quivered but kept her lips clamped shut.

"I guess not," he said, going for the little toe first.

He ripped the nail off with grunting pleasure. She screeched and writhed. A small splash of blood found its way into his mouth and mottled his lips. He licked them, then tore three more nails off the same foot, struggling to keep her flailing limb steady. More crimson droplets flicked onto his face, giving Johnson a cluster of red freckles across the bridge of his nose.

"No . . . No more . . . please," she whimpered. "I beg you."

Her next scream slashed through the air as Johnson finished pulling her toenails off one foot and moved to the other, gripping the nail on her second big toe with the pliers. "Ready to talk yet?"

"I can't! I fucking can't, you motherfucker!" she shouted, laughing maniacally.

Johnson nodded at Max, who swiftly exited the room. He returned seconds later with a bottle of vinegar from the kitchen and handed it to Johnson.

Johnson splashed her wounds with the brown liquid, which set her off shrieking anew. She thrashed in her chair as the fluid soaked into her mutilated flesh. "Drink up, bitch," he said. "This is what you get for harboring a fugitive."

"Stop it, you fucking piece of shit!"

He smashed her across the face with the glass bottle, tearing a gash down her cheek. Her godawful screeching and grating voice died out and she went limp.

Johnson laughed. "I think she's finally out cold, Max!" He lit a cigar. "Looks like we're going to be here a while. We'll move again in the morning. Hopefully we'll have something to go on by then. Have the men stand down for now."

"Sure," Max said, leaving Johnson alone with Gail.

"Gail, Gail, Gail," he said, circling the woman. "There's no need to play possum. I know you're not out. It's not going to buy you time. I will get the information I need."

She murmured.

He smiled. She was playing the game well.

He yanked her head back by her hair as hard as he could with his free hand, fearing her neck would snap on the back of her chair. She wailed, spat, and cursed him.

"That's more like it," he said, staring at her bloodied toes. The sight sent a shiver through him. "Shall I start pulling your fingernails off now? Is this really where we want to go?"

"Do what the fuck you like, arsehole. I'm sure that's the only thing that gets your little limp dick hard," she said through gritted teeth.

He took a puff on his cigar, released his handful of her hair, and moved around to her front. "We'll get started on the fingers as soon as I finish this. Can't waste a good smoke, you know?" He winked, inhaled another cloud, and exhaled roughly. "I really can't see why you would protect such a man, by the way. He's scum."

"I already said he'd do far worse to me than you and your goons. And family don't shit on each other either."

"Fair point," he said. "But if you should give me his location, I can offer you protection."

She scoffed. "Good one. Nothing could protect me from him."

"I'm serious. Once I have tracked him, I *will* kill him."

"You and that ragtag bunch of arseholes you call an army don't know shit. You have no idea what you're up against. He'll murder you all, rip you apart, and when he's finished, he'll celebrate by drinking your goddamn blood."

He chortled. "Well, you do paint a vivid picture."

"You won't be laughing when you come face to face with him. You'll be begging for mercy. My only regret now is that I won't be there to see your agonizing end."

He took another long drag and spoke with the fumes still in his lungs. "Touching. You know, after I've killed you, Venom, and whoever else he's with, I'm going to make it my priority to wipe out the rest of his family." Holding her gaze, he grinned wide and forced the smoke through the gaps in his teeth, out his nostrils. "Even the infants."

This removed the smile from her face.

"Maybe I should have your sister brought around here this evening? How old is she again? Twenty? Twenty-one?"

"You leave Jesse out of this!"

"Oh, I'll go after anyone and everyone close to you. I'll go through you *all* until I get what I want," he said, finishing the last of his cigar. "So you'd better start talking." He threw his cigar butt onto the carpet and stamped on it, grinding it under heel.

"He'll kill me if I say anything—if any of us do!"

"And what do you think I'm going to do to you, hmm?" He grabbed the pliers again.

"No . . . No!"

He started with her pinkies. The nails ripped clean off with ease. Her shrieking caused him to judder—it prickled the hair on his arms and at the back of his neck. Once both little fingers were done, he stood back, watching her writhe and spit. "Do we stop? Are we ready to talk?"

"Go fuck yourself!" she screamed.

Enraged, he tore the rest of her nails free, one after the other, with no break in between. He thought the pain would make her pass out, but still she was persistent. He slapped her once, twice, three times. "Talk to me, bitch!" He was losing control. If he didn't reel his emotions in, he'd kill her. Then he'd know nothing.

He shoved the pliers into her mouth and grabbed at one of the few teeth remaining. He yanked it out of her gob. A squirt of blood ensued. "Talk!"

She laugh-cried. "Fuck *you*!"

Johnson was done pussyfooting—he needed the information she had. If Venom was close by, the opportunity could be missed. "Insubordinate bitch!" he yelled in her face, letting loose a flurry of blows to her stomach: left, right, right, right, left, left, right.

She giggle-sobbed the entire time but still refused to cooperate.

"Fine, have it your way." Breathing heavily from the effort, he cupped his bloodied, bruised hands around his lips. "Max! Bring that other bitch and her boyfriend in here!"

Less than a minute later, Max dragged another woman into the room by her hair. She was no more than twenty years old. He forced her onto a chair opposite Gail and restrained her with ropes. Three more thugs brought a bloke into the room behind him, and, like the women, he was roughly shoved onto a dining room seat. He looked to be the same age as the new girl and wore nothing but boxer shorts. His body was covered in tattoos, his nipples pierced. He'd been gagged, and he grunted and growled under the tape to no avail.

"Jesse," Gail whispered. "Please don't hurt them. It's me you want. *Please!*"

"Well, isn't this cozy?" Johnson patted Gail on the head. "I'll hurt whomever I see fit, Gail. Especially if I don't get the information I seek. And you haven't been talking, so . . ." He nodded at Max. "Get the drill. And you three," he said to the thugs who had hauled in Tattoo Boy, "may leave, but tell Dawn to come on in."

They all grunted and left the room.

"Is this about Uncle Venom?" Jesse squealed.

"Shh, Jesse! Don't say another word," Gail warned.

"Ah, a talker, huh?" He glared at the new girl. "Well?"

The pupils in her wide eyes flickered between fear and uncertainty, but she obeyed Gail.

"One of you will open your flap soon, no worries," Johnson said, grinning wide.

Max was first to re-enter the living room, a Black & Decker carry case in hand.

"Non-blood first," Johnson directed him.

"Looks like your number's up, lad," Max said, clapping a hand to Tattoo Boy's shoulder.

"No! Gail, do something!" Jesse pleaded.

Gail pressed her lips together and looked away from the carnage.

"I don't think so," Johnson said, clapping his palms on either side of her head and forcing her to witness the grisly events unfold.

Max opened the hard plastic box and dug out the power tool. He pressed the trigger and the ten-inch drill bit whirled around and around. With an evil smile, he placed the cool metal tip to Tattoo Boy's exposed left knee.

"Well?" Johnson asked, easing his face close to Gail's and talking low into her ear. "Are you ready to spill the beans or what?"

"Gail, tell them what they want to know! Please!" Jesse shouted.

Tattoo Boy grunted and growled as his chest, arm, and leg muscles flexed impressively against his restraints.

"Don't do this," Gail pleaded, her voice soft, as though she had finally been broken. "I *can't* tell you anything. I don't *know* anything."

Johnson sighed in disappointment and gave Max the silent order to proceed.

Max beamed. The drill whirred as it kicked life.

The vicious tool bore through Tattoo Boy's knee. It rendered his flesh as easy as someone peeling an orange. Bones splintered and cracked, drowning out his stifled screams. Blood bubbled and spurted like an erupting volcano. The stench of drilled bone wafted through the room.

Max pulled the rotating bit out of the wound. Bits of ivory and leg hair and white-pinkish meat clung to its curves. Tattoo Boy's whole body shook, stiffened, then relaxed. Strings of bloody saliva oozed out of his mouth as his head swayed on its plinth, his eyes rolling like marbles.

"You motherfucking son of a fucking whore bastard shit fuck cunt—I'll kill you!" Jesse screamed, bucking in her chair.

"My, my, such language," Dawn said, entering the room. She looked doped up.

"Had a nap, my dear?" Johnson asked.

"Yes, but I'm sure glad you woke me for this."

Johnson chuckled. "It would seem we're having trouble extracting information from this trio."

"You can go to fucking hell!" Jesse screamed.

Dawn crossed swiftly to her. "Can I cut this one's tongue out?"

"Of course, if you think it will get us somewhere," he answered.

"You and I are going to have some fun," Dawn told Jesse.

"Right. Max, carry on," Johnson said.

His right-hand man was eager, and the drill bit was off on its path of destruction again as it bored through Tattoo Boy's other knee.

"I'll tell you what you want to know!" Jesse hollered over the grating whine. "Just leave Peter alone. Please!" She stopped bucking in her chair. "I'll tell you."

Johnson called Max off and clapped once with twisted amusement. "Finally, we have a winner!"

"Be quiet, you fool!" Gail snapped. "You know what will happen if you talk!"

"Dawn, shut that one up, please?" Johnson said, pointing at the elder woman. "She's clearly useless to us now that we have this pretty little thing."

"My pleasure, sir." Dawn pulled her Walther PPK from her holster and shoved the muzzle into Gail's face.

The woman didn't have time to gasp before Dawn squeezed the trigger. Four bullets punched through Gail's face and plowed into the wall behind her. Bits of shattered bone and mucus splashed the carpet.

Johnson cut the ropes binding Gail to her chair, shoved her body off, and sat on it, lighting another cigar. "All right, spit it out, Jesse."

She nudged her chin toward Tattoo Boy, who was crying and shaking. "Can't you help him before I start?"

Johnson thought about it for a moment as he looked into her green-grey eyes and puffed away. The way in which her hair flanked her young face made her look sexy, especially with the torn pajama top exposing some of her pasty flesh. "Max will see to it that the bleeding is stemmed. We'll also get him to a hospital, but only *after* you have given us some information."

She gulped. "Can you promise us safety from Venom?"

Johnson nodded. "He will never harm either of you. Now, get on with it already."

"Fine, okay." She sucked in a sharp breath and lowered her voice. "Do you know the old section of motorway between here and Manchester that leads to Newcastle? The section of old A5?"

"Yeah. What about it?"

"There's a pub out on that road by the name of the Rack and Cue. It's been in the family for generations. You can bet that's where Venom has gone. He was very close to that side of the family."

"Who are they to you?"

"Distant uncles," she answered. "Porky and his two brothers—I can't recall their names. I think they have a daughter and son out there with them, too. He'd go there for sure. They'd protect him."

The girl was sweating profusely. Johnson believed her, though he'd thought the road abandoned and uninhabited save for farmers these days. "Is that all?"

"No, there's more. Do you know . . . *what* Venom is?"

Johnson nodded.

"Well, he has a nephew who's worse. One who's more wolf than man," she said.

Dawn and Max burst out laughing.

"This ain't *An American Werewolf in London*, love!" Max teased.

Jesse's face was cold, expressionless. "Don't say I didn't warn you. That part of my family's dangerous."

Johnson blew smoke free of his mouth and leaned forward. "In what way, my dear?"

She told them what her sister Gail had told her: the family was killing people out there, selling their organs. "They've been doing it to keep the pub open. The place is a fortress of mazes and weapons and torture rooms, Gail said. And if you lot go there, you will all die trying to kill Venom."

"And you believe your sister?" Johnson asked, toeing the body on the floor at his feet.

"She would not have lied to me."

"No, you're probably right, my dear. Is there anything else my associates and I should know before we venture out there?"

Jesse's eyes lit up. "No, nothing else. Please, untie us and get Peter some help."

"Sure thing." Johnson nodded at Dawn, who again un-holstered her Walther.

She put two bullets in Peter's head and did the same to Jesse before the girl had enough time to draw another breath.

"Burn the place," Johnson said, walking out the door.

Dawn followed close behind as Max dispensed the fuel. "Shame we had to kill her. She had nice tits," she said, cackling.

Johnson laughed along with her.

* * *

By the time Johnson and Dawn were back in the four-by-four, Max emerged from the semi-detached house, balls of frolicking fire visible through the open doorway. The curtains were quick to catch, and the windows began to crack and blacken as the fire licked the roof. As the convoy started pulling away, the front door caught alight. Thick black smog polluted the night air.

Sirens wailed in the distance.

"Some nosey neighbors have alerted the authorities, no doubt. Best we step on it," Johnson said. "I may have some clout over the powers that be, but this would be a little hard to explain."

Before the ambulance, police, and fire services arrived on scene, Johnson and his band of merry men had vanished into the night.

CHAPTER TWENTY-SIX

Lying on his back on a bench in the pool tournament lounge, Diesel tried but couldn't sleep. *What are they doing up there with that . . . thing?* he wondered.

After the discovery on the top floor, Venom had told Diesel to get some shuteye so he'd be refreshed for his shift on the roof early in the morning. He'd had no problem leaving. Sleeping was the hard part. He felt vulnerable. Alone. The things upstairs could kill him at any given moment. Snuff him out.

Diesel wanted to run away. But he'd never backed down from anything or anyone before, no matter how hairy the situation or imposing the person was. His mind whirled. *What should I do? If I stay, I'm going to die for certain, either at the hands of Venom or the people coming for him. But if I leave, the same fate will befall me.* An early death was imminent in his career, but he'd never expected it to be *this* early.

The boards above him creaked. They were on the move. That meant dawn was fast approaching.

Seeing little point in lying there any longer, he got up. He needed fresh air, along with coffee and a smoke. He flung the flimsy blanket he'd used on the roof aside, arched his back to chase away the restfulness, and made his way out the door. He avoided looking at the carcass on the pool table—the smell was reminder enough. Once in the primary bar room, he stood behind the counter and put the coffee pot on to boil.

Fuck it. If I'm going to die, I'm going out with booze inside me too, he thought, pouring himself a brandy. He slugged it and downed three more helpings before leaving it there.

The hot water in the pot started to bubble. Diesel pulled down a cup from the highest shelf. An etching of Porky Pig graced the mug. *No guessing who this belonged to*, he thought. *Well, that fat bastard won't be needing it anytime soon.* He chuckled and spooned coffee into the cup. He held the milk and sugar, deciding on black. *Tar in a mug! Can't beat it.*

"How can you drink it that hot?" Toni asked.

The sudden appearance of another would normally have made him jump out of his skin, but he was getting used to all the surprises. They'd sharpened him. "Cast-iron gut, me," he said, winking and turning to face her. He couldn't help but think how hot she looked. Her tight-fitting jeans showed off a slightly plump bum and meaty thighs. He cast his gaze over her tits. They were small but pert. Suckable. Her nipples jutted through the thin fabric. *Cold?* he felt like asking her.

She grinned. "No. Are you?"

"Huh?" he said, his mouth dry. *Did she just read my fucking mind? Not possible, surely?*

"Very possible," she said, winking back at him. "Drink your coffee, beaut. We're going to need you on guard in ten minutes."

He was so gob smacked all he could do was gawp at her.

She pushed past him. "Come on, you ain't got time to stare. Bring your coffee with you. I'll bring you a fresh one later."

He nodded and followed her out the door and up the stairs to his side of the attic, his steps leaden. He was trying his damnedest to stay in the moment and avoid internal thoughts. What if they had already guessed his lies? How much had they gleaned from his mind? "Is Venom with Richard?" he asked, knowing speaking would keep his brain busy and unreadable.

"Yes. They're getting their rest."

"Will you be joining them?"

"As soon as I've seen you to your post, yes. Why?"

"I just fancied some company, that's all. It was a long day up there yesterday," he said.

"You aren't going to fuck me, Diesel."

"Who the hell said I wanted to?"

"You don't have to say anything."

"I was being serious. It *was* lonely."

"You won't have time to get bored because they'll come at some point. Venom is convinced about that. Says he can feel them nearby."

"Okay," he said, making his way up the ladder to the attic floor.

"Diesel," she called up to him.

He poked his head through the hatch. "Yes?"

"I'll bring you a fresh cup in about twenty minutes."

"Great. Thanks."

"No problem. Just get yourself settled. I'll leave one at the bottom of the ladder. A bite to eat, too."

He nodded and took off to set up his post.

* * *

By the time Johnson and the team found the turnoff for the old A5, the sky was aglow with daybreak. The weather-worn sign for it had been covered in foliage and grime, but Johnson had been quick to spot it. He'd used the road a few times, before leaving his third wife and daughter behind for good.

"Looks like it's going to be another glorious day," said Geraint, who'd been silent much of the whole trip. Dawn was slumped over sleeping next to him.

Johnson turned in his seat. "A good day to die?"

"As good a day as any."

"Who says we're going to bite it?" Max jumped in. "You don't really believe all that shit we've been fed by Hun, Gail, and all the others, do you?"

"Maybe. Maybe not," Johnson said.

Max smiled. "I think you've been reading too many ghost stories. Did her tale spook you or something?"

"Not at all, my boy. Nothing scares me, not after what we've seen and been through."

Max waved his hand dismissively. "Right. He ain't nothing but a damn petrol-head anyway, this Venom character."

"Yeah," Geraint said. "We aren't chasing any fucking monsters, ghouls, or ghosts. Nothing but mortal men and women walk this world."

That last remark iced Johnson's bones. He shivered.

"All I know," Geraint continued, "is that I'm looking forward to a cold beer after this shit's done and dusted. It's been a long outing this time, boys."

Johnson lit a cigar and snapped the Zippo shut. The loud clang reverberated within the vehicle, waking Dawn abruptly. "Well then, let's hope we're not shit out of luck for last orders over at the Rack and Cue." He dragged on his cigar and let out a massive cloud of smoke.

Max and Geraint both laughed and lowered their windows as Johnson's cigar fumes overwhelmed them inside the jeep.

"Hey, you remember that fucking badass from Swansea?" Max said.

Johnson guffawed. "You mean that dipshit who thought he was possessed by that Mexican deity?"

"Who?" Geraint asked.

"This would have been before your time, Geraint," Max said. "It was our first job together outside the military. Some dude named Lucas Owens changed his name to Santa Muerte because he believed he'd become possessed by the ancient god of Mexico."

"Yes, some nasty people wanted Lucas—Santa for short—dead," Johnson said. "Rival gang members were spooked by his antics and felt he was dangerous. He was definitely off his hinges. We'd heard a shitload of stories about him: how he'd been seen slaughtering sheep and goats in the name of his god, drank blood. Fucking madness.

"We killed all his men and generals and had him pinned, when he randomly started speaking in a different tongue. Ripped open his shirt and said 'No amount of bullets can kill me!'"

"What happened?" Dawn asked, sounding groggy still.

"I sprayed him all over the walls," Max said, smiling. "So much for him being invincible."

"I'll never forget that loopy fuck," Johnson said. "Batshit crazy."

"This Venom guy reminds me of Santa Muerte—that's why I brought it up," Max said. "He's probably nothing more than an old man, living off a reputation he's built up."

"Well, I'm sure we're going to find out quite soon by the look of things," Johnson said, pointing ahead.

On the horizon, the faint outline of a massive building peeked above treetops. The sunlight hadn't yet stretched that far, so the pub stood in shadow. Even though they were a fair distance away, the place managed to loom over them.

"Max, get a little closer, then pull over," Johnson ordered. "We'll walk the rest of the way from there."

"Makes sense," Dawn said, stretching and yawning beside Geraint. "That way we won't warn anyone of our presence."

"Exactly," Johnson said, flicking the butt of his cigar out his open window. "You don't get as far as I have in this game without vigilance."

"I hope we get the drop on them," Geraint said. "I'm busting for some action."

"That's what I like to hear. I want my hounds thirsty for blood," Johnson quipped.

* * *

Diesel's eyes quickly adjusted to the dawning morning and soon he was able to see all around him. After stretching once more and yawning, he made his way to the chimneystack.

First, he double-checked that all the guns were still loaded, with one in their chamber. Happy with his weapon inspection, he then did a long, drawn-out scan with the binoculars. He meticulously swept the whole area, doing a full circle. Nothing moved.

He set the binoculars to one side, dug his box of fags out of his pocket, and lit one. It felt majestic, standing on the roof with such a view before him. Not a sound except the wind assaulted his ears. He took deep breaths, holding the smoke in before releasing it into the morning air.

"Diesel?" he heard a faint voice call.

"I'm coming," he yelled.

By the time he got to the attic entrance, Toni had gone. In her place was a tray filled with coffee, sandwiches, and the all-important bottle of brandy.

He retrieved the goodies and shuffled back to his spot, noticing a note attached to the liquor bottle. He settled onto his blanket and read the little slip of paper: "Not too much, we don't want you falling off the roof!"

He chuckled and rammed a bacon sandwich into his mouth, washing it down with a big gulp of coffee. Toni had supplied him with not only a mug of fresh brew but also a full pot of the tar-like liquid too. *I'll be pissing like a racehorse!* He picked up a second sandwich and devoured that one, too. He burped, finished the rest of the coffee in his mug, and tore through the rest of the food.

Done eating, he stood and sipped the hot coffee, taking his time and admiring the view. Once his thirst was slaked, he placed the mug on the chimneystack and picked up the binoculars. Nonchalant, he surveilled behind him, left, and right, zooming over objects and empty space. *Boredom is going to kick my arse today,* he figured, setting his sights on the area directly in front of him.

A fleet of cars rumbled slowly down the roadway.

His jaw dropped. *Oh, fuck!*

* * *

The jeep trundled along at a slow pace. Johnson didn't want to dash down the road in case the sound of his oncoming convoy alerted Venom and any other person with him. Although the sun was rising in the sky in front of them and Venom would supposedly be powerless at this point of the day, Johnson didn't want to lose the element of surprise.

Even though Max drove with sleepy eyes, he was alert. Dawn and Geraint were both eager in the back, their weapons cocked. His soldiers were ready, and so was he.

This was war.

They drove another half-mile or so before Johnson pointed and said, "Right, Max, let's go ahead and pull over in that—"

A bullet tore through their windshield and hit Max in the throat. He slumped forward. Blood poured and spurted over the wheel. The four-by-four swerved, hitting the barrier of the dual carriageway. The vehicle flipped violently, smashing through a hedge and coming to rest upside-down in a field.

Something in his shoulder popped and Johnson roared in pain. He maintained his composure, undid his seatbelt, and threw the passenger door open. It groaned on its hinges as he dragged himself out of the wreckage. He gulped down copious amounts of clean air and staggered to his feet in time to witness the biker behind also get caught by a bullet. The slug smashed through his visor and caved his face in. He back-flipped off his bike and crashed to the road. The driver of the jeep behind him rolled over the body. The jeep's brakes locked up and the corpse of the biker tangled in the wheels, causing the car following to plow into the vehicle's arse-end.

Other bikers skidded and crashed into the pile-up.

A stray bullet caught a fuel tank and the whole thing blew, sending thick blankets of choking smog into the air.

The driver of the jeep exited his cab. His high-pitched screams ripped the morning air as others scurried out of the carnage around him.

* * *

The rifle clicked on empty and Diesel ducked behind the chimneystack. His breath exploded out in short, sharp bursts. He wiped the sweat from his brow— some was dripping into his eyes, making them sting.

He removed his cut, listening with a smile at the crackling of roasting metal and flesh. Glass popped. As the expected yet unexpected visitors tried to get their bearings, Diesel reloaded, convinced he could kill them all, now that he'd caused so much damage with his first attack. He was also sure their leader or leaders would have been in that first vehicle he disposed of. That was an extra bonus. Venom would be pleased.

Not wanting to give his position away, he slowly got back to his feet and cocked his weapon. He took aim. A man wearing grenades was helping others douse a woman aflame. Aiming true, he struck one of the guy's bombs, which blew him and the others around him apart. A cloud of red mist scattered and sprayed the ground. Through the scope of the rifle, Diesel could see a fair few running around on fire too. He laughed. *Fuck 'em. Let the bastards burn to death.*

He cocked another round into the chamber and aimed anew. This time he took down a woman who was behind the wheel of a car. Her head exploded like a dropped melon.

Then automatic weapons opened up all about him and returned fire. Bullets chipped away at the roof; slate, brick, and chimneypot erupted.

He ducked and cowered in his little space. "Christ!" he yelled, grabbing the brandy bottle. He unscrewed the cap and took down mouthfuls at a time, draining the bottle of its contents.

With renewed vigor, he stood, screamed in rage with his trigger finger squeezing, and emptied the rifle's entire magazine. He managed to hit a few who were giving return fire before needing to duck to reload again.

* * *

Johnson coughed and hobbled back to the jeep. Considering the spill it had taken, he was surprised to be alive. Except for his shoulder, which still screamed in pain, he seemed to have gotten out unscathed.

One look at Max confirmed the first bullet fired on them had killed the man. He gulped down his anger and brief grief (emotions had been bred out of him in the military) and shouted into the wreckage, "Dawn? Geraint? Are you okay?"

No reply.

Fuck, fuck, fuck. "Geraint! Dawn!"

"She's dead, boss," Geraint uttered from inside.

Fuck! "What about you, lad?"

"I think my leg's broken, along with a rib or two."

"Right, okay," Johnson said. "Can you crawl out?"

"Yes, my window's broken."

"Good, then get free," Johnson told him. "They must have a sniper posted on that roof. Take him down right away."

"Okay."

Johnson heard his man shuffle out of the metallic ruins as he took in the full scope of destruction. His manpower was down to under half, easy. Bodies lay scattered about the old road and vehicles smoldered in steaming heaps. Some of his soldiers were already returning fire, some were stumbling about in disarray, and yet others were fleeing the scene, likely thinking him dead.

Johnson caught a glimpse of Geraint clambering through the disheveled hedge their jeep had careened through. He bent, snatched his bag from out of the crumpled jeep, and followed. By the time he caught up, Geraint was getting into his rifle-firing stance. He'd been a crack shot in the army.

The gun bucked in Geraint's hands and kicked his shoulder backward.

Johnson grinned as a silhouette atop the roof of the pub disappeared.

CHAPTER TWENTY-SEVEN

THE BULLET CAUGHT DIESEL IN HIS NECK. Blood ejected from him quickly. He kept pressure on the wound as he clawed and struggled to the attic entrance. He knew he was spent—he just didn't want to die alone.

He made it to the hatch and peered down. The ladder was out, and he launched himself through the opening anyway, knowing the fall would hurt him further. But what did it matter?

The impact was hard. His sight blackened for a moment. When he came to again, Venom, Toni, and Richard were waiting for him in the darkness. Venom knelt at his side and held the hand Diesel offered him.

"I thought I had them," he gargled.

"You did well," Venom said.

Diesel choked, wheezed, and spluttered. "I . . . I think I . . . I . . ."

"Shh," Toni said, wiping his brow. She then removed his hand from the bullet wound, allowing his blood to spurt free.

The last thing he saw before closing his eyes was the bulk of Richard standing over all three of them.

* * *

"I'm scared," Toni said, staring down at the now dead Diesel. "Now what are we going to do?"

Richard roared, beating his chest.

"No, you can't go out there alone," Venom said. "They'll kill you."

But there was no stopping the huge beast, as he sprang through the hatch in the ceiling and disappeared into the daylight.

"Nooooo!" Venom bellowed. He whirled on Toni. "Quick, downstairs! We have to try and help him."

"But Venom, its daylight! We're . . . powerless, baby."

His jawline tightened. "We have to try."

* * *

"Hold your fire!" Johnson yelled. "Hold. Your. Fire!" he repeated. Whoever had been shooting from the rooftop was no longer a threat. He ordered his remaining soldiers to divvy out weaponry, and once they were done, he said, "Right, move forward."

As a cohesive unit, his team marched closer to the building. As they neared it, they ringed the front entrance and started lighting Molotov cocktails. Silence enveloped them, and only the harsh pops and crackles of their wrecked vehicles broke above the din of quietude.

"I'm giving you one chance to get your arse out here, Venom," Johnson finally bellowed. "Or we're going to smoke you out!"

"You'll have to come in and fucking get me, you piece of shit!" a muffled voice answered from somewhere just beyond the front door.

"That won't be necessary," Johnson muttered.

He nodded at his front line of attackers and one of his men threw his firebomb. A woman wearing punk garb followed suit. Glass broke and rained down in sheets as the Molotov cocktails crashed through the lower windows of the Rack and Cue. No blaze ensued.

Frustrated, Johnson lobbed his bomb, then ordered the rest to be hurled. Windows shattered and caved in all about the pub as the makeshift grenades smashed through them.

"We'll burn you out, you bastard!" Johnson called. "You may as well—"

Geraint roared somewhere behind him, an agonized yelp filled with terror. Johnson turned. His marksman was being held overhead in a powerlift by what could only be described as something inhuman.

Johnson gawped, arms hanging limp at his side. "What the . . . ?"

The ape-like wolf threw Geraint at him and his remaining soldiers, who dodged in front of the flailing human projectile to protect their leader. Johnson avoided getting smacked by the corpse but his team wasn't so lucky.

As they worked to untangle themselves from the heap of limbs, the giant beast-thing bounded to them and began shredding them with its long claws. Arms, legs, and heads ripped from bodies before Johnson could order them to get inside.

Unable to find cover and unwilling to leave his soldiers behind, Johnson threw his bag to the floor and rummaged around inside until he found it: a barrel of special bullets designed to stop the toughest of enemies.

With the beast still preoccupied with maiming his remaining troops, Johnson loaded the ammo into his revolver and took aim. He emptied the bullets into the beast's chest. Covered in gore and blood, it slouched to the ground and lay still.

Cautiously and with his weapon still raised, Johnson sidestepped over body parts and dead soldiers until he stood above the beast. He stared into the thing's eyes as it low-growled. The flicker in its humanlike pupils faded. It was slipping away, fast.

"What the fuck were you?" Johnson muttered as the creature took one last breath.

Johnson surveyed the scene. Nobody was standing save himself.

He holstered his gun and rushed to Geraint, kneeling at his side. "Lad, are you okay?" he asked, slapping the fallen man lightly on the face. Geraint didn't rouse. He attempted to wake him a few more times before admitting the entire team he'd brought with him was gone. His trusted friends and former subordinates had given their lives for his cause, one and all.

He stood, slouching, glimpsing viscera and crimson and twitching limbs in his peripherals.

He would have to go the rest of the way alone.

He clenched his jaw. "I'm coming to get you, Venom."

He reloaded his handgun, removed a wooden spike from his bag, and headed to the pub's entrance. He kicked the door open and entered, his mind singularly focused on destroying Venom. It wasn't even about the money or Hun anymore.

"You killed my nephew!" the same voice from earlier boomed from somewhere inside the pub. "You'll suffer for that."

"Where the fuck are you? Show yourself!" Johnson shouted, exiting the foyer and making circles on the spot inside the bar area. He was damned if he was going to get blindsided. "And if you hadn't noticed, you killed *my* men too. Good men, not like you, you . . . you . . . fucking *outlaw*!"

The one he assumed to be Venom laughed but still didn't appear. "What would you know about that?"

"Plenty. I've dealt with your kind before."

"You've never seen anything like *my* kind before. I guarantee it."

Johnson spun toward where he thought the voice had come from, deep in shadows beyond another entryway. "Then show yourself!" he bellowed, wiping sweat out of his eyes and slowly stepping in that direction. "I want to know!"

"Know what?"

"The truth about you."

"Is that why you choose to stick with your pathetic mission: to find out the truth, to see if I am some clichéd thing of the night?"

"Yes, if you want to put it like that. I did. I thought Hun was full of shit," Johnson said, knowing he'd pinpointed the fucker's location. *Got ya, bastard!*

"Ah, so it was that crazy bastard who sent you? I thought it may have been. He has sent others—who all failed, mind you. Just like you're going to."

"Huh. We'll see about that," Johnson said, dashing into a room with what would have once been a sturdy, eye-catching pool table. A rancid pile— *flesh, maybe? Guts and other innards?*—lay atop it though, marring it's once pristine baize. The smell overpowered his senses.

He coughed, then swallowed vomit. "Holy shit," he muttered, shielding his nose. "What the fuck have you been doing here?"

"I'll tell you all."

Venom stepped into the open, his large frame filling Johnson's escape route. He looked exactly as the pictures had all depicted through the decades.

"There you are," Johnson said, not intimidated by the slightly bigger man. He cocked his gun. "Ready to die?"

"That won't do you any good, Johnson," Venom said, stalking closer.

Johnson's eyebrows connected in a downward V. "H-How do you know my name?"

Venom smiled. "I know a lot of things. I see them in my mind."

Johnson's nostrils flared and he emptied the contents of his gun into Venom.

The biker didn't even flinch as the bullets ripped into his body. Vapor escaped the six bullet wounds in his chest, and the skin sealed over almost immediately.

That . . . That's not possible! Johnson sneered as he quickly reloaded his gun. *Must be a bullet-proof vest or . . . magic or sleight of hand or something.*

"It might be magic," Venom said, smirking. "But it wasn't some trick, and it's definitely not Kevlar. I don't need to wear one of those."

Johnson screamed, spilling some of his bullets onto the floor. Sweat poured out of him as his mind raced.

"I have one more surprise for you," Venom said, stepping aside. "And I think you're going to love this one. Came as a shock to me, too."

A woman walked out from the darkness, her pallid skin and jutting bones similar to Venom's. But there was something else about her facial structures and gait that caused Johnson to quirk his head sideways, digging through memories.

His eyes widened. He stopped fumbling with his ammo and weapon, more concerned that his faculties were about to give out altogether. "T-T-Toni?!" he blurted. He hadn't seen her in years, not since leaving her and that bitch she called a mother behind—his third wife, the one he'd had murdered for stealing from him.

"Hello, *Daddy*," she said. "We've been expecting you."

"It's a small world, isn't it?" Venom said, chuckling.

Johnson blinked tears away. "Toni," he said, voice quavering. Regrets crashed down on him. "I . . . I never meant to—You didn't deserve—"

"To be left behind like a sack of shit after Mam left you?" She walked toward him, holding his gaze. "From the stories she told me, I'm sure you were glad I was out of your life. And no worries, *Dad*. No harm came to me after you had Mam killed." She cocked her head to the side. "You *did* have her killed, right?"

"S-stay back," he yelled, waving his gun.

She stepped right up to him, her pretty facial features contorting slightly.

Johnson panicked and stabbed his stake through her chest. She collapsed to the floor, taking his best weapon with her.

"Nooooo!" Venom roared, flying across the room.

He hit Johnson with an uppercut, which lifted him off his feet. He crashed down on top of the gory pile on the pool table.

A small burst of blood erupted from his mouth as he coughed and caught his breath. "Son of a bitch," he said, rolling off the table and staggering to his feet.

"Toni!" Venom cried, rushing to her.

Johnson fired all the rounds remaining in his gun. The bullets bored into Venom's exposed back, sending the biker to ground. "I'll fucking kill you, you filthy pig!" he yelled, running at Venom and kicking him hard and repeatedly in his ribs. Bones cracked and Johnson smiled maniacally. "Ha! You're only a man like the rest of us!"

He spat on the downed man and spun around to Toni's body. He yanked the stake out of his daughter's chest and wheeled back to the biker.

To his shock, Venom was already standing.

Johnson growled, lost to the rage, and plunged forward with the wooden weapon. Venom grabbed his arm midair and twisted.

Johnson's elbow blew out and his wrist snapped. He roared in agony. But his pain quickly segued into a breathless whimper as Venom's face corkscrewed into something disgustingly stomach-churning. His teeth grew to a point and his fingers sprouted hair and talons.

Venom pulled the battered man close to his face. "I'll see you in hell."

Johnson cracked and started laughing.

His guffaws were cut short as Venom bit, clawed, and tore at his flesh.

* * *

Toni came to while he was still angrily feasting on her father. The stake had missed her heart. Barely, but she was alive, and Venom had never been happier in the past few decades.

It seemed the man upstairs hadn't entirely cursed him after all.

He helped her to the corpse so she could take in the blood and heal, and together they finished off their impromptu meal, leaving behind less than what they'd left of Simon. Then they cuddled and slept the day away, finding comfort in each other's embrace.

After dusk set in, they set to work pushing all the vehicles off the road and dragging all the bodies into the pub. They repacked their bundles and tied them to the motorcycle before Venom set fire to the Rack and Cue.

As they sat on the bike staring into the licking flames which consumed the pub, Toni was first to break the silence. "Where are we off to now?"

"Wherever you want to go. I just have two things to take care of first."

"And they are?"

"We're going to hunt down those truckers and the girl. We have to dispose of them—not just for killing my family, but because they could link us to everything here."

"I suppose you're right. They do need to die," she said. "And what's the second thing you wanted to take care of?"

He pointed at one of the packages on the bike. "I have to send this parcel off to my *friend*," he said, laughing, and Toni laughed too.

Once the pub began to collapse in on itself, Venom kick-started his motorbike and they pulled off.

EPILOGUE

Footsteps clopped down the length of the prison corridor at a hasty pace.

"Out of the way," the guard yelled at Shark, who stepped aside. The man dashed into the cell, face pale, breath escaping in rapid bursts. "This is for you, sir."

Hun smiled and took the discolored package from the guard. The thing reeked. "Has it been tampered with?"

"No, sir. We don't inspect your post. But I will have to wait here while you open it."

"Have it your way," the old biker said, gingerly sitting on the lower mattress with the box in his lap. His heart raced and he felt twenty, thirty years younger. *I've been waiting a very long time for this gift*, he thought, undoing the bow with a wide grin on his face.

He lifted the lid and frowned.

Johnson's decapitated head rested inside, the former soldier's dead eyes staring vacantly at him.

"Damn it!" Hun yelled, letting the box drop to the floor.

Johnson's head jostled around, and Hun noticed an envelope at the bottom. Carefully, he plucked it free and opened it.

Dear Hun,

I do hope you like the gift I sent?

Take heed, old man: I won't be sending another warning. Let the past lie. Any more attempts on my life will be met with brutal consequences.

Yours, Truly Forever,
Venom

Hun shook with anger and let the note flutter to his feet.

ABOUT THE AUTHOR

David Owain Hughes is a word-slinger of horror and crime fiction who grew up on trashy B-movies from the age of five which helped rapidly instill in him a vivid imagination. He's had multiple short stories published in various online magazines and anthologies, along with articles, reviews, and interviews. He's written for *This Is Horror*, *Blood Magazine*, and *Horror Geeks Magazine*.

Hughes is the author of six horror novels, four short story collections, and a plethora of novellas. Although he predominately writes within the bracket of horror and its multiple sub-genres, he's recently branched out into crime fiction and is slowly carving out a superb series of crime/noir thrillers under the umbrella title of *South Wales*.

Connect with him at:

https://www.facebook.com/DOHughesAuthor

https://twitter.com/DOHUGHES32

http://david-owain-hughes.wix.com/horrorwriter

Amazon UK: https://amzn.to/3MJlNc5

https://bit.ly/DOHughes_Goodreads